Praise for *Where The Sleeping Lady Lies*

"*Where the Sleeping Lady Lies* brings an interesting and refreshing scenario to the Eco-thriller genre, with plausible modern-day science… a subtle yet exciting environmental thriller that skillfully explains scientific concepts and findings in a way that makes it accessible to readers without losing the details that are important to the plot."
—CHANTICLEER BOOK REVIEWS

"*Where the Sleeping Lady Lies* is a compelling thriller that starts with what seems like a natural geologic event in Alaska and quickly evolves into a sinister human-caused plot that carries across the globe. A good read that is hard to put down."
—JOE MOORE,
GEOLOGIST/REGIONAL SOIL SCIENTIST ALASKA

"*Where the Sleeping Lady Lies* is smart and gripping, yet its bedrock is clear: greed corrupts and we should all be paying attention to preserving what is truly precious. I've never been so entertained by a wake-up call!"
—REBECCA BLOOM,
FOUNDER/ADVOCATE | WHEN WOMEN GET SICK
STORY DEVELOPER | HOLD THIS WHILE IP PRODUCTIONS
FOUNDER & STORYTELLING COACH | BLOOM YOUR STORY

"*Where the Sleeping Lady Lies* is a captivating read
that intertwines the fascinating natural world, we
live in with the darker forces that can exploit it. It
highlights the resilience and determination of humans
to protect mankind from impending destruction."

—LORI KOIDAHL,
AUTHOR, *GARDEN OF GRIEF - CULTIVATING A NEW LIFE AFTER LOSS*

"This international thriller explores the chilling consequences
of using nature as a weapon of revenge. A gripping read! I
loved this story and can't wait for the next book in the series."

—JULIE DAHL
THRILLER READER, ANCHORAGE, ALASKA

"*Where the Sleeping Lady Lies* is a globe-spanning thriller
inspired by Schuman's experience as a scientist in Alaska.
Blending scientific intrigue with high-stakes action, the
story follows a small band of friends as they race to protect
the innocent lives threatened by angry terrorists."

—APRIL DÁVILA
AWARD-WINNING AUTHOR, EDITOR & WRITING COACH

WHERE

THE

SLEEPING

LADY LIES

First edition February 2025

ISBN: 978-1-7379206-2-5 paperback
ISBN: 978-1-7379206-3-2 Ebook

To Those Who Breathe The Dust

Whose Bodies Ache

For Others To Have And To Take

But man is a part of nature, and his war against
nature is inevitably a war against himself.

—Rachel Carson

WHERE THE SLEEPING LADY LIES

A THRILLER

M. E. SCHUMAN

An Environmental Thriller

This story is fiction. The characters are fictional. The impacts of mining, climate change, and social injustice are factual.

THE LEGEND OF THE SLEEPING LADY

Many millennia ago, a clan of gentle giants inhabited the Great Land, now known as Alaska. Among the giant people was a beautiful young lady and a handsome young man who fell deeply in love with each other. Their unbound devotion was so joyous that all the villagers admired them and preparations for marriage were underway.

On the day before the wedding a messenger brought dreadful news that a fierce war-like people from the north were invading the country and destroying everything in their path. The village gathered in council to decide what to do. Some suggested going north to attack. The young love-filled man proposed taking gifts to the enemies instead of weapons, showing their interest was in peace and not bloodshed.

By morning the brave volunteers were ready to leave.

The young lady had tears of sadness when her lover came to say good-bye. He gazed softly into her eyes and whispered, "I shall return soon with news of peace. Meet me by the slender body of water with two arms." With one gentle kiss he turned and joined the departing men.

The young woman hurried to the pool of water, known today as the Knik Arm, and began the wait, confident that she would soon be back in her mate's arms. For many days and nights, she busied herself while waiting until finally she grew very weary and laid down to rest. She fell into a deep sleep.

While she slept, tragic news reached the village that their young men's pleas for peace had been in vain and a terrible battle had broken out. Most of the giant men were killed or captured. When the village women approached the young lady with the tragic news, they could not bear to disturb her from her peaceful sleep, and left her as she was. To this day, the sleeping lady lies there dreaming of the moment her beloved will return to her side and peace once again rules the land.

~ DENA'INA LEGEND

**THE FIRST PRINTING OF THE LEGEND WAS WRITTEN BY NANCY LESH, 1962*

JACKSON

"LATER, BRO." CAMDEN gave a thumbs up as he opened the door of his rental car. With a slight turn of his head, he looked at Jackson and yelled. "We will get 'em." And then, he got into the driver's seat and drove off disappearing into the forested driveway. It was the last time he saw his friend. The tracker went dead a day before the earthquake struck. The birch and aspen leaves were a golden red.

Rubbing his throbbing temples, he concentrated on every detail Camden had told him about ARKose over the last three months before he drove away that morning.

When Camden called to meet him, it was July in Anchorage, Alaska. The rainy season had begun in late May and except for that one night; the sky was blue and the midnight sun was shining. It had been thirteen years since he had last seen his college buddy and rugby mate. And there he was, sipping the same beer piss with his shaggy, blonde hair nearly to his shoulders, basking in the sun on the deck of the Snow Goose Bar.

"It's been way too many years, fly-half." As he sat next to his friend, reaching for the foamy stout waiting for him. Camden grinned, as he recognized the nick name. He played the position of fly-half on their university rugby team and the nick name held since the day he met Jackson.

"Yeah, and this is not Golden Colorado." He clanked his glass against Jackson's.

"Somethings don't change," he looked at the translucent beer in his glass. "Beer piss and your adversity to a barber."

"Yep. But here we are. Another bar, a different city and under entirely different circumstances." Camden paused, taking a sip of his beer.

"Wow. Thirteen years. If I recall, prop-man, which isn't much, we imbibed heavily after getting our doctorate degrees from the School of Geology and Mining."

"Oh yeah. Wild night that was." He paused. "And how is bush life treating you, my friend? At least I got a text letting me know you were in my State." Jackson teased. "You sent that in June."

"The scenery is fascinating. The lead geologist is quirky," Camden took a sip of his beer. "Damn, I barely had time to get from the Anchorage International Airport to Merrill Field when I arrived in Alaska. The woman that hired me was flying in by helicopter that week. Man, that feels like months ago instead of a few weeks since I arrived there."

"Why the hell are you staying in a hotel room tonight? Stay with me. It would be like old times."

"Yeah, that's what I'm afraid of."

As the two men chatted about their days playing rugby, Jackson noticed Camden keeping a close eye on people as they wandered onto the deck.

"Jackson, my gut is telling me something ain't right with this job." Camden shook his head. "Fuck, I need a haircut."

After paying the tab, Camden whispered to Jackson. "Let's find a quiet place to chat."

As they walked towards 4th Avenue on H Street, Camden pointed at Jackson's unlaced shoelaces.

"Yep, some things never change."

As he bent down to tie his hiking boots, Camden noticed the same guy who had followed him into the Snow Goose. He was stocky, quite a few inches under six feet with black shoulder length hair and wearing a black ball cap with a red symbol. The man crossed to the other side of H Street when Jackson bent down to tie his shoe.

When he stood up, Camden slapped him on his shoulder.

"Remember when that dude came after you because you were flirting with his gal?"

"Shit yeah. He was crazy. What made you think of that?"

"Remember what we did?"

He nodded, then whispered in Camden's ear. "Meet me at the bar on the first floor of the Captain Cook Hotel. I will take the backway off 4th Street. You can turn left here. The entrance is on the right." He glanced over Camden's shoulder. "The guy with the black ball cap? Faded Carhart coat. Mustache. Black hair."

"That's him," Camden said slapping his friend's shoulder. "See ya the next time I am in town." He yelled as he turned left while Jackson continued straight on 4th Avenue. Camden kept an eye on the man and when the man disappeared, he slipped into the side door of the Captain Cook Hotel.

"What the hell was that about? Did you get frisky with some guy's lady at camp?" He sat down, as he reached for the glass of scotch.

"You might say a blonde with exotic eyes and a stone heart got me a bit worked up."

Huddled over their glasses of the pale straw-colored liquid, Camden ran his hand through his hair and grew quiet. "You know how tricky it is to discuss particular aspects of a job with a signed non-disclosure agreement."

Camden took another sip as he gripped his glass. "My expertise is developing techniques to stabilize rare earth elements. That is what I was hired to do."

"Some of the most dangerous of the rare earths are the least stable."

"Exactly," he gazed into Jackson's eyes. "And the most unstable are radioactive."

He nodded as he mentally teased out the information that Camden was not disclosing. It was unusual to see his friend skittish and paranoid. Patiently, he uncrossed his arms on the bar counter and picked up his glass, twirling the golden liquid, and listened.

"Especially a rare earth element such as francium."

"Shit." He turned his head and looked at his friend. "Element 87? No way. It is so rare no one has been able to develop it."

"There is a shit load of francium below that mine over there." He nodded his head in the direction of the Cook Inlet. "I am contracted with a small company. You ever heard of ARKose?"

He shook his head no as he drained his glass in one gulp.

"What do you need?"

While they were talking, Camden air-dropped two photos that he took at the mining camp to Jackson's phone. One was of Daniel and the other was Peiling.

"Daniel, the head geologist is expediting some very specialized and expensive equipment to the mine site." Camden grew quiet. "The guy is from Pakistan. Went to Oxford. I very much doubt his real name is Daniel." Camden looked at Jackson.

"Last name?"

"Biel is the name he gave me. Dr. Biel. He is setting up a remote location to test the stability of the element once I am finished with the stabilization process. And when I was leaving the mine this afternoon, he mentioned that the owner of ARKose is investigating another facility to develop the element." He paused as he ran his hand through his hair and whispered. "That was in the NDA I signed. Hell, all of this could be legitimate. Shit, it could be history changing, to quote the blonde."

"You mentioned earlier something about a blonde. Who is she?"

"Her name is Peiling. One of the photos I sent you is her. My impression of her? She is important and at the top of the food chain with ARKose. Extremely intelligent. I assumed she was the owner when I first met her in June. She is Asian with long blonde hair," Camden answered. "A looker, but…" He paused. "If I can find a way to use the excess energy safely, element 87 could be the next solution to our energy crisis and end fossil fuel dependence. The possibilities of research development firms fighting for samples of this element to synthesize could be staggering. If the calculations are correct, this vein is so damn rich it is beyond what anyone would or could expect."

"How much are we talking about?".

"Enough to blow up all of Alaska and some." Camden looked at Jackson. "We are talking about an element that has the potential to radiate the entire Northern Latitude."

He shifted his gaze around the room.

"But you don't believe that. The doing good part?"

"Hell no. There is more Jackson. A lot more but not here," Camden swallowed. "This is risky, man. That dude with the ball cap is proof. I believe ARKose is intending to use this element or maybe sell it but I don't believe their intentions has anything to do with green energy."

"I've got a buddy at JBER — are you familiar with the joint military bases of the Elmendorf Air Force and Fort Richardson Army here?"

"Of course."

"Well, I can reach out to him and see what he has on ARKose. He is on a special operations team that deals with the transfer and transport of dangerous metals. And next time you are staying at my place. It will be quiet and secluded." He deliberated on how much information he should reveal.

"Get a burner. Text me at this number." He slid a torn napkin with the number.

Camden smiled. "A buddy huh?" His handler let him know that Jackson was the team leader of the special ops team he was referring to. "This could a bit dicey, Jackson."

"It always is. That is not up for discussion. I am in." Then added. "Maybe the dude following you has nothing to do with ARKose. Hell, maybe he recognized you from a previous fling with his girlfriend. You always did like to flirt with beautiful women. A scorned husband by chance?" Jackson snorted. "On the other hand. You are messing around with a nasty element and if 87 got in the wrong hands? There is no fucking around."

"I wish it was a spurned hubby," Camden winked. "The symbol on the cap that guy wore is the logo for ARKose. A red dragon. I am going to play it cool in the hotel tonight, make some work phone calls. Maybe even make an appointment to get my hair cut." Then he smiled. "I met this red-haired beauty on the plane when I first flew into Anchorage. She is into wild animals especially wolves," he arched his eyebrows. "I am meeting her tomorrow afternoon — do some exploring at the zoo, then dinner and…"

Jackson shook his head as he finished his drink. "You always were fast on your feet."

"Peiling is flying in this week."

He got up. "When will you be back?"

"I am shooting for the end of August."

"Watch your back. No hotel. My place. That is an order." He slapped his friends shoulder and left.

Chapter 2

SHELBY

WAS IT THE warmth of the morning sun on his face and the freshness of the air that was invigorating? Or, Camden thought, was it the anticipation to see Shelby again that made his heart skip twice as he walked along 7th avenue. He admired the rugged slate colored Chugach Mountains as ravens, the large bluish-black bird and cousin to the smaller crow, screeched as he disrupted their scavenging along the sidewalk.

According to Google maps the tiny, purple and green house was tucked between an automotive shop and an espresso vendor near his hotel. As he entered the one room barber shop, decorated in purples and blues, the young female with purple and blue hair, and rings in her eyebrows and nose, smiled as she guided him to the single chair in the room. She chatted as he watched his hair fall onto the black cement floor. She stood back studying her creation then grabbed a razor and trimmed the stubble and told him to keep the goatee. He laughed when she told him it made him look distinguished. "Right," he mumbled as he walked by the old cemetery with uplifted, black stained head stones. "A nice way of saying old."

While approaching the polar bear exhibit at the Anchorage

Zoo, he saw the tall woman with long red hair in a green jacket and blue jeans, wearing mirrored sunglasses. She had a small bag of peanuts and was watching the young white bear playing with a large fishing float. She kept her gaze on the massive youngster, its claws the size of a santoku knife, as he walked up next to her.

"Shelby." He whispered

"I always think of Binky with the tennis shoe in his mouth. Humans are such idiots," she said, glancing at Camden as she inched closer to him.

"Binky?"

"A 1200-pound male polar bear alone in a pen. Stubborn and independent like most males," nudging Camden. "One day, this Aussie gal jumped over two safety rails to get a close-up of the bear. He didn't care for that and grabbed her through the steel bars. He got her tennis shoe. She got stitches and a broken leg. For 3 days that bear kept the shoe in his mouth." She shook her head. "That image went global."

"What happened to Binky?"

"He died in 1995 at age 20."

"Aren't those for the critters?" Camden pointed to the bag of peanuts.

Her soft, un-ostentatious laugh was near a whisper. "This place has changed a lot since I started coming here as a kid. I planned to be a zoo vet, but the older I got the more zoos depressed me. These animals should be free, not in cages. Humans, however," she plopped a peanut in her mouth. "Most of them should." She bit on a nut. "Belong in cages."

She adjusted her sunglasses, sliding them down the bridge of her nose, and locked her gaze with Camden's, revealing the deepest shade of forest green. It was those eyes that stole his heart the first time they met while working a case together as FBI field agents two years ago. As they continued walking along the path, Camden never underestimated a woman of her height. He was 6 foot and her head reached above the top of his shoulder.

"Any more surprises last night after visiting with Jackson?" she asked.

"No, all quiet. Rather stupid for the guy to wear that ball cap. The red dragon was easy to recognize."

They slowly walked to a large wooded pen.

"ARKose has been on our radar for over a year, Camden."

He smiled. "And now you are my handler. Makes it a little more complicated, Shel."

"My supervisor is good with it. We are professionals," she mimicked. "And the FBI recognizes you are the best field agent in the world in the field of rare earth elements. And…"

"And you are the best geochemist they have. Not to mention, you were a field agent for 8 years until you met me." He looked at her. "I fear the promotion might not be quite as exciting for you."

"I disagree," she smiled. "And it allows us to see each other more. Between our field assignments we never saw each other. Now we can. And here we are."

"ARKose has been lurking in the shadows behind some of the largest mining operations worldwide – in the Congo, Malaysia, China, and Russia. Someone powerful is backing them. What they are doing requires cash. A lot of cash." He whispered, his lips nearly touching her ear. "They're keeping a close eye on me here, so whatever they're planning, I have them spooked."

"We need Jackson and his team. Charles is going to his boss for assistance. Knowing Jackson, as I do, he should hear it from you before our boss spills the beans as to what your real job is."

Camden knew their boss at the FBI wanted this group as much as he did.

"What about you? Will Jackson know you are my handler."

"No. Not yet. When the time is right, I will let him and Sam know."

"All those years I wanted to tell him the truth about me being a secret agent," he grinned. "And then to find out he never quit the military." He paused. "I sent him a photo of Peiling and one of Daniel. Maybe Jackson's team will have better luck in finding out who they really are."

"Yeah. Jackson is one of the good guys. I have known him for years through Sam. Alaska is a big state, but it is small when it comes to connections." Shelby murmured. "I have a feeling when this is over, there will be many secrets revealed," she looked at him. "Camden, don't mention my name. Sam does not know I am FBI. She will be relentless with questions if she finds out before I can tell her. If I must."

"I look forward to meeting her after the stories I have heard from you."

"You will," she rubbed her index finger across his new beard. "Jackson and his wife Winter will be fine. He's military. It's you that will be harder to protect at the mine site." She shook her head, concern in her voice. "I don't like it, Camden, but we're working on that. The remoteness helps as it limits who can get there. We have 24/7 surveillance on the airspace, but we don't have a comprehensive report on all the employees with access there."

They walked in silence, pausing to observe two wolves pacing in their enclosure.

She squeezed his hand as she slipped the bag of peanuts into it. The bag was heavy and looking down, he saw a device at the bottom of it.

"A new toy?" He smiled.

"Yes. It will pick up any listening device within two miles."

"Impressive."

"We will chat later," she said kissing his ear before walking away. "See you at dinner. My place."

He dropped a peanut into his mouth, as her musky scent of spruce and damp earth lingered.

CHAPTER 3

CAMDEN

HE WAS RESTLESS when he returned to his hotel room. He unpacked his laptop and began reading about the history of Stoney Mine while gazing out the window from his hotel room, captivated by the dusky blue-gray twilight with the midnight setting of the sun. After two years of being with Shelby, he was still infatuated with her beauty and strength. Her mind was analytical and her sense of humor was enchanting. He had fallen for her on their first assignment together in the isolated desert of Nevada.

"Who are you Peiling?" he whispered as he thought back to the day, he secured a contract to work for the company in Western Alaska. It was over three weeks ago when he texted Jackson as he caught the cab from the airport to Merrill Field. Seeing him the other night felt like old times as the two talked about rugby, geology, and beer in downtown Anchorage. Next time, he hoped to see Jacob, his twin who worked for the USGS as a glaciologist. He had not seen him since the graduation ceremony for their doctorates thirteen years ago.

Jackson advised him to stay vigilant at the mine, before he left

13

the bar the other night. He snickered however, when he warned him that his wife Winter would be relentless to obtain the real stories about Colorado the next time he visited.

"How does anyone sleep in this State?" He said to himself as he laid in bed.

The next morning, he waited in the small room at the charter flight's office, at Merrill Field for the plane to shuttle him back to the mine. Sitting there, he closed his eyes as he thought about the twin brothers, and how different they were raised compared to his childhood. Jackson and Jacob got their college paid by the GI bill. He on the other hand, grew up in a military family. He was groomed from a young age, first ROTC in college and then high hopes he would be recruited as an officer in the Air Force; following his parents and his grandfather's footsteps as a fighter pilot. He shuddered. *How quickly plans change and his life was thrown in turmoil.*

At the age of 10, after his father was killed when his F-15 Eagle crashed while conducting maneuvers, he knew the military life was not for him. His mother understood as she knew all too well how he had suffered at the loss of his father at such a young age. And he knew what his mother sacrificed as she climbed the ranks to be the second female general in the Air Force. Eventually, his mother retired from military duty to teach at the Air Force Academy in Colorado Springs.

He was grateful for the military life as his childhood took him all over the world where he explored every mountain and every rock he could find. He was fascinated with rocks and rock climbing. While his mom was stationed in Italy, he explored the Finale Ligure, the largest climbing area in the country. With over 3,000 routes to climb amidst verdant hills and lush green valleys, he could not contain his excitement. He had made it clear to his mom, that a military career was not in his career path.

After graduate school where he earned his Ph.D. in Geochemistry and specialized in developing analytical procedures for rare elements, he kept in touch with Jackson through postcards from his adventures all over the world. With sandy blonde hair and green eyes with an athletic build, he had no problem in finding beautiful women, according to his buddy Jackson. Jackson was no slouch in that arena either, with his tall muscular frame, and exotic dark features. He was anxious to meet Winter, and there was little doubt that his good buddy would find out who his handler was and Shelby's true profession as an FBI agent.

He thought about the twists and turns in his life. Camden embarked on a career in mining while devoting his spare time to analyzing and searching for rare elemental rocks while Jackson found employment with the USGS, where he specialized in earthquakes and seismic activity in Anchorage, Alaska. And yet, they both ended up in a position where their true passion is to make the planet safe, especially for those underserved, by studying the very foundation of the earth — the rock below. He knew his father would be proud of his vocation.

He opened his eyes, when he heard his name and a few minutes later, he was walking on the tarmac to board a Cessna 206 from Merrill Field, one of the world's largest small-plane airports. His father's crash was never far from his mind when he was in a plane. This time his pilot was a Yupik native. After going through the take-off instructions, he buckled himself into the co-pilot seat as they soared across the Cook Inlet heading west towards the mine site, which was 200 air miles away.

Although this was his second flight, it was no less magnificent than his first. As they ventured deeper into the wilderness, a world of rock and ice enveloped them at an elevation of 2500 feet. Magnificent spiring peaks adorned with snow caps and turquoise cirque lakes surrounded them in every direction. Lush green valleys and cliffs, sculpted by ancient glaciers, created a breathtaking landscape carved by Mother Nature herself.

With a sly smile, the pilot alerted him to a welcome party of sorts as they approached Lake Clark. The tall mountains of Lake Clark pass can modify strong winds aloft to create waves and large eddies on the lee side of the mountains. The turbulence is well known among small plane owners. This time he was ready, as the plane shuddered violently in the wind, as they made their way towards the Nushigak-Mulchatna watershed, the birthplace of Bristol Bay. Miles and miles of sloping green hills and small ponds reflecting blue sky and white streamers like mirrors were scattered among the winding river: the artery of life. He was in awe of the vastness before him as if nature was painting the scene before his very eyes.

As they circled over Stoney Mine, he couldn't help but feel a mixture of emotions. The view of gentle green hills sloping towards the mine site was awe-inspiring, but he also realized the potential devastation a mining operation could bring. An overwhelming sense of despair washed over him.

Amid his conflicting emotions, he spotted a majestic sight. A golden mass appeared amid the branching green alder below, and as they circled, his eyes met with those of a massive brown bear. For a moment, time stood still as the bear gazed back at him, standing on his hind legs, nose twitching in the air. His heart beat rapidly against his chest. The creature then lowered its front paws, revealing its sheer size and power before gracefully disappearing into the alder thicket once again.

As chills ran down his spine, he couldn't help but share the encounter with the pilot, "Did you see that grizzly? He was beautiful."

The pilot shook his head. "A bear. Hmmm. You see moon bear? Bear means strength, and courage to fight for your family. As he must," he said in English, heavy with Yupik dialect, pausing between words. He noticed the pilot's grin had vanished.

After landing, the pilot removed his headphones and looked at him with a serious expression. After a few seconds, he smiled and pointed to the passenger door.

After dropping off his gear in the nondescript modular, self-contained building that housed several dormitory-type rooms, he set out to find Daniel, the head geologist for the project. He was still surprised to see the armory of guards. Having worked in the Middle East, he was astounded by the level of security protocols at this mine considering the coordination it took to get to the remote mining site.

Finally, one of the security guards jumped into the driver's seat of a military-style off-road vehicle, pointing to Camden to get in the passenger seat. A few minutes later, they stopped in front of a heavy steel-like structure where a man with dark hair and a bronzed complexion stood with a wide toothy grin.

"Welcome, back. I hope your visit was relaxing?" Daniel asked. His coal-black hair was close trimmed, and he wore black-framed glasses that matched his dark eyes. With a short, lean stature, he barely reached his chest. He chuckled as it was beyond his apprehension how the man always looked so neat.

"Please, follow." Daniel said with a British accent as he turned and placed his left thumb on a reader outside the access door.

The door disappeared into the wall of the steel building as they stepped into a small entry room, imbued with a bluish light. Daniel placed his ID card over a card reader, and another door opened. As he was instructed the last time he was in this room, this core room is unique. He was still shocked at the sophisticated and well-secured core room, and again, the room was sterile without the normal stacks of the typical cylindrical rock cores. This time, however, they also were not alone.

"You will be surprised at the amount of francium we have acquired." Daniel illuminated.

Daniel introduced the technician dressed in the black lab coat as he smiled, trying not to look distracted, but he was. His radar was on full alert as he had never seen this man before. He was holding a black rock, the size of a walnut, weighing it and reading the result into a portable computer pad.

Daniel walked over to a steel door, which he opened with his ID card. This time he knew the drill as he stepped into a decontamination area. The door closed with a loud swoosh and inside, they each grabbed a sealed package containing a Tyvek suit with booties and plastic gloves.

As they donned the Tyvek coverings, Daniel pushed a glowing red button, and the steel door opened. Once he entered the darkened room, his throat itched from the dry air and like clockwork, within seconds, his nostrils burned. The bluish light cast an eerie glow on a shiny steel table in the center of the small room. It reminded him of a morgue, not a core sample room as Daniel walked over to one of the walls and grabbed two lab aprons, giving one to him.

"Safety precaution." Daniel said with a large smile on his face. His teeth were eerily white as he stood next to the table. The four walls shined with the same eerie glow as the table, and several red glowing lights lined the walls.

Each wall was gridded into compartments and when Daniel touched one of the small red lights, a drawer slid open. He withdrew a small metal box from inside and placed it on the table. Inside was a silver-gray rock about 4 cm in diameter that reminded him of obsidian. As they put on leaden gloves, Daniel picked up the rock and handed it to Camden. It was surprisingly heavy considering its small size.

"Yesterday, we found this in between two core samples of rock. It is beautiful, is it not?" He nodded remembering that there was no mention of this rock in any of the previous documents from the past owner. Daniel punched a red button, and another compartment opened. He grabbed the metal box inside and set it on top of the table. Inside were two core samples.

"These were among the several core samples that were sampled at the same location where this rock was found. There was nothing unusual or reported in the analysis. However, if you look closely using an electronic microscope, there is a difference. In fact, in this core, you can visibly see the difference."

He looked closer and he could see a slight change in the layer near the top of the core. It was smoother with a grayer tone. It would be easily missed.

"I see it. And this is why we need the lead apron's. You can feel the heat even with the heavy gloves. Even a small amount in the raw form is highly radioactive."

Daniel smiled again as he put the containers back into their compartments and responded. "I will show you what we have found since you left two days ago."

"I read your paper on new techniques for rare earth element deposits," Daniel said as they walked back to the camp center. "The one you recommended. Very interesting."

"I thought you would like it considering what we have discovered here. Or, you have discovered, Daniel."

As they walked to the mess hall, Daniel asked Camden about his expertise with on-site measurements for detecting rare earth elements.

"The numerous applications of rare earth elements have led to a growing global demand for the search of new REE deposits. One promising technique for exploration of these deposits is laser-induced breakdown spectroscopy. We had good luck with this technique to perform on-site measurements without sample preparation in Malawi." He paused as he stopped to look at the expanse of tundra.

"Where was I?" He continued. "Oh yeah. The exploration of a deposit relies on analyzing various geological compartments in the surrounding area. One of the challenges lies in the analysis process."

"That is the problem we have had in China." Daniel added as they entered the mess tent.

"Wow. I swear, this place smells like a five-star restaurant."

"Indeed, the smell here is overwhelming, considering our location. One reason why we have a bear fence surrounding the camp. I suppose you must be starving." Daniel chuckled. "Tonight is fresh silver salmon flown in from a local village. And of course, moose burgers," he said walking towards the row of steaming dishes. "The cook made an excellent fish chowder."

As they ate, he counted seven people eating in the mess tent. Four were locals, black hair, high full cheekbones, and lean. They spoke in their native tongue.

"Ah, you also mentioned neutron activation analysis in this paper," Daniel grinned. "We now have both mass and emission here, as well as reflectance spectroscopy."

"Ahh, the equipment arrived. That is excellent news," he paused to sip his rosehip tea. "The ability to ground truth for future remote sensing datasets is essential, and for that, we need known REEs."

"The challenges in REE detection using remote sensing primarily stem from geological factors rather than instrumental limitations. We can now estimate the size of the deposit, and lithological heterogeneity. The style of outcropping play crucial roles."

He chuckled as he was all too familiar with this technical-laden discussion with Daniel. The man needed to prove his expertise. He was the project geologist and each time, he reminded Camden of that fact. This would not be the first time he was brought into a project where the Project Geologist was left out of the hiring process. He was accustomed to the potential complications and risks of bringing in an outsider into a project, especially one as controversial as Stoney Mine.

With a smile, Daniel said. "It's getting late."

CHAPTER 4

DANIEL

CAMDEN WONDERED WHAT happened to August as he ran his hands through his thick hair, now shoulder-length, as he sat in the dimly lit lab. The light from his monitors cast dancing shadows on the walls, accompanied by the blinking red beeps of the state-of-the-art spectrometer equipment. Lost in thought, he wondered about what he discovered in this remote, untouched wilderness, and the ramifications.

"Have you been here all night?"

Daniel's voice startled him as he was leaning back on his chair, precariously balancing his feet against the edge of the desk. He nearly fell backwards out of his chair.

"You scared the shit out of me."

"I suggest you take a break and get some coffee. And some fresh air. And a shower."

As Camden stepped out into the cool morning air, winter was approaching with only a skeleton crew at the mine site.

As Daniel approached later that morning, Camden was still tired but the fresh air had revived his confidence about his ongoing analysis.

"Are you prepared to discuss the findings with our shareholders?"

"Yes. The data I have will provide answers about the deposit's size and the peculiar rock they have discovered."

"Any news on the element?"

Camden shook his head while swallowing the coffee.

"How is the correlation proceeding? Will it provide some answers?"

"It will." Camden responded confidently. "With samples from the last five drill sites in addition to what has already been collected, I will have the size of the deposit verified."

"What about the rock itself? When will we know?"

"Soon. The analysis will be done soon." Camden said as he stood up. "But Daniel, don't take that rock out of the box. You show them only the core samples at the drill shack. You understand?"

Camden noticed Daniel was too eager to please. He was brilliant but the man was easily intimidated and introverted. For the last week, Camden noticed the man was even more nervous than normal. One minute, the man was anxious and withdrawn, but the next, over confident and demanding. And with the shareholders arrival? Camden was not taking any chances with element 87.

"With company visiting, I better go take a shower. As ordered."

"I know the protocol, Camden." He yelled as Camden walked away. "I developed it. Meet us at the pad when you hear the helicopter. It should be around mid-noon." He said as Camden refilled his coffee and headed to the door.

His hair dripping wet from the shower, he stopped in his office to go over the results of the element francium. He ran the data three times resulting in the same answer. He still could not believe what he was looking at. The 87th element on the periodic table. A naturally occurring but rare, radioactive element. It forms and decays so fast that it has no practical use other than in scientific research. Francium is an element with no known stable form with the largest atomic radius. Many elements on the periodic table are abundant on Earth such as hydrogen, helium, oxygen, and carbon. Others are far more elusive such as promethium and thulium being the two most uncommon. Francium rests very much at the elusive end of the spectrum.

Camden remembered an expert in the field of francium, a postdoc in chemistry from Sydney, who presented his research at a conference in South Africa. The expert had suggested that Francium-223 can form in nature during the radioactive decay of other elements, but it is estimated that there are fewer than 30 grams, which is less than one ounce, of francium in the entire crust of the Earth at any one time.

He picked up the data analysis report on his desk. According to the data from the two new drilllogs he held in his hand the concentration of element 87 exceeded amounts anywhere found on the planet. Comparing the rock cores previously studied at five locations utilizing remote sensing data—ground penetrating radar and satellite images — the francium from the glacial deposit sitting below them was 20 times the total amount estimated in the earth's crust. He couldn't fathom why such a valuable and highly radioactive element would be found here. If element 87 encountered even a micro-drop of moisture, it would explode releasing radiation.

"Fuck, Alaska would be a nuke zone." He whispered. "And who are you really working for Daniel."

There was something about the man. He was like a weasel, always around. In his gut, he knew something was off. ARKose was unknown and so was the CEO and owner. Even after a year, the FBI had no information about this small, unknown company. Follow the money, his handler always told him. *Who is funding this endeavor?* After talking to Shelby late last night, he was relieved to know that Jackson's team is fully onboard.

Camden sauntered to join Daniel as the helicopter landed. The man stood still, his hands folded behind his straight back, smiling his toothy smile. Except for the gold serpent and red symbol on the doors, the helicopter was solid metallic black. When the blades stopped, he saw Daniel walk to the rear door as the long-legged blonde dressed in black leather pants and hiking boots stepped out. Two stocky Asian men followed her dressed in dark casual suits.

The woman intrigued him, with her long blond hair, blowing in the breeze. He certainly caught her attention as she focused her deep set, black eyes on him as she walked past Daniel and focused on Camden.

"Camden, nice to see you again," she said in perfect English holding out her gloved hand while waiting for the men to join them. "I hear you have made much progress since you arrived. The man talking with the pilot is Shing and that is his comrade Yong-Sun with Daniel," she never took her eyes off Camden.

Introductions were made as Daniel ushered the group into the mess tent. Peiling asked Camden how he has adjusted living in a remote camp, and offhandedly, questioned him about his personal life. What did he like to do when not in the camp? Where did he go for fun? All while the two Asian men sat without speaking a word, sipping their tea, their dark eyes unblinking like a pair of tigers toying with their prey.

Camden was no stranger to this strategy after working in places like Indonesia, Myanmar, and Mongolia. Besides, he would rather flirt with Peiling. She was mysterious and the fact that the FBI had not been able her find anything more about her was intriguing. She even looked like a ghost with exception of her cheeks which were the color of peaches. She was a fascinating challenge to his male ego.

After lunch, the group headed back to the helicopter for an aerial tour of the mine site. Camden excused himself claiming he had work to do in the lab. However, as he had hoped, Peiling insisted he join them. The mountains in the background were covered with dwarfed forbs and shrubs, turning red with the cool temperatures and decreasing light. The contrast with the white dusting of snow on the ridges could be a painting.

The quiet sleek A-star helicopter landed on a flat, rocky clearing next to a metal shed the size of a single car garage. Inside were a dozen smooth cylinders of solid rock, about a foot in length, with a swirl of gray and black material.

Shing, the elder, beefy man picked up one of the cylinders, and held it close to his face. With a Chinese dialect he asked Daniel what was in the center of the core. Daniel, puffed up his chest and explained that the small, silver rock the size of a walnut, was the raw form of francium. "Be careful Dr. Shing. There is some, although slight, radiation from this sample." He told the man.

Peiling and Yong-Sun joined the Dr. Shing.

"Peiling, it is safe so I recommend you take off your gloves. You can feel the coolness of the cool stone. And if you close your eyes, there is a slight vibration coming from the stone." Camden said.

Unbeknown to the group, he was able to take several pictures without them noticing. He also snapped a picture with Daniel standing behind the three people. Photos were restricted in any area of the mine site. As they walked to the helicopter, Camden said he wanted to check something, and ran back to the core samples. He found the one Peiling had touched and placed it in a plastic bag they always kept on site, and hid it in his backpack under his extra clothes he always carried with him when he flew in the helicopter. Spending the night wrapped around a tussock to keep warm was always a possibility flying in the bush of Alaska.

Back in the conference room, Camden prepared for his presentation on the analysis of element 87. He needed to be assertive and respectful, but not submissive. Trust was not expected at this level of business, but he sensed that making a shit load of money might not be the primary goal here. They were interested in the amount of francium they had discovered. Camden felt compelled to maintain control of the data and the rare element until he could uncover the true intentions behind this enigmatic project.

"Bore them with minutia. Increase their frustration until they make a mistake. You know how to play this cat and mouse game of theirs."

With a deep breath, he entered the conference room, ready to navigate the high-stakes game that lay ahead. He reminded himself he was the scientific expert in this field. And for him to succeed he needed answers. He suspected they knew more than they wanted him to know.

With a black marker, he drew a large circle and then added several smaller circles within the large one. In the center circle, he wrote "Fr," then proceeded to add dots to the surrounding rings.

"Elemental francium is a very rare element, ranking among the ten rarest elements on Earth. Its scarcity limits its practical use in commercial and industrial applications. Francium does exist in the Earth's crust, but it occurs in minuscule quantities. Consequently, scientists must synthesize it in a laboratory setting to study its properties." Camden paused looking at his audience.

Continuing his lecture, he elaborated. "Francium exhibits a low melting point, high instability, and a silver-gray color in its solid form. It is categorized as a dangerous reactive alkali metal."

He interjected. "We don't need a history lesson, Camden. Tell us how to mine and synthesize it."

Camden nodded. "The rate of decay changes with the remaining substance, resulting in a constant flux. For instance, francium's half-life is 22 minutes, meaning half of the original amount remains after 22 minutes, and a quarter remains after another 22 minutes. This is crucial to understand." Camden again paused, with his intention to cause an increase in anxiety in the room. He was reading the reactions of his audience. A tactic he learned from a FBI profiler in Quantico.

"Considering francium's short half-life of 22 minutes compared to other radioactive elements, like Uranium-235 with a half-life of 703,800,000 years, francium is highly toxic for a very short period of time. This toxicity is a significant concern. Because of its very short half-life, it is extremely radioactive and unstable. Up until now, francium has never been observed with the naked eye due to its scarcity. But that's about to change."

Peiling smiled, her curiosity piqued. Camden studied her posture, her facial expression. She seemed to understand the risks but needed further reassurance as she asked. "How easily does it explode because of its' half-life?"

"If a tiny drop of moisture, including humidity, comes in contact with elemental francium it will immediately explode. Working with francium carries two main risks." Camden began, adopting a more serious tone. "Firstly, there's the issue of radioactivity. As it decays, high-energy particles are released, which can ionize surrounding human tissues, leading to burns or even breaking DNA strands, causing cancer. However, due to the extreme difficulty in producing enough francium, it hasn't posed a significant safety concern." As Camden continued his explanation, the room seemed to hang on his every word. "There is another difficulty."

"Radioactivity." He answered.

"Yes, Daniel," Camden confirmed as he walked over to the whiteboard and wrote down a number: 0.000000001% of a gram.

"The largest amount of francium ever isolated is less than this. To put it into perspective, it is equivalent to the radiation found in a brand-new smoke detector. The crucial difference is that francium's much shorter half-life means that most of this radiation would be emitted within a few hours, compared to the years it takes for a smoke detector to emit the same amount. Now, let's address the second risk." He continued, pausing again for effect.

"It is lethal," Camden looked directly at Peiling. "If there were enough of the element gathered in one place, its high reactivity would make it prone to catching fire. But with fewer than 30 grams of francium in the planet…"

Peiling interrupted, alarmed. "30 grams in the entire earth's crust. You have said this many times. But the initial estimates here indicate a much larger deposit of francium." She glared at Daniel.

Camden smiled. She took the bait. "Daniel was indeed correct. The deposit is substantial. However, if I can continue?" he asked. *She knew element 87 was here and in a quantity that was inexplainable.*

She nodded eager to hear more, her frustration starting to decrease.

"Data from drill site #1 and #2 have confirmed there are substantial amounts of francium. Based on the information we've analyzed I estimate that there is 20 times more francium in the granite below than anyone could have believed. This discovery is unprecedented for a REE deposit."

With a cautious nod from Peiling, he continued. "The rock beneath us contains enough francium to hypothetically, obliterate the North American continent." Camden paused. "If that was our intention. The reason it has not exploded in the raw form is the instability of the element. Francium 87 spins so fast that the energy is basically absorbed. The atoms are too unstable to do any harm."

Before addressing the newfound challenge, he turned his gaze towards Shing.

"There has been a breakthrough by a group of researchers who managed to remove excess energy and trap francium by converting ions into neutral atoms." Camden highlighted the significance of this discovery in studying the atomic structure of the heavy element. Another long pause.

"With new technology, this rare element can be concentrated and confined allowing the ability to study the atomic structure of this very heavy element."

Shing couldn't hide his excitement. "The scarcity of francium has been the limiting factor. It burns itself up. We can deal with the radioactivity if what you say is true."

"The game changer." Camden nodded with excitement evident in his voice. "If our estimates are correct, and because we have a sufficient amount of francium coupled with access to laser technology capable of slowing down its high energy to the point of trapping it, we could harness that energy. Daniel has already reviewed the quantity analysis, and as the head geologist on this project, I'll pass this over to him. His expertise in geology and familiarity with the core samples from all the drill site locations will determine if we should proceed."

Daniel stood up and headed towards the whiteboard. "Every core sample from the fifteen drill sites has shown a solid layer of the igneous rock type that contains francium. We've isolated the seam and taken samples from five of these sites. Camden has verified these samples, and they all indicate the presence of francium. We have enough of the element to proceed to the next phase: isolating the francium and stabilizing it for energy production. The beginning of a new form of sustainable, green energy. This is our chance to make history."

As Daniel spoke about making history, Camden noticed a smug smile on Peiling's face as she glanced not at Shing, but at Yong-Sun.

Two weeks later, Camden was stabilizing nearly 3 grams of Element 87. While the stabilization of the element was processing, it was the perfect time to make a trip to Anchorage.

CHAPTER 5

SHELBY

"ANY LUCK WITH the photos?" Camden asked Shelby as he talked with her on the phone as he walked to pick up the rental car in Anchorage.

"So far, the only person we have existing information on, is Liu Shing. He is the CEO of a North Korean mining company called LSRE, Ltd. He holds the patent for the laser technology. Dr. Shing was born in China. His business is legit according to everything we have found. He is a contractor for ARKose. I am surprised you have not run into him before?"

"I was thinking the same thing. His laser is for drilling and acquiring rocks and rare elements. I normally am not involved with the finding of the elements so I am not familiar with him or his work. He did mention one of the reasons he took this contract was he has heard of me."

"The other man, Shing's companion — Yong-Sun? He does not work for Shing. That is clear but we cannot find anything on the man."

"Another ghost. That is interesting." Camden responded. "He looks more like muscle. Maybe Peiling's hired henchman?"

"Three ghosts so far; Peiling, Daniel and Yong-Sun. And whoever owns ARKose is hidden deep."

"I am heading to Jackson's now after I get the car. I sent him the same photos you got when I landed. I also have the core with Peiling's fingerprints. I will give that to Jackson as a union of our working together," he chuckled. "Apparently, he will barbeque some deer steaks. It should be an interesting night."

"Do you have the detection listening device I gave you when we were at the zoo?"

"It is activated now. It will be a long night so I will stay at Jackson's."

"I am heading to an interagency meeting with our boss, Charles, and the Commander of Jackson's team, Kent. We will be reviewing strategy, Camden. With you being this close to the last stabilization process of francium, stalling any longer may be off the table. According Charles, ARKose is moving to the top of the list of potential security threats. And yet, we cannot apprehend anyone until there is an actual threat. We now have the resources of the FBI and DOD investigating ARKose. People are uneasy with the fact that we cannot find any background information on our three ghosts. And with the new information that you provided on the quantity of such a dangerous rare element with the word radiation attached to it, well both agencies are listing ARKose as a potential threat." She shrugged. "Damn, we need more to arrest."

"I agree. I will update you tonight."

"Keep that burner phone Jackson gave you. For now, having one with a direct line to Jackson and one with a direct line to me, is proactive."

"I am next in line for a car. Chat soon.

Chapter 6

Jackson

BEFORE ENTERING JACKSON'S address into Google Maps, Camden used the device Shelby had giving him previously hidden inside the peanut bag, to ensure no one was listening or watching him nearby. He drove along a narrow road ascending through a dense white spruce forest, leaving behind the McMansions growing like weeds at the lower elevation. As the road opened to a vista that reminded him of Colorado, he saw a home crafted from corrugated black steel. A 6-foot-tall black metal fence adorned with intricate panels of bear, eagle, dragonfly, and a mountain with a moon rising to the sky stood before him.

"Incredible, isn't it?" He said, pulling up in his truck. "Winter is an artist with a torch and hammer."

"Amazing. Where did she learn this?" Camden asked while walking the perimeter of the fence. "Is that a wolf howling at the moon?"

"There is a story behind that." He said. "Her grandfather was a farrier and a blacksmith. He worked as a welder on the pipeline. When he passed away, he left her everything he had. She spent summers at fish camp with her grandparents and fell in love with blacksmithing the moment she saw her grandfather work the forge.

She pursued the art after taking some blacksmithing courses. Her studio is over there, next to the garage. That's also one of the reasons I chose steel over wood for this house," He chuckled, leading Camden inside through a set of French doors at the rear of the house.

"These mountains are incredible." Camden said, gazing at the breathtaking scenery.

"My granddad bought this land when he was first stationed at the army base here. They advertised it as a remote parcel under the Homestead Act. When my dad was stationed here, he put in a road and built this small log cabin." He pointed at the log cabin.

"We fixed it up but maintained the rustic appeal."

"Winter's words?"

"Yep. It's basic but we've maintained it. There's a rain catchment system on the roof for an outdoor shower, and the wood stove heats the water in winter while solar panels take over in the summer. The outhouse has a compost toilet. Mom wouldn't come up here without water, so Dad had it witched."

Camden took the beer as he handed it to him as they stood in silence, savoring the moment. Old friends relishing the beauty of the mountains not unlike those peaks that had brought them together long ago in Colorado.

"What did your buddy at JBER give you today?" Camden asked quietly, as they moved inside and settled on the comfortable living room sofa.

"You won't believe it." He grabbed a metal pelican case. He opened it and showed Camden some photographs and a folder stamped confidential. He placed them on the table in front of him.

"I bet I will." Camden mumbled.

"My buddy said ARKose has been on their radar for a while. He couldn't say much, but the words 'chemical' and 'nuclear' came up several times during our conversation. They have ties to the military in China and North Korea, but nothing concrete." He took a swig of his beer. "And Pakistan."

Camden pointed to the image he had taken of Peiling and her comrades. "What about the three guys?"

"My team is still investigating, but we have some leads. That older Asian man is the head of a corporation that designs lasers with several patents. He was seen with the President of China. His name is Shing. Doctor Shing. As for the younger Asian man, we believe he is Chinese, but we have no concrete information on him."

Camden took note of the words 'my team'.

"What about the guy in the background? The one I couldn't get a clear photo of?" Camden asked, holding up the blurry image of Daniel.

"We're drawing a blank on him. There was no hit on his name either. Facial recognition didn't turn up anything. If he did leave Pakistan for London at a young age, there's no record of it."

"Not surprising. What about Oxford? There must be a record of his graduation. And my description of him is…"

"Too generic. No record under Daniel Biel. We need fingerprints."

"Well, I can help you with that," Camden reached into his pelican and pulled out a plastic bag. "Inside is a rock with Peiling's fingerprint. I recommended she take her glove off so she could feel the coolness of the granite. This is the rock we have been finding element 87. And, this," Camden pulled out another plastic bag. "This is a piece of paper that Daniel handled."

"You have not lost your touch. Peiling and Daniel may no longer be a ghost."

"As far as the muscle man, Yong-Sun, we assume his name is an alias or," Camden concentrated. "I never had a chance to get a print from him. He never touched anything as far as I could tell."

"We will check on that. Now for ARKose. On the surface, the company appears to be a small mining corporation, scavenging through the remnants left by larger companies in search of rare earth elements. But their sudden appearance in Alaska raised eyebrows.

One of the guys in charge of Stoney was a retired head of the Alaska Department of Natural Resources."

"First Stoney Consortium and now ARKose. It never made sense to me until today. Someone knew there was a large deposit of francium. That mine is low grade gold." He took a sip of his beer. "Not worth the energy to mine it."

As the midnight sun settled behind the mountains casting a bluish violet on the snow, he handed a document to Camden while preparing T-bone steaks for the barbecue. The document was a summary from NPR based on an interview with Siddharth Kara, shedding light on the dire conditions of cobalt mining in the Democratic Republic of Congo (DRC).

"I thought you would be interested in this information."

Camden leaned back in his chair, sipped his beer, and delved into the troubling details.

The text revealed Siddharth Kara's extensive research on modern-day slavery, human trafficking, and child labor related to cobalt mining. The DRC, with abundant cobalt reserves, was deep in a supply chain tainted by the exploitation of artisanal miners working in hazardous conditions for meager pay. Kara's description painted a haunting image of these workers toiling with archaic tools, hacking and scavenging cobalt from trenches and pits, while the mining industry caused massive environmental devastation in the region. It destroyed the very livelihood for these subsistence peoples, forcing them to work the mines.

Camden understood the dark side of mining all too well, as he remembered the man who recruited him after he graduated with his undergraduate degree.

"Steaks are ready," his voice broke the silence as Camden sat down. "Dig in."

"Wow. This is deer?"

"Yep. Fuck me, this is one helluva tasty steak. You cannot beat kelp-fed deer from Kodiak," He chewed. "Spill it."

"You know this article reminds me of a man I met during my summer break after college. His name doesn't matter," Camden paused. "But he changed my life. It was before I went to Colorado."

Camden began his narration about an encounter with a man in Arlington, Virginia after returning from a three-week hiatus climbing a series of rocks in Krabi, Thailand. He was visiting his mom, who semi-retired from the Air Force, who lived near Virginia at the time. The man presented him with a stack of photos documenting a mining operation in Malawi. Along with the images, there was an old article that highlighted the exploitation and suffering of miners in Africa. The story revealed how the term 'artisanal mining' had evolved from illegal mining, raising debates on regulating small-scale mining to prevent revenue loss in mining communities.

"I must be an easy mark because he used an article to get my attention, just like you did now." Camden stammered, then continued the story. "That man worked for the FBI. He became my handler. After receiving my doctorate, I became an undercover FBI agent investigating potential illegal mining operations. My cover is a geochemist specializing in dangerous rare earth elements."

"Fuck me. No way. You worked for the FBI when I met you? In Colorado?"

"Yes, I did. Boy, was I green. Remember when I spent a semester in Virginia? On a research project?"

Jackson nodded.

"I was at Quantico. No one knew this. Not even my mom. She was not a second general yet but that was her next rank." Camden paused as he got up and grabbed two beers.

"Do you think people have a clue where the components of smartphones, computers, and rechargeable batteries for electric vehicles come from? That those batteries are powered by cobalt mined by workers laboring in slave-like conditions in the Democratic Republic of Congo. Women and children breathe that toxic dust."

"What do you think?"

Camden's mind was flooded with thoughts. He stared out the ceiling-to-floor windows as a dusky glow from the mountains snow filtered into the open living area.

"You wanted to tell me first before my boss did." He smiled.

"Yeah, man. I had to hold my tongue during those alcohol induced discussions we would have after rugby," Camden shook his head. "Especially on the injustice of labor practices within the mining world. You knew this article would hit my moral core."

Jackson smiled as he stood up and cleared the plates from the table. "Follow me. We have a lot to talk about and there is something you need to see."

The giant of a man, stepped into what appeared to be, a walk-in pantry in the kitchen. And then he vanished behind a door that slid open behind a shelf of canned goods. Camden approached as he saw him going down a set of stairs.

"Watch your head."

"You have a safe room?"

"Man cave," he said, "I showed you what my source gave me. How about your source, the woman?"

Camden walked around the 200 square foot room among computer monitors, shelves of food, a small shower and toilet tucked into the back corner, a large sink, and a solid wood bookcase with stacks of documents. He picked up a familiar photo of Jackson and himself in their rugby uniforms. Arms around their shoulders and huge grins on their muddy faces. As he set it back down, he noticed miscellaneous firepower lining one side in the corner of the room. Military lockers were stacked next to an old, well used couch near three large computer monitors on a desk.

"I never said she was a source." He mumbled. "And wait a minute? You are special ops with the military."

"Yep. Back to your source. You have always been a babe magnet, but this was planned. The timing, the mine, and that element. She is a source. It is obvious, now that I know you are FBI. You and this lady have something personal going on," he smirked. "But she is a source. Show me what you got from your lady friend. What was her name again?" he said as Camden slung his metal pelican case onto a worktable.

With a sly grin, he teased, "She does have magnificent red hair and the most seductive green eyes." He whistled as he pulled out a handful of classified documents. "I do not believe I mentioned her name." He handed the documents to Jackson as he sat down.

"Wowzer, your no name gal friend ain't no lab geek with an oil company. This is more than lab data with calculations and shit." He confirmed. "FBI is what I am assuming."

Camden looked into Jackson's eyes. "She is my handler." He paused.

"My first handler knew he had his recruit when he showed me a similar article you did just now." He reached into his wallet and unfolded a piece of yellowed paper.

"I carry the first few lyrics of a Zulu song by Hugh Masekela called Stimela. My first handler gave it to me. It reminds us of why we do what we do." He gave the faded yellow paper to his friend. "He was killed in the Congo two years ago helping a group of children escape from a mine."

Camden reflected on what he saw in Malawi. He could taste the bile in his mouth, when he remembered the images so many years ago, of men, women, and children, covered in dust, swinging heavy picking axes that weighed nearly as much as the human with those axes in their thin, hands.

Camden sat quietly as his friend read the few words. "I know about the coal trains crammed body to body of hundreds of people into dirty cars. Not unlike what happened to the Jewish people in Europe. They worked 16-hour days. Is that train still running from the surrounding countries, Namibia and Malawi? You were in Malawi." He stated as he handed the piece of paper back to Camden.

Camden sat quietly then nodded yes. "Keep it," Camden said. "Look up the song. The lyrics are powerful."

"There were indications you were not just a contractor. You have been working as a geologist and an undercover agent for the FBI." Jackson stared at his friend in disbelief. "I get the geologist gig but agent. Hell, you don't like guns. Do you even know how to shoot a gun?" he chuckled.

"Yep. I do." He replied with a half-cocked grin. "Here is what the FBI has on ARKose." Camden spread out more documents and photos. "Peiling's heritage is quite a story, but we believe she is North Korean, not Chinese. We need those fingerprints. With DOD and FBI this should be basic spy stuff 101. We do not believe ARKose is a Chinese-owned company but we are still searching the layers of shell companies. That guy there?" Camden pointed to the dark-skinned man wearing the pakol. "We suspect him of being the terrorist leader of a Pakistan Taliban offshoot group. But we have no concrete connection between ARKose and the group." Camden went quiet. "Daniel told me he was born in Pakistan but left when he was young, migrating to London. And yet we can't find any records of him. Coincidence? We don't know." He went quiet again. "Daniel is the connection but we have nothing on him."

Camden sat down. "So, my friend, let's talk about you and your team. I am guessing you never left the military."

He chuckled, looking at Camden. "Your handler did a search on me."

"She did but all she said was I should not worry about you and your wife."

"I need to be more careful," he mused. "I did leave the military, for a short period of time after Winter and I got married. Full-time geologist with the USGS. I was perfectly content until my commander came to see me one night. He handed me that article I gave you earlier."

"I lead an operation team much the same as the one I was

on," he contemplated. "More sophisticated in scope. Our team investigates the mining and transport of radioactive and dangerous reactive minerals. REEs were gaining interest among radical groups." He paused to take a breath. "Our mission involved tracking little-known mining companies that were purchasing low-value ore mines and using local labor – slaves – to transport the minerals to countries like North Korea, China, and Russia." Another pause. "My commander wanted me back because of a situation in Russia. Anyway, I said yes."

"So, when Stoney sold out to ARKose?" asked Camden.

"Nobody knew about ARKose until I showed my team your photos. We were aware of an unknown company that had invested in Stoney, but we couldn't identify the investor. Still can't. There was no suspicious activity to warrant military attention at that point. Stoney was just one of many mining operations in the State that piqued our interest." He replied. "But when I presented those pictures you gave me, some of them matched within several of our databases. However, there was no record of Peiling or Daniel. Like you said, they both are ghosts." He shook his head. "Like that third man in the photo."

He got up and walked to a nearby cabinet and grabbed two glasses by the sink. He poured the golden liquid from a bell-shaped glass bottle. "How about a brandy?"

"Hennessy. Nice. To old times." Camden clinked Jackson's glass.

In the darkness of the safe room, Camden and Jackson discussed strategy between the two agencies — the FBI and the DOD.

"I fly back to the mine in the morning. I assume there will be a series of meetings with your boss and my boss." Camden smiled.

The next morning, he waved good bye, as he watched Camden drive away, shortly before he left to his day job at the USGS.

*There is sufficiency in the world for man's
need but not for man's greed.*

—MOHANDAS K. GANDHI

CHAPTER 7

CAMDEN

IT WAS MID-SEPTEMBER — a month since he had seen Jackson. The birch and aspen trees had turned golden yellow and red. A bright contrast with the dark green spruce trees. He had just arrived in the Anchorage International Airport after four days on a remote unchartered island in the South Pacific. As he got out of his rental car, a bottle of scotch in his hand, he noticed Jackson had installed a gate and a sophisticated security system. The front door swung open as Waylon Jennings filled the air, as he walked up the stairs to the wide covered porch.

Noticing his friend's tanned face as he hugged Camden, he bellowed. "I see you got some sun."

"It was a nice break." He lied.

This time, when Jackson scanned Camden, it confirmed the presence of a listening device planted in Camden's phone. Rather than removing it, they used it to their advantage. They engaged in a jovial conversation, talking about football and country rock music, all while enjoying their scotch, Jackson explained that Winter was away on a weekend ski and ice climb with her friends.

"The pregame is on in a few minutes. Seahawks are predicted

42

to win but the Broncos have a talented new quarter back. Should be a close match up."

"The game is in Seattle, right?" He asked as he turned the large screen television.

"Yep. Should be a good one." Jackson winked.

After a dinner of grilled halibut and local veggies, they moved to the living room as the darkness enveloped the room. Jackson lit the soapstone fireplace as he spread out a series of photos on the carved wood and black metallic steel coffee table. As they conversed quietly about the game, with one of them yelling about a missed catch by a Seahawk running back or an offsides slam by a Bronco linebacker, he wrote notes by each photo.

At half-time, he scribbled one gram of 87, on a piece of note-paper by one of the photos showing only blue violet ocean with scattered white caps.

Jackson crossed his arms, sat back in the couch, and stared not saying a word.

As he stood up he dropped his glass. "Oops, sorry about that. This scotch went down way too smooth my friend. I had a few Singapore slings while on vacation but man, it appears I can't handle the booze anymore," he yawned. "I am exhausted after a long flight from Australia."

"Don't worry about the glass. Australia? What were you doing there? I assumed you went to Hawaii for a vacation. Was your gal friend with you? Pleasure by chance?"

"Nah. This was mostly business. A potential client who owns a mine north of Perth. But I did take advantage of the weather and do some fishing."

Jackson got up and pointed to the pantry door while turn-ing on the faucet. "You know where the spare room is, go crash. I'll clean up. The hawks are cleaning up the broncs but I think I will stick it out to the end. When do you have to head back to the mine?"

"Late shuttle tomorrow afternoon. Thanks, Jackson." He replied as he headed to the safe room.

Into the wee hours of the morning, huddled in the safe room, the two geologists analyzed the data that Camden had provided from the trip to the South Pacific.

"After I stabilized nearly 3 grams of the francium, ARKose planned a test of the element first to ensure, it can be transported and second, what it can do in the sense of releasing energy."

He sat down at Jackson's computer and tapped some keys.

"This is one of the many islands of Tonga, east of Australia, in the South Pacific where the Hunga Tonga and the Hunga Ha'apai volcano at one time towered above the waves as a pair of narrow rocky isles. In 2014, an eruption built a third island that connected the three rocks into one landmass and the island grew as rock and ash built new land." He pointed to the image on the bottom as he explained the process of how they tested francium using a highly precise laser to drill a shaft 2 miles below the sea water to a thrust fault near their target, a volcanic island.

"Before he went to the ARKose mine," he explained. "Shing was on this isolated island at a small facility to test the robot and the laser." He paused. "With less than one gram of element 87 contained within a small robot, the robot was intentionally destroyed, allowing water to contact the element. We were over 500 miles away."

"Shing's laser?" Jackson asked.

"Yeah. He was in the South Pacific before he spent the last month drilling a channel with the laser at the ARKose mine. This was how ARKose found the vein that contained twenty times more francium than anywhere in the world. He also designed the robot." He pulled up another image.

"This is the result," He pulled up a recent image. "Less than one gram destroyed the volcano and the island, leaving those small outcrops of rock visible just beneath the waves."

"Holy shit, Camden, you can't go back. It's too dangerous," Jackson said. "That island in the South Pacific was a test of things to come. They obliterated the volcanos. You were 500 miles away? Can, you imagine if the target was closer?"

"You sound like my handler."

"She's right, Camden. We've got enough. "Three volcanoes are underwater because of francium. I think it is time for you to pull out of this."

"I need to find out what the real target is. The FBI has spent over a year planning my infiltration into ARKose. Once we have the intel on who and why, then I'm out. Otherwise, they could go underground, and we'll never have those answers." He sat back in his chair with arms crossed. "This time they used francium to blow something up. The next time? It won't be some remote rock in the middle of the ocean."

"Damn it." Jackson shrugged. "Anchorage sits on two thrust faults. The mine is across the inlet from one of the most strategic military bases on this continent. JBER. Remember Russia is just right over there?" He grimaced. "Seriously. JBER, Greely and Richardson could be blown up with element 87."

"For now, we assume the bases are the target. Any information on our 3 ghosts?"

Jackson rubbed his face and shook his head no as he explained no finger prints matched for Peiling or Daniel. "We have not found any substantial lead and that is with both our agencies working on this."

"There is no tie to ARKose for destruction of those islands. You know, if anything Shing or me could easily be set up for that disaster. ARKose — Peiling and Daniel would walk away."

"Military is aware of the potential threat by ARKose to our National Security. After this explosion in the south pacific? We know it was not a natural occurrence. My team will have all hands on high alert." Jackson swallowed. "We don't know when or why but we know the what."

"Who is the who, Jackson," he pointed to the images. "Those waters are not considered a US territory. Unless you have something that links them directly to the explosion, I am not ready to pull out. For our benefit of where we stand, let's say ARKose admits they blew up those rocks. So what? No one was killed. They could explain the whole thing away as a malfunction of a new type of robotic laser for mining the ocean floor. No permits are required. It was in international waters. It would be a solid year lost except for one fact that we now know. They have a dangerous element that someone, if not me, will stabilize."

"Then we'll track you. Take it or you're not going back. The bug we found in your phone proves they're suspicious."

"I believe you just gave me an order, friend?"

Jackson shrugged and nodded his head, chewing on a pencil.

"My handler said the same thing. I have had a tracker and a listening detection device on me since I returned this morning." He smiled. "She is taking me caribou hunting tomorrow across the Inlet. The pilot will be FBI and will drop me off at the mine site. She wants a look at the operation."

"I agree with this strategy. I look forward to meeting this lady."

"Yeah well, if we see anything unusual, she will pull the plug. We need intel on who is funding this operation, Jackson. If she pulls me out tomorrow, all of this might be for not." Another pause as he ran his hands through his hair. "If I stay, I cannot stall the stabilization process any longer. The first phase will be complete when I arrive. There will be more to process but, over ten grams will be ready with another ten grams being processed." He crossed his arms. "My next step is to do some creative manipulation of element 87."

"You have a process to do that? To keep it from exploding."

He discussed his hypothesis is disrupting the atoms from exploding with contact to moisture using a microbe. With Jackson's help, he felt more confident that his process could work.

Early the next morning, he turned and gave a thumbs up to Jackson before getting into his rental car.

"Shel, I am just leaving Jackson's. I should be at the rental car drop off at the airport in 20 minutes. See you there." As he left a voicemail, he contemplated the plan she had proposed. "A caribou hunt. What the hell do I know about hunting caribou." He said to himself.

Thirty minutes later they were boarding a float plane from Lake Hood. Shelby introduced the pilot as he went through the safety precautions and soon, they were flying over gray waters of Cook Inlet heading west to the Alaska Range. The pilot was a seasoned navy pilot before joining the FBI ten years previous. Eight of those years flying in Alaska and overseas missions.

"Weather is building out of the west so be prepared for a bumpy ride." He announced.

Chapter 8

Shelby

S TARING OUT THE plane's window, she noted the stark contrast of the bright red leaves of the arctic bearberry against the blanket of bright green heather on the treeless mountains. A sure sign of an Alaskan winter approaching.

The pilot buzzed the mining camp 100 feet below as he rolled the red and white Cessna 206 while snapping photos of the mine site from a built-in camera on the lower right wing. Sitting in the passenger side, she clicked her headset asking the pilot to get close-ups of the drill site. He nodded while glancing at the map on his lap and banked the plane.

Camden was quiet with his eyes focused on Shelby as the pilot pointed to an oblong dull brown metal tote in the one-oh clock position. Daniel, with a keen sense of where to drill for the largest vein of francium, had directed Shing where to use his powerful laser to drill a shaft deep into the earth's mantle. She turned her head to look back at Camden as he nodded his head. This time with a smile. She smiled back and looked through the front window of the small plane. She knew Camden was not happy with her plan, especially when she trumped him with the chain of command remark.

After a few more clicks of the camera, the pilot circled while relaying the call letters of the plane to a security guard at the mine informing him that they were landing on the nearby lake. As they flew low over the lake, she saw the reflection of the plane; as smooth as looking at a mirror. The pilot flew into the wind using maximum flaps just enough to avoid a full stall, maintaining a slightly above normal attitude of the nose as the floats skimmed the water. With a turn of the rudder, the pilot delicately manipulated the allerions, the moveable flaps of the wing tips and glided the plane next to a small pier where a six wheeled, fat tire tundra vehicle was waiting. The driver remained in the open vehicle, smoking a cigarette. As Shelby and Camden jumped out, the pilot grabbed Camden's bags and set them on the pier, when a mayday call was heard on the planes radio. The pilot immediately jumped in as the voice on the other end repeated the mayday. There was an accident at a nearby hunting camp and they were in need of immediate assistance of a float plane. The pilot was the closest. With a nod of her head, Shelby understood he would let camp security know his ETA when he could pick her up.

As they got into the tundra vehicle, their driver mumbled that it was hunting season and this was a normal event in bush life. He looked at Camden and relayed the message that Daniel was waiting in the mess hall as he turned the switch of the vehicle. Turning his head towards Camden, he added that the man was not happy with the surprise visit of a guest.

"How about I get acquainted with Daniel and you go unload your gear," she arched her eyebrow at Camden. "Join us when you are finished."

Camden watched her disappear into the mess tent as he walked to his office, making a stop first at Daniel's office. Once, inside he glanced at the neatly stacked papers and the perfectly sharpened pencil atop a notebook on Daniel's glossy desk. His eye caught the scribble of three sets of numbers on the notebook paper. Camden grabbed his own notebook from his rucksack and wrote the three numbers down. He then reached into the hidden pocket of his pack and pulled out his i-phone and took a picture. After leaving his bags in his room, he entered the mess tent and saw Shelby, holding a steaming cup of coffee, in what appeared to be a deep conversation with Daniel as he walked to their table.

"Oh, Camden," she sipped her coffee. "I didn't see you. Daniel and I were talking about the chemical components of the rock samples they are finding here."

"An enlightening conversation" the man remarked. "However, you should have let me know about your planned arrival."

"Sorry about that, Daniel," Camden sat down. "It was unexpected. Last minute trip and since we were only thirty minutes flying time from here it was a great opportunity to see more of this area."

"There are protocols but it is refreshing to discuss what we are finding with a chemist familiar with the geology of this area. Shelby provided me with a stimulating conversation on her background and refraction of granitic rock that they use in the drilling of oil."

"She does have an expertise in that aspect of geology in Alaska." He smiled. "It won't happen again, Daniel."

"No, it won't," Daniel admonished. "I mean considering the news. Amidst the arrival of the unexpected, but delightful, company," he nodded at Shelby. "I forgot to mention that Peiling has found an incredible facility." Daniel's eyes conveyed the message with a smug grin. "ARKose wants us out of here by tomorrow. There is lots to do, Camden. You will need to secure the element."

Daniel stood up, nodded to Shelby and excused himself.

Camden reached down and took an envelope out of his rucksack along with his notebook. He tore a page from his notebook, slipped it into the envelope and gave it to Shelby.

"You're coming back to Anchorage with me," she whispered. "If they are closing this facility, you are done here, Camden."

He shook his head, touching her hand resting on the table. "No, Shel. This is the next step. We are wrong about their intention of destroying the military base here. If they are closing camp, that means it is not the military installation in their crossfire. If I don't go with them, we will lose them. I need to finish this." He slipped the envelope under her hand. "Find out what these numbers are. They are our first clue as to what ARKose intends to do with the element and that laser. The three sets of numbers appear to be latitude and longitude. Three locations that are not in Alaska much less North America. The envelope is addressed to my mom, just in case someone asks. As soon as you are on the plane find out where those locations are. And one other thing, the guy that picked us up at the lake? I have never seen him before. Why bring in someone new if the camp is closing?"

"Then damn it Camden," she grabbed his arm. "We have them if those numbers represent their targets. You are coming back with me."

And then the tent grew dark and shook as a gust of wind slammed the heavy, insulated material as if it was built out of paper. A few seconds later a piercing snap of light ignited the darkness followed by a thunderous boom a few seconds later. She felt as if she was sealed in a drum as hail pounded the tent. She clasped her ears when Camden wrapped his arms around her as the air temperature dropped. Two guys ran into the tent as one yelled to get the heat on while the other warmed his hands hugging a hot mug of coffee. Both looked like drowned rats. And then the generator went dead.

Standing in the dark she heard one guy yell shit as she heard things fall off a table and onto the wooden floor. The other guy screamed 'where is that damn flashlight! Fuck I just smashed my knee.'

"Come on," Camden said as another crack and pop exploded outside the tent. The inside of the tent lit up for a brief second. "We will run to my office."

Shelby put her hood up on her fall parka as thunder boomed. "That was three seconds Camden. Less than a half mile away."

Standing water covered the compact ground as rain and hail pelted her coat. Her skin stung when she glanced upward to see where they were running towards. The sky was black and the visibility was difficult to see anything a few inches in front of her face. "Camden?" She yelled.

"Here," he grabbed her shoulder and pushed her into the open door of the building where his office was. "The fuel stove is working on manual but not the fan."

A few minutes later Daniel rushed through the door, soaked and visibly shivering. He explained the pilot is stuck in Dillingham and will not be returning until the storm blows over.

"How long?" She asked.

"Tomorrow mid-morning. Maybe. It is a huge storm coming out of the southeast. Air traffic is stalled."

"Hunting Season." She cocked her head, looking at Camden. "During 9/11 all aircraft was grounded including air charters flying hunters in and out of hunting camps. The sky around Anchorage was silent. Hunters had no idea what was going on because the weather was clear and sunny." She warmed her hands standing as close to the stove as she dared. "Looks like none of us are going anywhere."

Camden understood the meaning of her statement. "You will be fine here, Shelby. I need to go to the core room. Generator?" He glanced at Daniel.

"It will be up soon. The static energy from the lightning caused it to short. The electronic key code switches to battery power when there is no electricity from the generator. The outside door will need your badge but the interior doors will be open."

Camden nodded at Shelby as he walked back out into the sleet and darkness.

A hour later, the generator had been restored as Shelby snuggled next to Camden in the single bed. The dormitory room was one of several in a series of metal totes that were designed to be shipped individually and then sealed together. Smaller camps were temporary but the larger mining camps such as this one, were more or less, permanent features in the remote landscape in bush Alaska.

"What were you and Daniel talking about before I walked in?"

"I asked him about his story. Where he from, you know, small talk." She whispered. "Daniel said he was born in Pakistan but his Aunt smuggled him to England at the age of 8. Apparently, his father was a nasty fellow in the Taliban. When I asked him about his mother, he said she died. It was strange." She bit her lip, furrowing her eyebrows. "His demeanor, the pitch of his voice, it was as if he were in a trance."

"A trance?"

"Like he was hypnotized. His pupils got larger," she whispered. "He is an odd man, but brilliant. You know he studied at Oxford when he was 16 years old? His mother was a professor at the University before she died. That is an odd combination for a woman in Pakistan."

"How so?"

"She was a mother and educated - professor, and married to someone in the Taliban. It makes me wonder what happened."

Camden knew when she bit her lip and furrowed her brows she was strategizing.

"In the morning, you are leaving with me when the pilot returns, Camden. Did you check the locations?"

"I couldn't, there is no internet. We now have power but no internet and no cell service. Those locations might not have anything to do with ARKose. Hell, they could be anything; drill locations, the facility or…"

"Targets," Shelby interrupted. "Three separate areas. Three different latitude and longitude locations."

"Let's wait until we find out more in the morning. Meantime…"

The hail had switched to rain sometime during the long, dark night but the wind was relentless. The morning sky was dark but the wind was lighter and the rain was intermittent, but the ceiling was low.

"Oh my god," Shelby stopped and took a deep inhale as she entered the mess tent. "Pancakes and bacon. I am starving." She saw Daniel and walked towards him as Camden got two coffees.

"Shelby your pilot has gone back to Kenai. Anchorage is shut down and the ceiling is not lifting between here and Dillingham. There is an opening right now but it is closing fast and he needs to get back to home base." Daniel said as he was finishing his breakfast. "My pilot has informed me that there is a window of good visibility around 2 pm that he is estimating he can land here. There is a good chance he can get into Anchorage to drop you off."

"Well, if he can't, if you are in need of a chemical engineer, I am rather bored with my current job at the oil company analyzing oil samples." She half-joked as Camden arrived with coffee.

"What is going on? Chatter from the kitchen said Anchorage is socked in."

"Yep. My plane left for Kenai from Dillingham. Apparently, it is a very low ceiling right now from Dillingham to here as well as to Anchorage. Only jets are landing and taking off from International. Daniel, however, did offer me a ride to Anchorage on the ARKose jet that will be arriving here at 2 pm." Shelby sipped her coffee. "I am ready for some pancakes and bacon. Camden?"

Camden went quiet as he stared at her. "Go ahead, Shel. I want to talk to Daniel."

"We have lots to do Camden before that jet arrives. There is a narrow window and we need to secure all the francium, the stabilized and the raw form."

"I am aware of that, Daniel. I have all the core samples loaded and ready to go. The stabilized francium is also secure. I was afraid when the generator shut down last night the stabilization process that I started before I left a couple of days ago would have been affected."

"And?"

"It was finished and it is secured in a lead box along with the other francium. There are 10 grams in that box. Well, 9.5 grams to be exact." Camden drained his coffee. "I estimate there is another 20 grams in the rock core samples that can be stabilized." Camden rubbed his face. "This amount of raw francium in the natural state is mind blowing. Once it is stabilized, it will literally shake up the mining community." Camden took another sip of his coffee as he stood up. "I need food," as he started to turn away, he stopped. "Where is the new location, Daniel?"

"Peiling is keeping it quiet."

"Why the rush? Especially, with this weather. Why risk it?"

"You know as much as I do. I am only following Peiling's orders. She wants this place buttoned up. The weather is our problem to deal with." Daniel wiped his mouth and stood up. "When we get everything secured and, on the jet, we will have a better idea of our flight path. Right now," Daniel looked at his watch. "I have lots to do. We will leave the remaining crew here. They will secure the site and once the weather clears in Anchorage, they can take the charter back to Merrill Field. If Shelby wants to stay here, she can but the weather does not look good all week. First-priority on that charter is for ARKose crew." He started to walk away. "Know this, if Peiling finds out we allowed a stranger in this camp, Camden. Well, if it was up to her, she would leave your girlfriend here."

"And if that happens, I will stay with my girlfriend and you guys can find someone else to stabilize the rest of element 87." He mumbled.

"What was that about?" She asked as she sat at the table.

"Nothing. He didn't even hear me."

"Go get food."

The activity at the mine was buzzing with activity as winds

gusted and rain fell. Crew members were transporting the rock cores and samples to a staging area within a tote at the landing strip. Much of the ground was supersaturated with the heavy rainfall, which is one of the advantages of the large tundra vehicles as opposed to a truck.

While sipping her coffee, in the warmth of the mess tent, she found out the cook's brother was the pilot for the charter flight company that transported the crew and supplies back and forth from Merrill Field. She remembered Camden talking about a Yupik pilot he flew with. After another round of pancakes, she readdressed the letter Camden gave her, and when the cook grabbed a cup of coffee, she asked him to join her.

"Please, could you or your brother mail this for me when you get to Anchorage? Just in case I don't make it to Anchorage any time soon." She said as she gently touched his hand. And of course, he would, she thought. The indigenous peoples of Alaska understood the need of community, especially in bad weather.

He would keep her letter safe and make sure his brother would mail it if he was not on the first plane out of the field camp. She explained, with watery eyes, she was concerned for her parents, as they expected her back yesterday from her caribou hunt. Her father had been having heart issues and she hoped this would not aggravate it.

As the ceiling lifted slightly, a sleek, Lear jet landed at precisely 2 pm. The crew quickly loaded the rocks as Camden, Shelby, and Daniel boarded the plane. Shelby looked out the jet window but all she saw was the swirling fog as the jet gained altitude. The pilot announced they were heading west as the weather had once again turned tumultuous. The flight path would take them over Nome and into Russian airspace.

"Well, it appears neither of us are going back to Anchorage." She smiled as she grabbed Camden's hand with hers.

"Damn it, Irish," Camden shook his head. "This is quite a coincidence you being on this jet."

"I do have my ways, Camden."

"I swear, sometimes I wonder about your ways."

"It was a bit difficult, I admit. Controlling the weather takes a spell of considerable focus." She smiled. "Did I tell you that my great, great grandmother was considered an Irish witch? She was called a Callieach."

"No. I don't recall you ever mentioning that you have witch blood." He closed his eyes. "Sometimes, I swear, Irish, you never stop surprising me."

One day later, shielding their eyes from the bright morning sun, they stepped out of the jet in Southern China. As she struggled to breathe due to the scarce oxygen, he recognized the landscape. Two sets of symbols: one in Chinese with angles and straight lines 日喀则 and the other in Tibetan with curves གཞིས་ཀ་རྩེ་. They were at Shigatse Peace Airport. Camden focused on the mental map he had developed during his month in the vast, windswept plains of the Tibetan plateau two decades earlier.

CHAPTER 9

SAM

SHEETROCK STILL CLUNG to the steel beam bones of the shattered buildings like the dry skin of a corpse. Down was now up, and up was now sideways, and there was nothing left of the crumbled structures that made any architectural sense.

As if on cue, the left wing of the Alaska Airlines 737 Max dipped slightly. She felt goosebumps on her arms as Sleeping Lady appeared and then disappeared from her window as the plane banked steeply right, allowing a full view of the wide, churning gray waters of the Cook Inlet. And the remains of the City she once knew. With her forehead pressed against the plane's window she heard passengers gasp. Two of the three mustard-colored towers of the Hotel Captain Cook had been turned to rubble. Only the shortest and the oldest of the towers remained.

It was early September. Almost a week had passed since the 8.5 magnitude earthquake shook Anchorage, killing hundreds, including three of her friends, who were lost in the thirty-foot swirling water of the tsunamis.

The plane shuddered, rocking side to side, as she gripped the armrest of the empty middle seat. She held her breath, and then the wheels landed and the brakes grabbed, pressing the passengers forward as the plane slowed.

She combed her messy, sun-streaked hair with slender tanned fingers with unadorned short nails. With a deep inhale through her nose and a slow exhale out her mouth, she wiped her tears, grabbed her old purple duffel, and followed the half-full plane of passengers walk down the stairs onto the tarmac. Stopping briefly, she felt the cool September air on her face. Then, with a steady and determined stride, she searched for familiar faces in the crowd.

Winter, Jackson's wife, ran towards her with outstretched arms, wearing her usual brilliant purple wool cap. Taller than Sam at 5 foot 7 inches, her plump lips were framed with dimpled cheeks. Her lavender and teal fleece kuspuk camouflaged her muscular body, but her waist long purple streaked hair flowed out from under her beanie. She kissed Sam's cheek and hugged her tightly.

"Where is Jackson?"

"He's with the truck. It's hard to find a place to park these days," Winter said, as she looped her arm through Sam's. Jackson was riding home from work on his bike when the earth shook, throwing him onto the asphalt. His injuries were minor except for a head contusion and a slight concussion.

"How's his concussion?"

"It could have been much worse if his head wasn't as hard as a boulder."

Staring at the partially collapsed parking garage, she was speechless. Large chunks of cement were piled into slabs of pyramids, as if marking a place of time now gone. Black rebar protruded from the ground like daggers.

"The Airport and downtown took a heavy hit. Not surprising." Winter shook her head.

"No, not surprising. How quickly the '64 quake was forgotten. Only the oldest and the shortest of the three towers of the Captain Cook survived this one."

And then she heard her name as Jackson stepped out of his truck. She stood for a second and then quickened her pace towards the giant of a man. He smothered her in his long, brawny arms, and kissed her face. She saw the pink puffy skin on his forehead where his helmet had met the pavement.

"Conversation piece," he chuckled as he touched his forehead. He opened the door for her as Winter sat in the front passenger seat. "Glad to have you home, Sam."

Tossing her duffel into the backseat, she jumped into the back seat.

"The two earthquakes were not normal Sam," he muttered, chewing on a toothpick as he maneuvered the truck through the destruction of what used to be the International Airport Avenue.

"Jackson, you are dealing with a lot right now."

No doubt her friend was still in shock at the disappearance of his twin, Jacob during the tsunami that struck Prince William Sound.

"The seismograph is not wrong, Sam."

"What do you mean two earthquakes?"

"One epicenter near Tyonek causing a tsunami in Cook Inlet. The second near Whittier causing a tsunami in Prince William Sound. Both shallow, less than 3 miles deep and both hitting at the same time. No warning," Jackson paused. "We confirmed there were two epicenters not one. At first, because they were at the same time, we assumed there was a primary epicenter or two scattered centers with distinct areas of major impacts."

After being friends for almost two decades, she understood Jackson well enough to know he was holding back on the details about the earthquakes but he also was mourning the loss of his twin. She noticed a small black device the size of a TV remote in Winter's hand when she showed it to Jackson. It had a blinking green light.

"What is...?"

Winter interjected her. "When is Jon arriving?"

She noticed Jackson looking at her through the rear-view mirror.

"He's hoping to be here a day or two before the wake. He was ready to cancel an important meeting with the leaders of the local tribe I was working with so he could fly with me, but I said no."

Sam caught the grin on Jackson's face. Everyone knew Sam hated to fly and Jon had the permanent indentions in his arm to prove it.

"ARKose. Tell me about this mining company. Jon has never heard of them."

"That is something to ponder. Considering that is your husband's business to know who and what these small mining companies are doing. Jon's company, LUNA Inc is well known around the world and yet no one has heard of ARKose. Including my world-renowned geochemist friend who was working there on contract. He couldn't tell me the details because of the NDA, but he was working with a rare earth element that was highly volatile and dangerous. He was very concerned the last time I saw him." Jackson was quiet. "And then shortly after he returned to the mine, southcentral Alaska was hit not with one, but with two powerful earthquakes—simultaneously. Two earthquakes at the same time with precision. That is not geologically possible."

Winter turned in the passenger seat to face Sam. "Any news about Shelby?"

"No news. Her mom believes Shel is still alive. Her brother is not giving up. He has been hounding the coast guard, calling every flight charter company, hospitals and…" She could not say the word. "Despite being deaf, he is a bulldog in protecting and now, finding his older sis."

"I remember your stories about you and Shelby taking sign language to communicate with him. And for other things." Winter grinned.

"Yes. He is an amazing and accomplished advocacy lawyer. They refuse to give up until they find her."

She told them about the conversation she had when Shelby's mom called her. Her heart skipped a beat as she listened to the familiar soft voice with the Irish dialect of her best friend's mother.

"It's been a week since the earthquake." Jackson stated.

"Yeah, but she is a mother without closure." Winter looked at Jackson shaking her head.

She thought of the word Jackson used to describe the earthquakes. Two earthquakes that were not caused by nature — their strike was an act of precision.

"You never did tell me what fault the epicenter was for the Cook Inlet quake, Jackson."

"Castle Mountain Fault. Not far from your old stomping grounds, Sam. The other was…"

Jackson looked at Winter and shrugged. "The tsunami in Whittier was triggered by the landslide in the Barry Arm fjord." He paused. "With precision."

"That is the second time you have mentioned the word precision when talking about the earthquakes. What the hell does that mean? I don't understand. I thought the earthquake caused the landslide which caused the big wave in Whittier," she said. "I've lived amongst earthquake and tsunami warnings all my life, only to find out I have no clue what any of this means."

Jackson explained his hypothesis. "We believe ARKose intentionally used an explosive, radioactive, rare-earth element to target the thrust-faults beneath Cook Inlet and Prince William Sound. The impact caused the two earthquakes and the resulting tsunami in each body of water."

Radioactive. She contemplated what her friend was telling her as she stared out the truck's window. Nothing was recognizable. One of the oldest restaurants in mid-town, the Long Horn was a rubble of red wood. The sign was still laying in the moonscape of what used to be the parking lot. Block after block was rubble. The famous Peanut Farm was now two buildings; split down the center with one of them tipping into Campbell Creek. Bar stools, the remains of a pool table and a juke box were scattered among the cement debris.

"Radioactive. What the hell does that mean? There is no mention of radiation in the news. I see no one in Haz mat suits."

"No radiation leaked to the surface. It could have but it didn't. That was not the intent." He quieted. "This time. The amount of radiation from the explosion of the element was contained below ground. The intent was the earthquakes themselves, to do damage."

"Sam, we will explain it. I promise." Winter touched Sam's right hand, which clenched the cushion of her headrest.

"At least the Bush Company looks normal and in one piece. And busy for this time of day." She said. "Remember that retirement party we went to? Oh, man, Shelby and I had more fun watching you guys' flirt with the dancers."

"Logan, Shelby, Jacob and you. I remember that night well considering how much alcohol was imbibed," Jackson squeezed Winter's hand. "That was before I met Winter." He shook his head.

"Wasn't that the party where Shelby introduced you to Logan?" Winter asked.

"That it was. Shelby was a biochemical engineer and Logan a mechanical engineer for the same oil company."

"And Logan introduced you to me." Jackson interjected. "He was a good friend. I miss him every day, Sam."

Winter saw the tears running down Sam's cheeks. "Did you know they now have male dancers?"

"Oh my god, are you kidding? Well, the demographics are changing from the days of the pipeline era. We need to go. You do owe me a bachelorette party."

"We will and I do. That is a promise." Winter nodded with a broad grin showing her dimpled cheeks. "With Shelby."

"A mining company did this?" She whispered. "300 innocent people killed. All this chaos."

"Yes. And before you ask…"

"Why?"

"We do not know that yet." Winter answered.

Jackson looked at Winter as she nodded. "Jacob worried about the rapid change of Alaska's glaciers in the Sound. He was studying the Barry Arm because of a potential landslide from the remaining debris as the glacier receded. According to the sensors in the area, the landslide was stable. However, there had been an anonymous call from a boater…"

"So that was why he was in the Sound?"

"Yes." Jackson answered.

"How can a landslide be stable? I thought a landslide means well, the land slides."

"The Barry Arm landslide is not a normal landslide. The technical term is kite. It is the material left after the glacier has melted. It can creep a few centimeters at a time or not at all. It's movement is the result of the instability of the weight from the glacier. If there is a sudden melting of the ice, that can cause vibrations within the mountain and then cause the land to slide."

Winter interrupted, "And there was not just one, but three calls to the office."

Jackson nodded. "Three callers who reported rock and debris falling into the Sound from Barry Arm. You know how that works, Sam. If a federal agency receives a report that there is a dangerous situation from a constituent, bogus or not, we check it out. Jacob said the sensors showed nothing. No movement."

Winter shook her head as Jackson touched her hand.

After thirty minutes of maneuvering around broken cement, and giant sink holes in the asphalt it was a welcome sight to get off the main streets of Anchorage and start climbing up the forested outskirts of the City.

"And Jacob's boat?"

"The Heron just um, disappeared. No one has found the boat."

He looked at Winter. "You know Jacob, any chance to get on the water. The anonymous calls about debris with no sensor movement was all it took to get him out there. He was doing research using a new type of laser to detect melting ice in Blackstone."

"And then the earth shook." Winter interjected.

"And then the earth shook." Jackson looked at Winter.

Silence filled the vehicle as she bit her lip.

"ARKose intentionally triggered a quake in the Sound and the Cook Inlet using what was it called?"

"Francium. The 87th element on the periodic table. Element 87 is a radioactive and highly unstable rare earth element. Camden was responsible for stabilizing francium. That is his expertise."

"Camden. Your friend. Camden.?" She paused, thinking. "Wait a minute, he was the cute babe magnet. He would always get the women and you guys played rugby together. That Camden?"

"Yes, that Camden. He got the contract to do this work. But he didn't always get the ladies."

"He helped ARKose do this?" Her voice raised an octave or two.

"No. Oh my God, no. He figured something was up. That's when he came to me for help."

She rubbed her eyes, looking at the scenery as the truck climbed the upper hillside area in the Chugach Mountains. And then she saw the elementary school she and Shelby attended. She smiled as she remembered Shelby — the tall, gangly girl who looked like a stork — long, pale skinny legs and knobby knees. And feet the size of snowshoes. The local bully was making fun of the girl until Sam, with her right hand clenched in a tight fist walked up to the kid, who stood at least a head taller than she. The boy turned and ran.

"You okay, Sam?" Winter asked.

"Yes. A lot to take in. Why did the sensors not go off and yet, debris was falling into the Sound? None of it makes sense. Was there a small shaker before the 8.5?"

"It doesn't make sense because there was no debris falling into the Sound. The anonymous reports about rock debris causing huge waves that would sink a small boat, were lies."

Then the device in Winter's hand beeped as she placed her index finger to Jackson's lips and shook her head no. Then she wrote on a notepad: We Are Being Listened To.

Who the hell would be listening? She shook her head and stared out the window.

"I called Shelby's mom when I landed. She has no other information other than Shelby was hunting with this guy near Tyonek. She didn't know his name." She took a deep breath, looking at the spruce forest as the road snaked its way up the mountain. "The Coast Guard found their float plane and by the looks of it, they were taking off when it got hit by the wave in the Cook Inlet. They found what was left of the plane in some spruce trees, minus a wing and the tail."

There was little recognition of where she was as they drove from the airport through the city. The destruction was everywhere with slabs of broken asphalt in places it shouldn't be and buildings crumbled with large gaps where windows should be.

But here in the forest among the solid rock of the Chugach Mountains everything seemed normal. She could pretend the earthquake was nothing more than a nightmare.

"Home, Sam." Winter said as Jackson turned the truck off.

"Wow. This front gate is new. And impressive. A Winter design no doubt. So clever."

"Thank you."

The gate design was made of bronze and black metal with a silhouette of the Sleeping Lady. Along the lower part of the mountain were trees and above it all was the midnight sun.

"Look close, Sam." Winter motioned.

Sam walked closer and touched the cool metal. "You remembered?"

Winter nodded as Sam hugged her and looked at the artwork.

There on the mountain was a wolf howling at the midnight sun. She thought back to that day.

One night, with a few too many glasses of wine, Sam told Winter about the snowmachine fiasco with Shelby when they were 16. Now, this memory was forged in metal, a gate welcoming all. A vision that had been haunting her dreams since Shelby's mom called and told her Shelby was missing.

"Welcome home, Sam," Jackson stood on the front porch looking at his friend and his wife, walking from the gate to the home he built — steel, wood, and glass nestled on ten acres amongst the spruce trees. Jackson designed his house to withstand 120 mph winds and the roof to support 20 pounds of snow per cubic foot. His expertise in earthquakes also guided his design to build a home capable of surviving an earthquake with a magnitude of 9.5.

He squeezed her hand as she stepped through the front door into the arctic entry, the Alaskan version of the foyer. She instantly felt the warmth on her cheeks from the custom blue soapstone fireplace framed with large river rock from floor to the fourteen-foot ceiling, hand collected from Quartz creek. A carved bronze mantel glimmered against the rock wall. Rough-cut wooden beams were left open across the width of the house.

Home, she thought as she scanned the interior of the open room with the deep rich wood, the massive windows of glass, and sculptured metal of bronze and steel. It was designed so the natural world outside of the home would feel as though it was inside.

Toklat, the golden retriever-Bernese Mountain dog cross, who was sleeping in front of the fireplace, lifted her head and thumped her tail when they walked into the great room.

"Is that all I get ol' lady?" She knelt next to the brown, black and golden mass of fur, kissing her gray muzzle. Winter rescued her when she was a pup thirteen years ago.

"Alexa, Spotify playlist fifteen!" Jackson yelled as he and Winter were in the kitchen. Rock and roll filled the silence.

She zeroed in on the several pictures on the bronze mantel, picking up a black metal frame with figurines cut out of the metal, one of the many creations by Winter. She touched the faces looking back at her. Logan, Shelby, Jackson, and Jacob. With sweat-drenched shirts they had their arms around each other with smiles on red-tinged faces. In the background were layers of mountains and blue sky against the brilliant white ground. They had spent the day back country skiing on King Mountain in the Chugach Mountains near Chickaloon. She gently placed the frame back on the mantel and wandered to another.

A photo of Winter and Jackson at their wedding. Winter wore a sleek, ivory satin knee-length sheath with Jackson dressed in a casual linen shirt and pants. They were standing in the sand barefoot, with a bright red sun behind them, as they kissed. Waves, hearts, and mountains were carved in the bronze frame with a date and their names. It made her smile as she remembered the ceremony. She smiled as she recalled the name, she called their ceremony. Winter on the Beach.

As Jackson silently crept up behind her, she jumped.

"Good times," Jackson had brought her a large cup of steaming coffee, with a slather of milky foam and a swirl of cinnamon and sugar on top. Her favorite.

"A room full of memories, love, and happiness." She took a long sip, licking the froth from her upper lip. "Now what?"

He cocked his head, and she followed him and Toklat up the narrow black steel staircase. Sam stopped as she stepped onto the plank floor, noticing that the walls were covered with maps and diagrams. Three whiteboards had calculations and symbols she did not recognize.

"What is all this?" she said as she turned around.

"We need tell you something, Sam. And don't freak out." Jackson said.

"Freak out! Of course, I will freak out. That is what I do."

Winter disappeared down the small hallway that led to a guest bedroom and bath. When she came back, she was not alone.

"What the hell?" She ran to Jacob and he wrapped his arms around her. "You are real?" She pinched his arms and touched his hands.

No words formed putting her hands to her mouth. She could feel the warmth of his touch as Toklat whined, thumping her tail.

"Sam," Jackson said, breaking the silence in a hushed voice. "We could not risk telling you in the truck. I almost did before Winter gave me the stink eye." Jackson rubbed his face, before running his hand through his hair, something he always did when he was nervous.

"Um, could you add a finger of scotch to this coffee? Forget that, could you bring me a scotch, two fingers, no coffee."

Jackson saw Sam's hazel eyes change from less brown to greener. A sign that her temper was starting to boil.

"Sam, we decided to keep Jacob's sudden rise from the dead a secret."

"You couldn't trust me?"

Winter gave Sam a glass of the golden liquid as she whispered in her ear. "Remember, whispers over shouts. We are clear but we never know when we are being monitored." Winter put her index finger against her lips.

"Sam, we couldn't take the chance. We suspected the calls about the debris falling in Barry Arm were a hoax. In fact, we staged the idea as a test to see if ARKose was monitoring our conversations. I pretended to be Jackson." Jacob whispered while looking at Winter. She nodded, looking at the black remote-like device in her hand again with its green blinking lights.

"Ok, I am going to sit back down. Man, those meds I got in Quito for anxiety, ya know, for flying they must be wigging me out. Not that this isn't good news to see you, Jacob. Alive that is." She plopping down on the couch, taking a sip from the glass of scotch in her hand.

Her friends stood still, watching and waiting, giving her some-time to absorb the shock of seeing her dead friend that was now alive.

"Scotch before dinner. Scotch before." She looked at her watch. "Bloody Hell". As she swallowed the liquid in one gulp something wet and gooey was being spread on her hands. She looked down into the golden-brown eyes of Toklat, as the dogs' slimy tongue made its way up her arm. Her face would be next if she did not respond to the dog, as she scratched the thick fur.

"This is what we were alluding to in the truck. ARKose intended to kill Jackson. We think." Jacob paused. "By luring him to the Sound with a false tip that there was an avalanche of debris in Barry Arm. In fact, we could not tell you. It was to protect Camden, who is missing. We are sure ARKose has him." Winter grasped Sam's hand.

Jacob sat next to Sam. "As Jackson mentioned to you earlier, I got this call at the office from a boat captain. He refused to give me his name or the boat name. He said that the Barry Arm landslide was dropping boulder-size rocks into the water, nearly capsizing his boat." Jacob got up and walked to a diagram on the wall. "I immediately checked the sensor equipment. There was no move-ment being picked up."

"He called me," Jackson said. "I won't go into the details right now, but we lost Camden's tracker. It went dead just before the earthquake hit." Jackson shook his head.

Her head was a hive full of buzzing bees. *Tracker. Did he say tracker?*

"We knew Jackson and Camden had been followed several times when Camden visited. And we were being monitored by some very sophisticated equipment," Winter said as she held up the remote device. "This device detects anyone listening within a quarter mile."

"I found a listening device in Camden's phone on his... last visit."

Quietly, she was absorbing what her friends were saying.

"We devised a plan to bait whoever it was monitoring us by repeating a theory revolving around the Barry Arm. We stressed that if an earthquake struck Prince William Sound – specifically the inlet near Barry Arm, the landslide would give way, sending a massive wave directly at Whittier." Jacob stopped. "The truth is, the Barry Arm landslide has been stable for almost nine months. It has not moved a centimeter. When I got the message from an anonymous source, which was untraceable, we had to assume the bait worked. The man on the phone repeated what we had said, in this house, word for word. Then the office got two more calls saying the same thing. The callers refused to leave a boat name or name."

"Why would anyone want either of you dead?"

"We think ARKose was after Jackson. I was collateral damage you might say."

"Initially, it was going to be me. To go to the Sound." Jackson rubbed his face.

"Then I thought it would be better if I went. That way, they would still think Jackson a threat, and try again."

"Why?" Sam asked.

"I was a threat. A lose end. They were monitoring me. I don't…" Jackson paused.

"I lost communication with Camden after he left Anchorage on his way back to the mine, now owned by the mining company called ARKose."

"Jacob used my truck," Jackson continued. "He left right after we got the message from the first anonymous tip. I made a point that it would be easier for me to take the Heron and Jacob should stay and monitor the sensors in the lab. It was all show. That boat was never getting in the water."

"Say what? That makes no sense."

Winter saw Sam's eyes grow wide, shaking her head. "Later, after the quake we, Jackson and I, talked about how Jacob insisted it should be him that should check out Barry Arm. Not Jackson."

"And it was Jacob that apparently, disappeared and not me in the wave."

"And what happened to the Heron."

"A friend has a boat shed in one of the small inlets far from the main channel of the Sound. It did not even get wet. I hid in my friend's boat and when we got to the ramp, she hitched her truck to the boat and we drove away. The quake hit while we were driving back to the USGS office. That is when Winter called to let me know that Jackson was at the emergency room after a bike crash during the quake. I hid in the office until Jackson and Winter showed up. It was a bloody mess outside," he looked at his twin. "So was Jackson. I have been playing missing and presumed dead ever since."

"But why do this at all? What did they gain?"

"Right now, we suspect ARKose is owned by a para-military or group targeting US military bases such as JBER and disrupting transport centers, such as Whittier. Camden suspected, with the location of Stoney Mine, just across the inlet, that ARKose had the ability to use a trajectory system to deliver the element to stress fracture points such as the two thrust faults in question. It appears or they are wanting us to think, that their intent is to weaken the US military bases in Alaska and disrupt transportation. A strategic location when you consider Russia and Asia."

"Toklat, I think your human guardians have finally lost it. I suspect Jackson was not the only one who suffered a major concussion. Come on, girl," she helped the dog onto the couch, as Toklat licked her face with absolute, undeniable happiness.

"Sam, how about we get you fed," Winter said as she took the empty glass out of Sam's hand.

"We can chow down on the main floor. Then go down to the safe room," Jackson said as they headed down the stairs to the kitchen. "Alexa, volume up."

Toklat's big brown eyes watered as she scratched the dog's muzzle. Her pleasure showed as the drooling white slime spread on her pants. "Maybe I can have another miracle," she whispered. "I will find you Shelby." In her heart, she felt her friend Shelby was still alive.

"Sam, let's eat." Jackson yelled.

While attempting to peel the big dog off her lap, struggling to get off the couch, she looked at the dog. "Did he say safe room? God, I must be exhausted and delirious. Maybe the scotch." She mumbled. At that moment, the dog cocked her head, then with the speed of a hummingbird, planted her tongue on her face.

As she enjoyed the spaghetti dinner, and the chatter of her friends, the one glass of wine immediately had an impact on her. Exhausted, she kissed everyone good night and went to bed.

CHAPTER 10

SAM

DELICATE, IRIDESCENT BLUE octagonal flakes hung from the tips of olive-green spruce needles, limbs bending heavy with snow. Violet hues, shimmering off the white snow, melted into the morning glow, as the sun peaked above the spires of the Talkeetna Mountains. A peach haze swept over the sloping flanks of Sleeping Lady, as swirls of snow encircled the glacial abraded face of the asymmetric mountain.

She skied through the knee-deep snow leaving two pencil thin shadows. As she stopped, waiting for Shelby to catch up, she blew smoke rings as her warm breath condensed in the chilled air. Her long chestnut hair hung frozen below her wool cap, clanking against her blue jacket, as she bent down to clear balls of snow clinging to her bindings. The cold air stung her nostrils with the pungent scent of the lingering red berries on the waist high naked moose berry shrubs. The red berries clung to the bare branches, refusing to drop to their death.

"The snow is perfect," Shelby whispered as a cacophony of coyotes vibrated through the silence, announcing the sun's warmth on the mountain slopes. "Look at the size of those footprints. They are the size of a cantaloupe."

The two young women had been tracking the elusive lone wolf mile after mile.

"He is on his own." She pointed her ski pole into the direction of the single set of wolf tacks. Somewhat startled, a large brown mass stepped within an arms-length in front of her. The moose waded through the snow, unafraid, as he stretched his long sausage shaped muzzle delicately around the last remaining twigs of a birch tree. Two small velvety antler buds bulged between the large ears. Then the moose disappeared into the forest as quietly as he had appeared.

"Sleeping Lady is glowing in the morning light," Shelby whispered. Her pale Irish skin was flushed with rosy cheeks. Her single braid of mahogany hung below her multi-colored wool cap. "You want me to break trail?"

"Is that a hint?" She laughed at her friend. "Shel, you are always telling me to slow down."

Shelby ignored her. "Well, we will be running out of light soon. And we do have a wolf to find."

She laughed. At 16, feisty and independent, she and Shelby planned a weekend camping trip. It was late February and in the early morning darkness, they loaded snow machines, their back-country skis, and camping gear in the truck and drove to the groomed winter trail near Willow. On the map, the trail should fork to another trail and eventually to their destination — Mount Susitna, known by the locals as Sleeping Lady.

For twenty miles they bush wacked. Every few miles, a ski from the snowmachine would slide off the windswept trail, getting stuck in the icy crust. Humbled, unequipped to deal with down alders and broke branches from the spruce trees, they acknowledged their defeat. Tired with their long underwear, damp under their insulated snow pants and coats, they made it back to a turnout off the main trail, and made camp.

At least they had the sense to haul some of the broken wood littering the impassable trail.

With tent pitched and a fire built, they roasted marshmallows, and stuffed them on the gooey, melted chocolate squished between the graham crackers. Savoring each morsel, taste buds were stimulated as their muscles ached. Silently, they gazed at the silhouette draped in a velvet blanket of snow.

"Tomorrow, we ski." Shelby declared.

"Most definitely," she nodded. "Tonight, however we enjoy our view of the Lady."

Shelby snuggled in, weaving her arm through Sam's.

Under the moonlit sky as the northern lights danced over their Sleeping Lady's head, they made a promise.

"As long as the Sleeping Lady sleeps, we will always be there for each other — no matter what or where we are. Always."

"What if she wakes up?" Shelby murmured.

She laughed. "If she wakes up? It will be Armageddon. She will be one pissed off bitch."

"So true. She will search until the end of time for the killer of her dead lover." Shelby stood up, arched her back, and howled at the moon.

Startled, she sat up in bed. "Where the fuck am I?" Her body was damp. And then she remembered she was back in Alaska. At Jackson's.

"Wow. It's getting stronger." She whispered. "The dream is as vivid as the memory." She rubbed her eyes as she crossed her legs. "Always, Shel. I will find you."

CHAPTER 11

JACKSON

A FITFUL SLEEP LEFT Sam with circles under her eyes. She staggered into the busy kitchen following the scent of freshly roasted coffee and warm cinnamon rolls.

"Rough night," Winter hugged her. "Your mug is waiting."

Sam told her about the recurring dream that started after Shelby disappeared.

"We had so much fun on that crazy adventure, Winter. Maybe it was seeing the gate. Last night, the dream seemed so real. It is as though it is real. Like it is alive. When I saw the mountain, Sleeping Lady, for that brief second before the plane circled, I got this feeling. I know Shelby is alive. I just know it." Sam smiled at Jackson.

He walked over and gave his best gal friend a hug as he nudged her toward the living room. The four friends huddled around the warmth of the fire place while Celtic melodies filled the silence. He kissed Winter's hand, as he watched his brother Jacob and Sam licking their sticky fingers and chatting. Briefly, he felt a sprinkle of joy, taking in the normalcy of the moment of friendship and love.

With plates stacked in the kitchen sink, one by one they went upstairs.

"Right now, no unexpected ears. And if we need to," Winter pointed to the scattered pads and pens while holding the remote device in her hand. "Normal chatter among friends."

"Do you remember when you were working for that mine in southwestern Alaska and you told us about the super hummocks?" Jacob whispered as he twirled a red marker in his hand. "You said you had never seen anything like it before."

Sam nodded. "Yes, the hummocks on steroids. Really strange, like something from another planet. They were flat-topped rectangular mounds, made entirely of organic material but not rounded or built up in a cone shape typical of a pingo." She cocked her head. "Why?"

"Why did you notice them?"

"They didn't fit the definition of what a hummock is supposed to be. Or any vegetative landform on frozen ground," Sam arched her eyebrows. "Typical field work in the Great Land – the largest research project on the planet."

"But you researched them to find out why they were different, if I recall."

Sam nodded in agreement. "We even called in a specialist. He didn't have a clue. We finally hypothesized it was the location. The mine was located smack at the convergence of the cold interior climate and the wetter western maritime climate. It was fascinating."

"Think about the Barry Arm glacier as those hummocks on steroids. As the Barry Arm glacier melts, the landslide reacts in three ways — it moves forward, it diminishes, or it doesn't move at all."

Sam realized how much she missed these technical discussions with her friends. "It doesn't react like a landslide should."

Jacob nodded, holding his index finger upwards, another sign that the professor was getting to his point.

"The Barry Arm Glacier diminished at such a fast rate in the last decade that it caused the surrounding terrain to become unstable. Everyone agreed, if that slow-moving landmass were to catastrophically fail – becoming what we think of as a landslide – it would fall 3,000 feet into the fjord below, directly sending tsunami waves toward Whittier."

"And it happened. If it had been in the spring or summer when the Sound is crazy busy, who knows how many more people would have been killed by the wave."

Jacob contemplated. "A coincidence? Not likely and it didn't happen in the summer with warmer temperatures. By comparing satellite imagery from different periods of time, the rate and location of motion confirmed that the landslide moved almost three feet about 6 months ago. And then it stopped. Completely. Our sensors have showed no movement until during the earthquake."

"And that is what caught your attention? That it stopped."

"Exactly, Sam. That is my point. It moves at a speed depending on the weight of many variables — the shift of weight of a glacier when it is melting for example." Jacob looked at her. "Barry Arm Glacier was retreating quickly, more so than Cascade or even Harriman. But the sensors for the landslide were quiet."

"Yeah, but then a huge earthquake hit."

"Yes. My point is we have always been able to measure it. Sometimes it makes no sense, but we measured it. When it was slow, when it was fast, and when it did not move a fraction. Our sensors work. Our sensors, up to the minute the earthquake hit, showed no movement." Jacob was silent reflecting on the images that he had been studying for a month.

Sam stood up and her eyes got wide. "The call from this unknown boat captain said the slide was moving, dropping boulders into the water and nearly flipping his boat. That was before the earthquake."

"Bingo. In fact, there were three calls reporting a very dangerous rock slide at Barry Arm. Boulders the size of cars were falling into the water. None of those calls were traceable and all were anonymous. Before the earthquake. When the sensors were quiet.

There is always an explanation once you know where to find one. Like there was with your strange hummocks." Jacob sat down.

Sam looked at Jackson. He sat forward while resting his elbows on his long, muscular

"Whittier was constructed and operated by the military during World War II. The Army chose this area because the water is ice-free year-round with the deepest open water port accessible through the Gulf of Alaska." He took a sip of his coffee before continuing.

"Whittier was considered a secret facility. It even had a code-name: H-12 during World War II when Alaska was considered an overseas war zone. Whittier was a back-up location for the highest-ranking officials of the United States government, if necessary." He grew quiet, then added. "Including the President."

"Whittier went from a classified military installation to a pre-mier tourist destination." Winter added.

Sam listened, picking up the inflection of Jackson's voice and concentrating on the key points. Whittier — the deepest port in the state. The port was isolated and protected.

"To find the epicenter of an earthquake you need at least 3 seismographs. Find the distance from each seismograph to the earthquake focus, which is the intersection of the three circles – you find the epicenter." He stood up, grabbed a black felt marker off the whiteboard and drew a triangle near Barry Arm and another near Tyonek.

"With the information Camden provided me, I have calculated a trajectory from each epicenter originating at the ARKose mine site." He paused. "Before Camden left here that morning, he let me know that he was not taking the shuttle back to the mine site." He sat down. "A friend arranged a caribou hunt using a private charter flight from Lake Hood. After their hunt, the pilot would drop Camden at the mine site before coming back to Anchorage. The next day the two earthquakes hit."

There was a hushed silence in the room. Sam stood up and

walked closer to the diagrams, crossing her arms. "Camden has managed to get himself involved with a mining company that has intentionally caused two earthquakes using a dangerous rare earth element." Sam turned, sat back down on the couch, crossed her legs as she mumbled. "Crystal clear." She took a sip of her coffee. "But how did a rare earth element do this Jackson?"

"A sophisticated laser was used to bore through the rock below the Cook Inlet. It created a shaft of sort from the mine location to a thrust-fault below the Inlet." He paused. "Camden was hired by ARKose to analyze what appeared to be, a large granitic vein of francium. The quantity was estimated to be more in that vein, than the amount estimated for the entire planet. It was discovered by a geologist who works for ARKose. His name is Daniel Biel."

"Sam, we understand you have lots of questions. You have been thrown right into the middle of this. Right now, this is what we have hypothesized." Winter squeezed her friends hand.

"According to Camden," he continued. "It would take less than a gram of francium if exposed to a minuscule drop of water to cause a large explosion. We believe a small robot was used to transport francium through the shaft. The robot was then destroyed exposing the francium to moisture. That explosion caused the thrust-fault below Cook Inlet to become unstable causing the earthquake…"

"And causing the landslide in Prince William Sound." Sam responded. "But why would ARKose come after you guys?"

Winter spoke up looking at Sam. "We think ARKose got spooked when they saw Camden with Jackson. What we do know, is ARKose was listening and watching Jackson and Camden. After Camden's visit to the South Pacific where ARKose conducted a test of this element, Camden noticeably became very nervous. The dynamics changed after that trip. And then, Camden disappeared."

"What happened in the South Pacific?" Sam asked but did not wait for an answer.

"Camden is presumed missing because he found out ARKose

was doing some dangerous shit and rather than telling someone important, like I don't know, maybe the FBI, he instead calls his college drinking budding who works for the USGS." Sam sat down. "When did USGS become rock cops?"

"Sam," he got up and stood next to her and whispered. "Camden is with the FBI. And although I rather like the title rock cop," he thought briefly. "For now, we need the assistance of someone who knows how to mine. Someone with connections in high places and who has a guy with the skills to do some computer mining."

"You want my husband, Jon DuSuie. And Mik," Sam stated. "He is planning to be here in a few days for the wake for my, your," Sam gulped. "Missing but very much alive brother and two friends."

"More or less." Winter answered.

Sam grew quiet as the reality of the situation replaced the nervous joking. She was thinking about Shelby.

"Trust me, Jon will want to be part of this. And we need him." He said. "I think it is time to go to the pantry."

"Pantry?" Sam sipped her coffee, but blew off the remark. "Jackson, you do remember Mik, right? The gorgeous, blue-eyed devil with the skills of AI." Sam said. "I do recall at our virtual wedding, there was a vibe between your computer nerd," she winked at Winter, "and Jon's computer nerd." Sam paused and laughed as she added. "Mik. The guy who has nearly caused several international incidents, involving the wives of some powerful people." She caught the smile on Winter's face as Jackson's eyebrows arched.

"It was friendly teasing. However, I did enjoy your jealously, my love." And then Winter kissed his cheek as he blushed.

For a brief second, the burden that each friend felt with their current situation was eased with the memory of Sam and Jon's wedding.

Sam put her arm through Jacksons. "You do know, that Mik's

banter with Winter over Facetime after our wedding in French Guiana, was his way of showing his approval of you and Winter. Even if it was virtual. Mik is all about loyalty to his friends."

Sam trusted her life to these four people; they were her family. "When I was working for LUNA, Inc. in French Guiana, you guys believed me when I told you about all that shit. My conspiracy theories about what happened when I was kidnapped." She shivered remembering the toxic pollen of the mendewe plant. "That fanatic plant toxicologist LUNA hired and her plot."

"Yeah, when you told us it was a plan to disrupt the financial security around the globe by killing hundreds of diplomats with the International Monetary Fund in New York City using plant pollen?" He smirked as he revealed a hidden door to a metal spiral staircase in the pantry.

"Yeah, that plan." She stared into the semi-darkness. "Ok. Into the pantry we all go."

Winter teased. "Jackson's man cave is what I call it but he always called it the safe room."

"The safe room. Right," she shook her head, following Jackson as he disappeared into the darkness below her. "You all have been busy, very busy."

"Us, the FBI, and Jackson's special ops team." Winter declared.

"Jackson's what?"

"Winter. We agreed we would tell her later."

"It is later my love. The rock cop."

Sam breathed slowly. "FBI. And Jackson's own special ops team? I suppose this part of the story is in the details. Is there a sleek fast Batmobile down here too, because," she swallowed. "This room feels like a very small cave. A very small..."

"Sam, I built this for security during an environmental crisis," he explained as he winked at his wife. "And from Winter's iron work."

The house was sturdy, but even a building of steel, glass, and cement can burn. Wildland fires were a constant threat on the hillside of Anchorage with the increase in beetle-killed spruce trees. That was one reason for building a steel home, the other was the high winds blowing off the Cook Inlet converging with the Chugach Mountains in his back yard. Sam, who had lived for years on the top of a ridge near Chickaloon, understood the strength of the mountain winds after spending many sleepless nights waiting for her roof to blow off.

"I never thought this room would be used as a shield against someone trying to kill me and those I love." His face was a shadow from the bluish glow of the monitors.

As Sam stepped into the room, she couldn't help but think he looked like a giant standing in a Hobbit's cave; walls of concrete, low ceilings and no windows. She took several deep breaths, to slow her pulse, as her claustrophobia creeped in.

Completely underground, the small room was furnished with two bunk beds, a wet bath, survival equipment, and an array of firepower. Although Sam knew Jackson and Jacob were military trained with their education paid by the GI bill, she realized looking around the room, that there was much she did not know about the brothers. Triple monitors along with surveillance equipment filled one end of the small room, casting the eerie glow.

"Are you okay?" Winter asked, noticing Sam nibbling her nails. Although the basement was cool, her forehead was glistening.

While kidnapped, she was held in a dark tiny room in the basement of a research facility hidden on a private island in the Caribbean. She forced a smile. "Seriously, seeing this. You guys got my attention. I can handle it."

"Concentrate on your breath, Sam." Winter suggested. "Slow in and out."

"You know every yoga and woo woo person tells me to breathe. I mean. Really? I breathe. I would be dead if I didn't."

"Breathe slow and deep on the inhale, Sam."

"I got it."

Winter shook her head as she walked over to the computer and sat down while clicking the keys. Winter, with her maroon and purple hair was a mechanical engineer by training but her passion was in climbing and computers. The physical challenges of finding the right combination of rock ledges and crevasses were thrilling for the agile, strong Winter. And deciphering computer code was her mental challenge.

Sam watched as Winter tapped the keyboard, remembering the first time she had met the Yupik native. She asked if Winter was her given name. Sam smiled remembering the woman's answer. She had giggled and relayed the story that she was conceived in the middle of a blizzard at base camp on Denali. "Try getting that image out of your head every time you are winter camping."

And how true. Every winter camping trip she had taken, she remembered how Winter got her name.

Winter turned the left monitor towards Sam, allowing her to see the screen. She pointed to the top image, revealing two small islands with a crater on the larger rock, surrounded by shimmering blue water.

"Almost two months ago, a catastrophic eruption – without warning – destroyed the volcano and the island, leaving two small outcrops of rock visible just beneath the waves."

Winter turned the right monitor to show the others, which showed an image of light blue water with white caps surrounded by a hint of darker blue below the surface.

"NASA estimated the explosion to be equivalent to six million tons of TNT. An explosion that no one has witnessed in recent decades. The explosion sent a plume of ash 16 miles up into the stratosphere and a tsunami racing across the Pacific Ocean. The demolition of the volcano and island took less than thirty minutes. No one can explain it but a lot of scientists are studying it. Except for us." Winter hesitated. "Like the slide at Barry Arm, there were no signs — the remote sensors had no blips that something was happening until the volcano erupted and the islands disappeared below the water."

"What does this have to do with Camden? And ARKose?" Sam pouted. "And the…"

Winter looked at Sam with a brow arched and a slight nod.

Winter looked at Jackson who responded. "Camden was near the destruction of this volcano. ARKose tested one of the rare earth elements Camden was trying to stabilize."

"Francium." Sam responded as she saw Jackson's brows furrow as she stood behind Winter. He gazed at the monitor.

"What happened here in the South Pacific is linked to the earthquake in Alaska. It will make more sense after I explain the magnitude of what we are facing. No pun intended."

He grabbed a chair and sat down, rubbing his hand through his hair.

"In late June, almost four months ago, Camden texted me. His full name is Camden O'Connor," he chuckled. "He was contracted to do some work with a mining company in Alaska. He did contract work all over the world for mining companies including in the Middle East and Africa, specializing in stabilizing rare earth elements. His expertise was figuring out how to process them. When he got a contract to do some analysis for this mine in Alaska, he took it." Jackson rubbed the pink welt on his forehead.

"About three weeks after he arrived at the mine, he called and said he was in town. We arranged to meet at the Snow Goose." Jackson quieted. "I knew something was up. He was reserved and skittish. Hell, we played rugby, drank beer, and debated mining — he is brilliant. His Ph.D. was in Geochemistry. He is a fucking climber. He doesn't get skittish or paranoid." Jackson took a deep breath. "He was brought up in a military family. His parents were Air Force. His dad, a fighter pilot died when Camden was young. His mom eventually became a general."

"Wowzer. A female general in the Air Force." Sam exclaimed as she noticed Winter touch Jackson's hand, as he in return, squeezed her hand.

"We met at the Snow Goose, but then he insisted we walk to another bar so we went to the Cook. Camden looked tired and I swear his nervousness bordered on paranoia. Until he told me why." Jackson crossed his arms. "He was analyzing a specific element and this time he told me the company name, ARKose. Sam, when the Stoney Consortium failed, ARKose was next in line to buy the mineral rights. Unlike the previous company, ARKose is interested in REE's or rare earth elements; not gold. During his analysis he found some astonishing information." Jackson whispered to Winter continuing his story.

"After a couple glasses of scotch, we got serious. In this kind of work, as you know when you were a consultant, the normal business practice with a contractor is they must sign a non-disclosure agreement. Camden was juggling what he could tell me without violating that NDA." Winter turned the monitor toward them so they could see the screen.

"And much more than that," Winter whispered. "As we found out."

"Chemistry 101 - an abbreviated periodic table. The alkali metals in water are the most reactive metals and spontaneously undergo a chemical reaction with water. These include common elements like calcium, sodium, and potassium, which we encounter in everyday life. On the other hand, the more uncommon alkali metals such as rubidium, cesium, and francium are not commonly found and are considered rare. Hence, why they are called…"

"Rare earth elements."

He smiled at Sam. "Additionally, these elements are also radioactive and considered dangerous due to their instability, which is why they are scarce or rare."

"What is so important about francium?"

"It is highly radioactive. It is one of the most reactive and rarest of the elements in the periodic table. ARKose is interested in only mining francium, according to Camden. As we mentioned earlier, they discovered an unusually large amount of it, considering the element is referred to as artificial because no one has been able to synthesize it in quantities that have ever been produced. Cesium is the next, most reactive metal after francium. These substances are classified as hazardous materials."

Winter pulled up a shape that looked like the Rubik's cube on the monitor.

"Anyone who has had chemistry has seen this symbol — it is the white square of the diamond. If a vehicle is transporting a hazardous substance, they are required by law to post this symbol on the outside of the vehicle."

Sam recognized the symbol and at the same time, searched her brain trying to recall the element.

"Francium falls in the white square. When you see a letter with a horizontal line, the substance is hazardous and will cause a fire *but* you do not want to use water to put the fire out because it will explode. My point is, these are all nasty, and they are radioactive." Jackson paused.

"The Stoney Mine was not shut down when the consortium shut down," Winter said, thinking out loud as she was staring at the monitor. "It was bought by ARKose." Clicks of Winter's fingers flying across the keyboard broke the silence of the room.

"No one understands this process better than you, Sam. You spent nearly 18 years as an environmental scientist conducting environmental impact studies for large scale mines in Alaska," Jacob stated. "A mining company intends to mine, lies to the local people with the promise of good-paying jobs, and ensures the protection of the environment. Then that mine sells to another mine, and then to another. The false promises are forgotten while the politicians and shareholders become rich and the natural resources are trashed. They keep buying and selling until they get a political sweep buying everyone in the way so they get away with murder. In this case, literally."

Winter tapped a few keys, and an image appeared on one of the monitors. "The Stoney Mine is upstream and north of Lake Iliamna the largest lake in Alaska, which then flows through the Kvichak River into Bristol Bay. You were one of the wetland scientists that surveyed the vegetation and the soils at this mine. It is in one of the most remote, wild, and uninhabited parts of the Bristol Bay watershed," her normally quiet voice increased in pitch. "The villages of Nondalton, Newhalen, and Iliamna were all promised economic security and with Anchorage about 200 miles away, it was easy to schmooze politicians and regulators. The largest open pit mine in North America with deposits of copper, gold, and molybdenum, was lining the pockets of the shareholders while destroying the most productive fisheries in the world."

"My crew and I spent ten days rafting the Mulchatna River conducting vegetation and soil transects in that area. It was spectacular – streams full of fish, caribou herds everywhere, and grizzlies feeding along the river. Blue sky, pure water and nothing but wilderness." Sam reflected as she bit her lower lip.

"And my backyard," Winter stated. "My birthplace."

He nodded at his wife and continued with a geology lesson. Sam knew this process was leading to something big and this was no doubt a practice presentation for a different audience.

Sam bit her lip shaking her head. "Alaska's Department of Natural Resources pushed for this mine. Congress pushed for this mine. Not the most stable of locations to build the largest toxic pit of chemicals. It has never made sense considering the Stoney Mine holds low-grade ore, requiring a large-scale operation to recover it."

"When that environmental group from California exposed the corruption with the CEOs of Stoney Mine with the paper trail going from Juneau to Washington, D.C. — the payoffs from the mining corporation to the congressional office — that was when people started taking notice of what was happening." Winter said. She punched a few more keys and pulled up a document.

"In an interview with the Senate majority whip, she raised questions about whether Stoney mine officials misled Congress which is a crime," Winter's voice increased an octave.

"Allowing waste and destruction to an ecosystem is not a crime, but don't lie to Congress. People assumed the controversy would impact the 2019 re-election of the congressman in Alaska after the recording linking his campaign contributions from the Stoney Mine Corporation." Winter read.

"Far from it," Sam was now distracted from her discomfort. "He not only got re-elected, he is the chairman of this super cyber technology subcommittee in Washington D.C. They have oversite of technology in mining. The nick name of the group is called city which is spelled C I T I. It is beyond me why that is not considered a conflict of interest."

"Even though the state of Alaska's Public Offices Commission reported violations of campaign funding laws during the election." Jacob shrugged.

"There are no ethics in politics," Sam commented. "Only money."

"And one of the most fragile habitats at risk is the McNeil River Sanctuary and Refuge. Remember, when that new and upcoming young legislator proposed a bill to close the refuge to new mining claims?" Jacob chimed in.

"Because those magnificent grizzly bears would disappear along with their food source." Sam swallowed.

"The conversations you and your husband Jon must have." He grimaced. "That poor man."

"Just the opposite. Because he owns a mining company, he believes the only way mining will survive is to empower global environmental and social regulatory agencies." Sam responded. "But we do have some exciting debates. And lots of fun after the debates."

Sam sat forward, her elbows on her knees.

"Now that you all have intentionally distracted me."

"You were looking very white, Sam. And sweat beading on your forehead." Jacob responded. "Selfish really as we don't want you to puke."

Sam rolled her eyes. "I am not going to puke." She stuttered. "Ok, fine. I felt like it. Soapbox aside, explain to me why this element. And the connection to you guys and the quakes. Other than Camden is your old college friend, Jackson."

"ARKose now owns the mineral rights of the Stoney Mine Corporation. We just uncovered that ARKose was a silent investor in Stoney, and they have no intention to mine copper and gold. From a PR standpoint, this makes ARKose a poster child of mining to the public—no open-pit mine of toxic waste to kill off the Bristol Bay fishery." Jacob summarized.

On cue, Winter tapped the keys, and a slurry of documents filled the two monitors.

"Radiation, Sam. It is all about radiation." He said. "We believe the earthquakes were the goal here, incapacitating South-Central Alaska. Camden told me ARKose was looking for a facility to develop francium. For creating sustainable green energy." Another pause. "But what if that is not their intention?" He looked at Sam and then continued.

"Camden found some clues that ARKose knew there was a shit load of francium sitting below the Stoney Mine. He also observed some suspicious or inconsistent activities." he added as he handed Sam a pile of paperwork. Sam noticed two sheets each with a grainy-colored photo along with three sheets each with black and white photos.

"Camden managed to take these colored photos at the mine. The other 3 are stock images we gathered."

The first photo showed in the background the broad expanse of open tundra with mountains and a sleek black helicopter in the foreground. Sam could make out a red symbol 丼 on the doors and a red dragon on the tail fuselage.

"He took the photo of the two Asian men and the blonde, without them knowing," Jackson pointed to the photo.

Sam studied the photo with the woman. She was of an indeterminate age with long blonde hair, dressed in sleek black pants and a black jacket with the same red symbol on the upper sleeve near her shoulder. She was holding a core sample in her hand as the two Asian men were looking at it. There was a thin, dark-skinned man standing in the background.

The third image was a grainy, black and white photo of a Middle-Eastern man. Someone had written over the top of the image 'TTP' = Tehreek-e-Taliban Pakistan. He was wearing a cap, a pakol, that was rolled up around his forehead, exposing his dark hair.

The fourth was a stock photo of two men with black hair. One of the men had his hair shaved on the sides of a chubby face—the President of North Korea. The second man in the photo appeared to be one of the men in Camden's photo taken at the mine.

"What do those symbols mean? I am guessing the blonde and the helicopter belong to ARKose." Sam asked as she spread the images on the multi-use table.

Jackson smiled. "Interesting you focused on the symbols and not the men in the images."

Sam raised her eyebrows as she cocked her head sideways.

"Legends from ancient China describe a global catastrophic flood so vast that the waters reached the sun and covered the mountains, drowning all the land-dwelling creatures, including mankind. During this global calamity, there stood a legendary hero named Nüwa."

Jackson stood up, grabbed a black marker from the whiteboard on the wall, and drew two symbols on the whiteboard: 洪 舟.

"Nüwa turned back the flood and helped to repopulate the world. Analysis of the ancient Chinese Bronzeware, Oracle Bone, and Seal characters that are associated with 'flood' and 'boat' led to the present-day discovery of evidence for Nüwa's ark in the Chinese characters."

Jackson wrote "FLOOD" next to the symbol 洪 and "BOAT" next to the symbol 舟.

"Nüwa's ark housed eight worshippers or 'the remnants of the world,' and finally came to rest on a mountain. After the flood receded, the world began to be repopulated from the eight people on the Ark. The Chinese account of the flood has been dated to 1000 BC, suggesting that the Chinese possess one of the oldest written records of the flood. Although the world has experienced earthquakes, fire, volcanoes, and disease, a great flood is the one disaster that has been universally and consistently recorded in cultures, especially in reference to religious documents such as the bible."

"ARKose wants to cause a flood? I thought they were into earthquakes."

Jackson continued. "Notably, in Chinese history, this great flood was the result of the rebellion of a group of people about 2500 BC. In the text of Huai Nan Zi, which was written about 200 BC, the legend goes on to say that in ancient times, the poles - north, south, east, and west - that supported the roof of the world were broken. As a result, the heavens were broken, and the nine states of China experienced a continental shift and split. Fire broke out, and the water from the heavens could not be stopped, causing a flood. There is documentation that around 1000 BC, there was grieving and mourning all over the earth, as flood waters reached the sky, flooded the mountains, and drowned all living things. But, 'Nüwa' sealed the flood holes with colorful stones and repaired the broken poles using four turtle legs."

"You could have just said the symbol meant boat or Ark, short for ARKose," Sam smiled.

"True, but the legend is important. And you were more interested in the symbols than the people." He smirked.

"Bite me."

"Camden believes these clues from ancient times relate to current events. He said the past is key in understanding the intentions of ARKose. For example, fire and ice," he mumbled, biting the end of the marker. "And colorful stones." He looked at Sam.

Sam rolled her eyes. "I get it. Arkose is a sandstone with feldspar that comes basically from granite, if I remember."

"Yeah. And feldspar is a group of rocks that are formed from minerals such as aluminum silicates."

"Yeah, yeah. I get it, Jackson. We have the boat and the minerals and the..."

"Savior. All these biblical legends refer to someone who is going to save the world." Winter added.

"Perceived legends." Sam said.

"And how does fanaticism spread? But through religious doctrines." Jacob added.

"Before he disappeared, Camden gave me the two photos he took at camp, along with a document on the symbols and the culture." He paused, thinking aloud.

"When I put the pieces of this... puzzle together." He walked to the whiteboard and drew boxes with arrows connecting the boxes. Inside each box he wrote a word then stood back chewing the end of the black felt marker before he quickly drew a large circle encompassing the diagram. Satisfied, he grabbed the red marker he drew a zig zag starting at the upper left of the circle diagonally to the lower right of the circle. He stepped back nodding slightly.

"Since the beginning of civilization, we know this planet has gone through a massive continental shift resulting in the split of continental plates resulting in volcanic explosions of fire followed by a the cooling of the planet and ice. We know this, through geologic time, because human species have documented the sequence — first with the graphic language of petroglyphs to the written word for fire and flood. The flood swallowed the land leaving only the summits of mountains. Then…"

Sam yawned. "Noah's Ark. According to Christians."

Winter smiled. "Nüwa's Ark. According to Asian beliefs." She made eye contact with Sam. "The Stones."

And together Winter and Sam whispered. "The Hero."

Jackson stared at the whiteboard, then turned. "And then we witness two earthquakes and two tsunamis."

"ARKose is the Ark and the Stone." Winter looked up from the keyboard. She noticed Sam settle deeper into the couch, her legs curled. below her and not saying a word. "They create the continental shift. The volcano and the fire. And then the flood."

"Who is the hero?"

"ARKose." Jacob responded.

"Camden wrote in the margins," Jackson said as he wrote two words in capital red letters on the whiteboard. ARKOSE = PURIFY ???????

"On that last morning, before he got in his rental car, he whispered to me Arkose is the savior." Jackson wrote two more words. ARKOSE = SAVIOR

"The explosion in the pacific ocean was a test." Sam contemplated. "Purify? What the hell does that mean?"

"I am not sure, Sam.

"Clean the world of the military in Alaska? Is that the intent?" No one said a word.

"Okay, I think we need a break." Winter said. "Lunch."

"I will be up in a minute." He said not taking his eyes of the monitor. "I will make sure everything is secure down here first. Not that anyone cares." He mumbled.

Sam stayed behind watching Jackson as he picked up a picture.

She knew it was a picture of him and Camden in their rugby shirts. As she quietly walked behind him, she heard him whisper. "You had better be alive, my friend. I am going to do whatever it takes to bring you home. We are going to find you."

"I feel the same about Shelby." He wasn't startled at all when she squeezed his shoulders.

"Something is bothering you. Care to share?"

He grabbed the image with the blonde. "Dammit, Sam I am missing something. Or her. Something that he might have told me. It is gnawing at my gut. There is something about her."

"We will figure it out big guy. For Shelby and for Camden."

"Come on. I need food for some reason. It seems like we just ate, but that was hours ago." She nudged him out of his chair.

CHAPTER 12

SAM

AFTER FOOD AND a walk in the crisp fall air with Toklat and Winter, she settled into the well-worn, comfy couch next to Winter. She breathed deep through her nostrils, counting one, two, three, then exhaling through her mouth; four, five, six. Her pulse, matched the beat as the blue light emanating from the monitors, cast eerie shadows across the walls of the safe room, choreographed to the whirring of the computers. The group listened as Jackson revealed the chronicle of events since his first meeting with Camden.

Her mind raced, processing the information, but words eluded her. Her focus remained fixed on what Jackson said about Camden's contact; the woman with the red hair.

"What was the woman's name? Camden's contact?" She asked.

"Handler." Jackson answered.

"Whatever."

"He never said." Jackson replied, then hesitated before speaking. "She was more than just Camden's handler. His face was flushed after he met her at the zoo," Jackson shook his head, ran his hand through his hair. "They were seeing each other. Personally.

But he never revealed her name." He cocked his head, raising an eyebrow. "Why do you ask?"

"Shelby. The handler is Shelby."

"What? No. She couldn't be. There are a lot women with red hair, Sam."

"Shelby mentioned this guy she met. He was a geochemist, but she never gave me any details about him. It was strange, but not out of character for her. She was busy with work, and there were new guys popping in and out of her life." She shook her head. "I mean, I don't mean. That makes her seem…she was not like that. Christ."

"Breathe, Sam." Winter put her hand on Sam's knee.

"It was like two or three months ago when I noticed something was bugging her. We would talk every week but she never mentioned him again even after I asked about him. I assumed he was no longer in the picture. Then the blah blah about work. There was something up but she didn't provide any specifics." She paced. "I felt worry and concern from her. But she blew me off."

"Holy shit, Sam." Jackson flew out of his chair. "Camden mentioned she was a red-haired beauty with this sultry Irish voice and incredible forest green eyes."

"Jackson, it's Shelby."

"Shelby?" Winter asked. "From grade school, who signed? Her younger brother became deaf so you and Shelby learned sign language. She introduced you to Logan."

In that instant, everyone understood the significance of this discovery.

"That means." Sam sat down. "That means she is an undercover FBI agent."

Winter's eyes were shining as she looked at her husband. "Why did we not know this?"

"The FBI would not have revealed her name. None of us would have suspected Camden's handler was Shelby." Jacob interjected.

"Babe, I never made the connection. If she wanted us to know,

Camden would have told me." Jackson rubbed his face looking at the ceiling. "But this is good."

She shrieked as she sat back down. "It means she is alive and with Camden. I know it."

Jackson sat down. "I can guarantee Camden's mom does not know the truth about her son. And his mom is a retired General from the Air Force." Jackson shrugged. "I will say this, Camden and Shelby, if his handler is Shelby, Sam, have been working this mission for two years. They would not compromise it. For anything."

She stood up and began pacing, speaking rapidly, not paying attention to the conversation in the room. "Crap. She sent me a text. It was strange because it came out of the blue. She said she was going on an unexpected trip. With *a* guy." Sam grew quiet as she struggled to sit. "And then her mom called me to say Shel was missing. It was right after the earthquake."

Her mind was racing. "Her mom said Shelby had gone caribou hunting across the Inlet with a friend, and then the tsunami hit. I assumed the unexpected trip was the caribou hunting." Sam leaned forward, her head in her hands. "The plane they found, the one she was supposed to be in was empty. There was no sign of her or the guy she was hunting with." She slumped in the chair staring at the ceiling which only increased her claustrophobia.

"When did she send that text, Sam? The day." Jackson demanded.

She looked at her phone, her eyes widening. " It was the day before the earthquake. Shelby told her mom she went hunting."

"Show me the text." Winter read quietly. "But she told you, a friend who would understand the true context of her text. This is what Shelby texted you. 'I am leaving on an unexpected trip. Not planned. With C'." Winter looked up. "She did not have time to do anything but send a quick text to the person she trusted the most. She used her personal phone."

"The FBI. Where is the FBI?" Sam squealed.

"I will confirm with the FBI that Shelby is Camden's handler but I am guessing they have heard every word of every phone conversation and have seen every text you and Shelby have exchanged, Sam." Jackson looked at his friend, before continuing.

"Shelby knew the FBI would see that text she sent to you. If ARKose took her phone all they would read is a text to a friend by the name of Sam." Jackson stated. "The FBI has been monitoring ARKose for two years. It was a year of undercover work by Camden before ARKose took the bait and hired him to synthesize francium. Camden and Shelby met two years ago on an assignment in the desert of Nevada."

"Two years ago?" She was bewildered. "How could she not tell me?"

"After the explosion in the south pacific, his handler — Shelby suggested it was time to shut down the mission. I agreed. Camden refused because they need to find out who is funding ARKose. Remember, the FBI will not risk the mission and neither will I. Remember that. We, the FBI and my special ops team, are including you at my request. And believe me, over the last month, this has caused quite an uproar and heated discussion at the Pentagon." Jackson rubbed his eyes.

"Everyone must believe Jacob, Camden, and Shelby are dead. Sam, you came back to Alaska to attend a wake. The FBI believe Camden and Shelby are not dead, but have maintained their cover and have been taken to a new facility somewhere else. Camden mentioned that Daniel, the head geologist for ARKose and Peiling have found another place to continue their work. They still need Camden. The FBI want this mission to succeed including the rescue of their two agents. I will tell you as much as I can but not everything." Jackson paused again looking at his friends. He rubbed his hand through his hair and sat down, took a deep breath and continued.

"The plane found near Tyonek in the Inlet is not the plane that delivered Camden and his handler, who we now suspect is Shelby..."

"It is Shelby."

"Shelby," Jackson nodded looking at Sam. "The pilot that flew them to the mining camp was an FBI pilot in a plane owned by a charter flight company. Someone, we suspect Daniel from ARKose cancelled the flight to pick up Shelby. We assume Daniel used the storm as a reason why the pilot was not picking her up."

"Why did the pilot leave in the first place? Why not just stay there."

"Shelby wanted time at the mine so they came up with a diversion using a hunting accident. The pilot flew back to Anchorage when he got the message that someone from the mine cancelled the flight. Then the storm hit. He had no way to get hold of Shelby."

"No one figured in the weather?"

"Exactly, Sam. We believe Camden and Shelby left Alaska in a private jet the day before the earthquake." Jackson calmed himself. "So, for now, we need to proceed with the plan that three of our friends are presumed dead after being caught in a tsunami. And Sam," Jackson looked at her. "I will confirm if Shelby is Camden's handler."

"Thank you. Now, I need to text Jon."

"We know." Jackson nodded at Winter.

Realizing the need for caution, Winter urged, "Don't say anything specific."

"Trust me, after French Guiana, Jon and I have a code word to signal sensitive conversations," Sam remembered the code word. They came up with it the night Jon proposed. She pulled out her phone and texted Jon the word XUL.

"Deep in the heart of the Amazon rainforest, there is a tribe that worships the jaguar as the ruler of the jungle and the embodiment of the forest's spirit. The tribe believes the jaguar possess unparalleled strength and wisdom. XUL is the name for jaguar in their native language." She said nodding at Winter.

Winter smiled as she sent Jon an email with the relevant documents and moments later, Jon's face appeared on the monitor, covered in dirt and sweat, but his eyes locked onto Sam's, bringing a sense of relief.

For the first time since she arrived in Alaska, her anxiety decreased when she heard Jon's voice and then saw his face on the monitor. His sandy blonde hair was flattened from sweat as he took his faded ball cap off. And his blue-grey eyes locked on her eyes. No words were necessary.

"Camden O'Connor?" Jon asked. He had walked into his office at the mine site in Ecuador as Winter's message arrived on the secure link. He was one of those rare CEOs that preferred being in the field rather than in an office. LUNA, Inc, was restoring rain-forest habitat for several endangered species including the jaguar and the Uakari Monkey, after acquiring a gold mine that removed hundreds of hectares of the Manduvi trees, and left the streams contaminated with toxins.

Jackson questioned. "You know Camden?"

"We met at a conference three years ago in South Africa. He was a speaker on the technique to fine-tune the analysis of radioactive rare earth elements." Jon ran his hands through his damp hair, shaking his head in disbelief. "Camden. I will say this, his passion drives him. He is one of those scientists that is driven to succeed. He is respected across the mining community from environmentalists to drillers." Jon got quiet. "FBI. Wow. Shelby and Camden. What are the odds? Man, that is a duo I would not want to mess with. My bet is on them."

Jackson nodded.

"Anything on the blonde?" Jacob inquired referring to one of the documents Winter sent.

"I have never met her. Mik has all the information and I'll fill you in when I arrive." Jon replied, glancing at Sam. "And Winter, Mik will reach out to you."

"I look forward to working with Mik again." Winter giggled, looking at Jackson.

"Great." Jackson glanced at Winter. "Inside joke that everyone in the room seems to know about."

"Mik thrives on beating the establishment with his skills. She won't be a ghost much longer." Jon beamed.

"We need your expertise on element 87, Jon. It's the key to finding Camden and Shelby." Jackson said, choosing his words carefully. "The FBI is the lead on this right now, but Shelby's boss and mine, are treating this unofficially, as a joint mission. We have full support."

"Sam mentioned that you are still in the military. Team leader of a special operation team that monitors the exchange of rare earths, I believe."

"Yep, and already, we cannot keep up. We work closely with organizations such as the FBI." Jackson responded.

"It is about time the US took a military approach on this issue," Jon nodded. "What these groups are doing in regions of Africa, South America, and Asia is criminal. It is a step but we need an international law across all continents. Countries like the USA and China and my homeland, Australia are at the top of the list of drivers of this industry, Jackson."

"I am with you Jon. The demand for these elements like cobalt and the money involved is staggering. And soon, there will be mining of the ocean which means…"

"International water. A fucking free for all." Jon answered.

"In the meantime," Winter interjected, "We have a wake to plan. Jon, Sam will call you on an unsecured line to provide the details. We want anyone who might be listening to know that we are not searching for our friends."

"Babe, chat in a few. And Jackson, keep her safe."

"Always, my man." Jackson nodded before Jon signed off.

Everyone in the room understood the best way to protect Camden and Shelby was to go ahead with the wake that they had originally planned.

However, to convince ARKose, the parents of Camden and Shelby needed to be convinced that their son and daughter were not coming home. In the blue glow of the small room everyone agreed the next two phone calls were going to be difficult.

CHAPTER 13

CAMDEN

SHELBY MOANED AS he told her a story about three young guys with backpacks and climbing gear, uncut hair, and sunburned faces walking from Nepal into Tibet. And the British couple who were documenting monasteries, who gave the climbers a ride to Lhasa, making numerous stops along the way.

"As a climber I bet you have never experienced altitude sickness."

"No, I am lucky because it is worse than sea sickness," he kissed her warm forehead. "Many mountain climbers have not summited due to altitude sickness. Even the most seasoned experts can get it. It goes away with a decrease of altitude but unfortunately, we cannot go any lower."

"Keep me distracted Camden. Continue with the story."

He smiled as he reminisced about the time he was in Nepal and Tibet.

He described the landscape — the pass where they descended to Yamdrok Lake—a narrow body of water with brilliant turquoise hues, its shape often likened to that of a huge scorpion by Tibetans. Despite strong Tibetan objections, the Chinese constructed a hydropower plant there in 1997.

"For Tibetans, there's a profound spiritual concern. Legend has it that Yamdrok represents Tibet's 'life-power'— if the water were to vanish, all Tibetans would perish."

Slowly sipping green tea, he whispered in Shelby's ear.

"We have been in Shigatse for a week, Shel. I have that same nagging feeling — like we are missing something. I went through everything in my head from the minute we left the mine in Alaska to disembarking the plane, and driving from the Shigatse Peace Airport to here."

Shelby nodded, grabbing his hand, as she whispered in his ear. "We assumed ARKose was planning a terrorist activity against the U.S." Shelby replied. "That has all changed. We had it so wrong, Camden." She concentrated on her breathing. "Continue your story about walking along the Tibetan Plateau after climbing Mt. Everest," she hesitated. "You mentioned the geology and how valuable the water is. Telling me your story will focus you're mind."

"The Yarlung River flows along the Yarlung Tsangpo Suture, the fault line marking the boundary between the Asian and Indian plates. The rocks on either side of the suture hold distinct different pre-collision histories. The Lhasa terrane to the north is juxtaposed with metamorphosed sedimentary rock scraped off the colliding Indian Plate to the south." He went quiet.

"Crap, Irish. You are brilliant," he leaned in close to her "The Yarlung Tsangopo Suture."

The tea warmed his body as he kissed her ear and whispered. "Who initiated the conversation about you coming with us on the jet?"

"Daniel did. The plan was to drop me off in Anchorage. Why?"

"He was going to leave you at the mine. I made it clear if he did that, I was staying with you. And the remaining francium would stay in its' natural, rock state."

"You threatened him," Shelby concentrated. "You put him in a box with no way out." She snuggled against Camden's warm body. "I would have been fine there. The cook would never have left me with no food and no radio." Shelby sat up, rubbing her temples. "So, you are wondering why in the hell he even offered me a ride to Anchorage in the first place?"

"Yes. Peiling would have just as easily had you killed. Daniel took a huge risk by even having you on that jet. Why? He could have left you at that mine, alone, with no way home. I would never have known he abandoned you. He could have assured me you would be on the first flight home. So many options and yet he chose…"

"But he didn't. He wanted me on the jet."

He finished his tea, staring into those green eyes.

"Exactly."

"Because he can control you by using me. Me, you're girl-friend," she murmured in his ear. "Your beautiful witchy girlfriend. He will leverage me against you if you do not obey." Then she changed the subject. "What about this suture?"

"Suture is the name given where two plates are in contact. But it is the river that is important."

"The largest dam in the world and probably the most con-troversial," she laid back down, her head resting on his shoulder. "Three Gorges is situated on the Yangtze River."

"Precisely. A source of pride for China's leadership."

"Camden, are you thinking the dam is a target?"

No response.

"Camden?"

"What?" he mumbled brushing his hand through his shaggy, blonde hair. "This is what happens sitting in a dark room for ten hours a day." He apologized. "Yes, Shelby. I am betting one of those sets of numbers is the location of Three Gorges Dam."

"How much time do we have?" Shelby grabbed his hand, look-ing directly into his eyes.

"Element 87 has reacted to the reduced polarity shield. I can't extend the stall much longer and I am on phase 2 for the other elements ARKose is interested in."

"Cesium, promethium, and plutonium."

"Yes. Fortunately," he stated. "The drilling has encountered an impenetrable vein. The laser couldn't cut through it. We call that a rock burst—dense granite under immense compressive stress. This is one of the dangers of traditional mining using humans and pick axes deep into the earth. But with a laser, there is no danger since there is no crew. All Shing needs to do is ramp up the laser speed. For now, it buys us time."

"Shing's laser technology is poised to revolutionize global mining around the world."

"And we are back to my point, Shel. Peiling would just as soon have you dead. Why would Daniel take such a risk, even if he could use you to leverage me?"

Shelby bit her lower lip, concentrating. "He wants something. I can use that in our favor. What bothers me is why the urgency to leave Alaska. That dam isn't going anywhere." Shelby pondered. "And in that weather. I am simply collateral damage to them. But you? Why would they risk your life in a plane crash? Even if the low ceiling continued for the rest of the week."

"It's the numbers. We need to confirm what those three numbers represent." He said. "They are locations but where? They are not in North America. And why here in Tibet."

"The dam is one of them. And the other two? You were 500 miles from the volcanic islands."

"Tibet is one of the most seismic regions on the planet." He said. "It's the legend. I told Jackson the key to ARKose's plan is to understand the Chinese Legend of the flood. It is important. Peiling said she will make history. Not by creating a new energy source that will eliminate the need for fossil fuel. And the flood will cleanse the earth and the savior, Nüwa saves the people. She…"

"Peiling will be the savior. But that does not make sense unless…"

"She is not Chinese. And Daniel is not British. He is Pakistani." He looked at Shelby. "It's not just the flood. It is also the fire."

The natural world is our home. It is not necessarily sacred or holy. It is simply where we live. It is therefore in our interest to look after it.

—Dalai Lama

CHAPTER 14

JACKSON

"JACKSON, I SENT an encrypted email to retired General O'Connor at the Air Force Academy in Colorado Springs," Winter said. "She should have gotten it by the time you are on the phone with her."

While he was waiting to talk with the General, he thought about how reserved Camden would get whenever he talked about his dad. After a tough, muddy match of rugby, and after the two of them had a couple of beers, he had asked Camden about his father.

He closed his eyes remembering that night in the bar as Camden talked about his dad.

"It was a day I will never forget." Camden had told him.

With a slight smirk on his face, Camden described how excited he had been all day waiting for his dad to come home. They had planned a four day climb up Mt. Rainier while his parents were stationed at a base in Tacoma, Washington. Camden had been practicing his breathing with his climbing boots and pack on his back, going up and down the stairs in his parents house. Camden's father, an air force test pilot was doing maneuvers in eastern Washington when there was a malfunction. When his mom walked into his bedroom, her face was ghostly pale and her eyes bloody red; she did not say a word. He knew his dad was not coming home; they were not going climbing. Shortly after the memorial service, his mom was transferred to Italy.

He rubbed his eyes. *And now, he had to tell his friend's mother, that her only son is missing and presumed dead.* Winter walked over to her husband and kissed the top of his head.

"Remember, Camden is alive. You need to do this to keep him that way, Jax." A nickname she used when she knew he was in a tough situation.

"You are right, Winter. I need to convince her that it is time to come to Alaska, not for a search of her son, but to attend his wake."

When he first called Camden's mom to inform her about her son's disappearance after the earthquake, the General insisted on helping with the search. He dissuaded her for the moment at least, until he could find out more information.

"Hello Jackson," the General responded. "Any news on my son? And please, call me Enid."

It was as if Camden's mom knew this call would come.

"After his father was killed, I knew my son's desire to join the military ended that day his dad died. DNA has a powerful pull on one's psyche. I knew my son would serve his country and satisfy his passion for the environment. I remember the day he had returned from Malawi and he was so distant, silent. I sensed he was troubled so I suggested we grab our fly rods." There was silence on the phone. "We were fly-fishing on the South Platte. After a few casts, I asked him what was up. He told me about the slave labor at this mining site. He wouldn't, but now I realize he couldn't tell me about the company he worked for, but he did tell me about children and women covered in toxic dust. Men were so thin from lack of food they weighed little more than the pickaxe they were using twelve hours a day in the heat. You know, my son saw more depravity in the human soul at those mine sites than what I witnessed in my entire military career." More silence. "I will pack my bag and be there tomorrow." She paused. "Jackson, you were always my favorite of Camden's friends. I mean that."

"Enid, there is something I need to tell you about Camden. And me."

And so, he did.

"Thank you, Jackson for telling me the truth. And I swear, I do know something about keeping secrets. I will see you tomorrow."

After a few minutes of contemplation, he walked upstairs into the kitchen where his brother, his wife, and Sam were waiting. Along with a bottle of scotch and four glasses.

"Enid will be here tomorrow. Man, I feel shitty about this. I did tell her the truth..."

"What?" Winter said.

"No, not that. She told me a story about her and Camden fishing. When she finished with the story, I knew it was my turn to tell the General, I mean Enid, the truth about my real job, working with the military on a special ops team." He poured a shot of scotch in his glass and swallowed it in one gulp. "And about Camden working as an undercover agent for the FBI."

"What did she say? Oh my god." Sam responded.

"She knew he was with an Agency. She didn't know which."

"She not only is a general but a mother. Of course, she knew." Winter commented.

"I told her about the day when Camden came to me for help. It was the day we decided to be honest — no secrets. Camden's handler agreed to the proposition."

What he did not say, to anyone was the three of them concurred to keep their arrangement among themselves. And it was that decision that still haunted him. The burden of that decision was his to carry. If he had only told his supervisor or someone, maybe Camden would be here. And so would Shelby.

"Trust me I get it." Sam said as she poured a shot of gold liquid into each glass.

"I never in a million years believe I would be planning a wake for my bro. With my bro."

"Hey at least I can make sure you do it right? Cheers," Jacob said. "Wait a minute. Do we say cheers for a wake? That seems rather cold."

"Can't get much colder than having a wake at your own house, bro. The FBI said it will be easier for them to monitor the arrivals at your house, Jacob. They will have cameras everywhere and we will make it obvious you are no longer living there. And as I say that out loud, it is weird. This whole situation is." He shook his head. "Fuck me."

Sam was watching the twins, thinking how the brothers were not only identical in their looks, but their mannerisms. *The touching of the chin with the left elbow resting on the right forearm. Pupils dilated when focused in deep thought. Passion with intensity in their voice.*

"I am relieved our parents are not here to go through this." Jacob said as he glanced at a piece of paper Winter passed to him.

"This is the list of friends Sam and I are contacting for the celebration of life for Jacob, Shelby and Camden."

"The crazy of this strange plan." Sam said softly squeezing Jacob's hand. "We don't know if Camden and Shelby are alive."

"Sam, don't go there." Winter said touching Sam's hand.

"Okay, liquid courage gone. My turn."

Sam went outside to the deck to call Shelby's parents. She knew they still had hope. Their daughter had only been missing a week. ARKose had to believe no one would be looking for Shelby and Camden. For now, it was the best strategy they had to keep them alive.

"Shelby's parents are coming." Sam said, just as Jackson and Winter walked into the living room. Jacob was carrying the bottle of scotch as Winter brought in the glasses.

They stood in a circle, raising their glasses as Jackson toasted.

"Here's to good friends, never above you, never below you, always beside you."

He turned the music on. "I feel like this whole thing is an endless nightmare that I cannot seem to wake up from." He sat down on the sofa and took a long sip of scotch as Toklat walked over and plopped down with her head on Jackson's feet.

"Back to the beginning. We planned for a wake and a wake it shall be. In less than 3 days." Winter reminded everyone.

"And tomorrow, two FBI agents are showing up under the guise of mountain-climbing friends from Talkeetna who want to pay their condolences. They will be setting up surveillance equipment." He added.

"We can pull this off," Sam whispered. "Really, the only thing that has changed, is a few more unexpected guests." She swallowed. "And Jacob is not dead but alive but we pretend he is dead." She clinked her glass with Jacobs.

"The morbid thing is I can watch who shows up for my wake. Ug, guys, what do we tell everyone when I suddenly am alive? Fuck, will I still have my job? Hell, remember that life insurance we each took out when we signed up for the gov? I wonder how much that is worth now."

"Not enough, I am sure." Winter laughed as Jackson's phone buzzed.

He looked at his phone. "Camden's handler is Shelby. My boss confirmed it with the FBI."

The room was silent.

"She is alive. I knew it."

"Sam, do you have an ETA for Jon?" Winter asked.

"What? Sorry, with the news about Shelby." Sam closed her eyes and took a breath. "His jet lands around 7 am tomorrow morning, but in case there are headwinds, he said by 8 at the latest. He has transportation and prefers to drive here himself. But he will text me when he lands."

"What else did the General say?" Winter broke the silence.

"First, she wants to be called by her name, Enid. Second, just that her gut told her he was working for a federal agency. The long periods he was gone and no communication. Ya know, I have been thinking about this, a lot." He swirled his drink. "We will tell her the truth about Camden. When she arrives. She needs to know and honestly, I think she already knows her son is not dead."

After a hearty dinner, the friends gathered around the fire and talked about the preparations for their friends wake. At 11:00 pm, they called it a night.

The next morning, Sam caught Jackson smiling when her phone buzzed at 7:45 am as everyone scurried into the kitchen, grabbing coffee as Winter produced a big batch of muffins from the oven.

"Perfect timing, as always," Sam said as she and Toklat ran out the front door. She stood by the gate when a black SUV appeared in the long driveway. At six foot the lean frame of Jon DeSuie stepped out of the driver's side door. Toklat started barking as she got between Sam and the gate as the stranger approached, with a faded canvas, duffel thrown over his shoulder.

"Ahh Toklat, the protector in disguise," he said in a calming voice. The barking stopped, and her bushy, multicolored tail started waving back and forth rapidly. Saliva formed at the corners of her mouth, a sign of affection from Toklat. She had caught many in the crossfire of that drool as her head matched the speed of her tail. Jon did not care as he bent down and rubbed her head, keeping his eyes on Sam. He hugged her tight and whispered in her ear. "Damn, I missed you."

Tears flowed down her cheeks, with no words escaping her lips. "We will find them," he whispered.

Toklat started barking and running in circles when Winter and Jackson came out the door and wrapped Jon and Sam with open arms.

He let go as Jon whispered, "Good to see you, Jackson. For now, I need coffee, and I smell something incredible. Winter's doing, I presume?"

"Let's get you fed and caffeinated," Winter said, squeezing her hand tight on his forearm as they went into the house with Toklat following at their heels. Sam put her arm around Jackson as he kissed the top of her head. He turned and stared into the forest, then shut the door behind him.

They stopped and watched as Jacob quietly greeted Jon. A scene that could have been so different.

"Dam, you look good for being swallowed by the sea." Jon slapped Jacob's back

Sam looked at Jackson with moist eyes. Friendship and love were their secret weapons, and with two missing, nothing would stop them until the circle was complete.

"Enough, Sam, help me get these men fed. Jon, grab a mug and the coffee is in the carafe. We got work to do." Winter ordered as he kissed his wife on the cheek.

The friends kept the conversation uplifting but sorrowful as they each talked about Camden, Shelby and Jacob. After a conversation about the plans for the following day he yelled. "You two ladies, get. Jon, grab your cup follow me."

He disappeared, followed by Jon and Jacob, into the pantry leaving Toklat behind sitting in front of the pantry door.

"Toklat does not like the man cave."

"She will move to the living room after I close the door."

"The music also has conversations of our voices to keep the canine calm." Jacob said.

"Even Sam's."

"Wow, no wonder Mik likes to work with Winter." Jon exclaimed. "I was impressed with her skills pulling off our virtual wedding."

"Ha! I have heard enough about that lover boy," he smiled. "My lady is a catch, but she is my catch."

"Yeah, all true. He owns some of these gray hairs after a few near international incidents," Jon scratched the tawny growth on his face. "I admit, married women find him irresistible. There were a couple of countries, where I was not sure diplomacy would work because of those indiscretions." Jon chuckled. "It makes me wonder, is Winter on some special ops team?"

Jacob chuckled. "Join the crowd. I'm still in the fog on that one."

"You two sound so much alike. No doubt, that helped play a part in this strategy to let others hear what you want them to hear. Your poor parents. I can imagine the stunts you two pulled." Jon exclaimed. "Business?"

"Let's have it, Jon. The blonde." Jacob insisted.

Jon's expression turned serious as he opened his threadbare duffel bag and pulled out a folder. He then took a card from his wallet.

"So, this is what my lady couldn't stop talking about at night under the covers. Shit. Can I have one of these? Maybe a half-dozen? That little do-hickey would save my ass and prevent last-minute trips to the florist."

Jon handed the folder and the reader to Jackson. After following Winter's instructions, he signaled to Jon that he was ready. Jon placed his thumb onto the card sticking halfway out of the reader, and then the monitor came alive with data.

With their team assembled, hope and determination surged through them as they prepared to find where Camden and Shelby were.

Chapter 15

Shelby

S HE CONCENTRATED ON the details of the ARKose compound. On the outside, it was a simple retreat, not unusual in Shigatse, except for the fact it was carved from the natural granite cliff encapsulating it. From an aerial view, the compound appeared as a single large two-story rock edifice, complete with gardens and a terrace. It was an enigmatic blend of a penitentiary and clandestine haven, nestled in the heart of near-isolation, somewhere between nowhere and anywhere.

"Why here?' She whispered as she walked through the gardens and through the steel doors to darkness.

What made this building extraordinary, was what lay behind the massive steel doors on the main floor. Extending outward and downward in the shape of a V, were two tunnels that vanished into the granite rock cliff.

She stood at the bifurcation of the two tunnels. Each tunnel housed two modest-sized rooms equipped with steel doors that would be invisible if not for the intermittent red blinking light of a retina scan. In the west tunnel, on her right, the first room served as the rock room where Camden dedicated his days to slowing and stabilizing element 87 and other rare earth elements from the Tibetan plateau.

The second room, positioned halfway down the shadowy corridor, functioned as the drilling room where Shing operated the powerful ZEUSS laser which cut narrow channels into the rock deep into the earth's mantle. The location of the channels created by the laser required the skill of a surgeon. Unlike a surgeon who might remove a mass from human tissue, Shing would articulate a small robot to remove a cylindrical core of rock from the earth.

She had no access to either of the rooms in the west tunnel. She turned left.

Like the west tunnel, the east tunnel contained two rooms as she walked down the dim passage, passing the first room — the computer and image analysis facility. This was Daniel's domain, where he spent most of his time.

She stopped noticing the small red blinking light and then continued to the second room where she spent her days. Her room did not require a retina scan or any security access as she pressed the camouflaged button in the wall. The door slid open as she stepped into the small laboratory. Her job, according to Daniel was to sample the waters of the several hot springs as well as the rock cores.

"Rock and water." She said as she walked over to the spectrometer. The analysis for the sample showed an unusual high concentration of a rare earth element called promethium. The rock core sample that Shing provided for this sample site, showed the same ratio of concentration. She walked over to the small cooler. Inside, she selected a glass bottle with a sample plot location. As she opened the lid under the hood, a strong odor of sulfur permeated the room as she poured a small amount in a Petrie dish as the door swooshed open.

"Hello Shelby." Daniel said as he entered. "How is the sampling going for our two locations?"

"The water from the hot springs called DA20N is in the

spectrometer now, Daniel." She turned to look at the small man. "As you can see promethium is high. It corresponds with the rock core as well."

"And what about SE15N and KA13S?"

"Working on SE right now."

"Good. Good. As you know, I do appreciate your assistance in this analysis, Shelby. Peiling is not happy with me."

"Yes, you remind me of that every day, Daniel." She glared. "If I do not do as you ask then she will kill me and you? What will she do to you?"

She knew Peiling would kill the man and so did he.

"I am playing along but don't threaten me. You brought me here. I did not ask to be here. You could have left me at the camp. It was your choice to bring me."

"You did offer your skills as a chemist, Shelby."

She watched him walk around the small room. *What does he want from me.*

"Yes, I did but…"

"I cannot control the weather, Shelby. So here, you are. And you are a great help in this process. You have skills that I admire and if we play this correctly, Peiling will also admire. I only want to protect you. She can be very, um, dangerous when she is angry."

He likes control over me. His posture has even altered as he talks at me. He is like a puff adder ready to strike.

"Please, do not misunderstand me. I appreciate the fact that you are concerned for my safety." She walked closer to him. "Here, look at this sample. It is quite amazing the link between the water in the hot springs and the rock deep below."

"Yes. It is fascinating."

"What do you want from me, Daniel. Why am I really, here?"

"I must go. Please let me know when you are ready to process the site SE15. I am predicting a surprise in that water."

"A surprise? What the fuck does he mean by that."

She placed the petri dish with the water from the hot springs identified as SE15N in the spectrometer and picked up the rock core.

"What is so special about this rock? Surprise? We will see."

For the next hour, she prepared the small piece from the solid core. Minerals contained in rock can be identified based on several properties that can be visually observed.

First, she recorded the color, the type of streaking of the mineral, the shininess, and then hardness. Next, she placed the sample in the electron microscope for identifying the crystal shape before recording its' specific gravity.

"Wow, this is beautiful." The soft, pliable silver mineral was a complicated lattice in a cubic shape. "What are you?"

A few hours later she saw Camden standing in the garden on the lower terrace. She watched him as he stared into the sun high above.

She approached him from behind as she wrapped her arms around his waist. "What are you thinking about?"

"I am too tired to think." Despite having the freedom to roam within the compound, they suspected they were always under watchful eyes.

He gave a casual shrug. "How's the headache?" his arm encircling her.

"All gone. The Diamox worked.

She tilted her face to the sun, her eyes closed.

"Is there enough 87 to destroy Three Gorges?" She looked at him. "From your earlier reports, the mine in Alaska would stay open until element 87 was 100% stable and contained for transport. It wasn't completely stable when you transported the element to the South Pacific. What changed?"

"Let's walk." He grabbed her hand.

Camden whispered. "We had a small amount, barely a gram that we tested in the South Pacific. The drill location was shallow and the robot sealed and secure. It was a tightly controlled test. Shing knew the channel and robot would be sacrificed." Camden shook his head. "I estimated the stability of francium was less than 65%. I argued with Daniel about the dangers of transporting it. My anxiety was greater than any climb I had ever done sitting on that plane knowing what we were carrying. After that test in the South Pacific, I developed a new technique to improve transporting francium." Camden was talking fast. "Or I thought I did." He stopped in the hallway and, rubbed his neck.

"You need to stretch more when looking through the scope."

They continued walking.

"Once here, I calculated we lost close to 3 grams transporting the element from Alaska. It is haunting me. I do not understand it. But something caused it to destabilize. Maybe in the rush to leave camp." Camden shook his head. "Daniel's response was too casual when I told him. Peiling will be furious when she finds out."

"Who had access?"

"Only me.

"Are you sure?" She asked as she opened the door to their room. "I need to rinse my face and take another pill."

"Yeah. I could use a shower."

Once inside their small room they continued their conversation in the bathroom. Camden was quiet.

"Like you said, the answer is in the numbers," She turned the faucet on full blast. "ARKose does own the mine so they can go back and get more, right?"

"Yes, technically. What if something happened that would prevent them from going back?" He jumped into the shower.

"To Alaska?"

"What?" He asked as he cracked open the shower curtain. "Yes. Maybe ARKose does not want to go back to Alaska. They don't need any more francium."

"That makes sense. If the plan is for them to market the process not necessarily develop the field. The vein, or whatever you call that."

She heard the shower turn off as she grabbed a towel and handed it to him.

"Shit, if Daniel overrode my access key."

"So, Daniel could have had access to the francium. But why? Why would he only take 3 grams." She went quiet. "But it could explain the discrepancy of the amount of francium."

"Enough to cause…"

"What? Cause what Camden?"

"Two thrust faults lie between the mine and Anchorage. And Whittier," he looked at her. "That is more than enough to cause an earthquake. And not just one."

"We suspected they might target the military bases. What if they did? And we did nothing to stop it, Camden."

He knew that expression all too well on Shelby's face. The way she arched her eyebrows and rubbed her temples.

"Shelby, that is why we left Alaska so quickly. And maybe why Daniel brought you here. They did what they intended to do in Alaska. And now, they are intending to deliver element 87 to target the suture."

She watched him lean against the wall and slide to the bathroom floor.

"The missing 3 grams of the most explosive radioactive element on this planet. We have 7 grams of stable francium."

"It is time to make an offensive move." She kissed his head.

"Where are you going?"

"I have a plan. I need to find Daniel. Instead of being manipulated by Daniel, I will provide him a compromise if he wants my expertise in chemical analysis. No more waiting. No more trying to figure out who is behind ARKose. If they caused an earthquake in Anchorage that is on us. We are done collecting intel. We are now on the offense to stop ARKose. We need to let the FBI know where we are."

Camden caught a spark in those devious forest-green eyes. "Shit."

He snickered as he thought about Daniel. He knew first-hand what Shelby and her magical charm can do to a man. No one can say no to those eyes.

As he stared into the mirror, he reminded himself why the FBI's plan went wrong. He underestimated them. Daniel was one step ahead of him the whole time. He dried his hair with a towel as he said to himself, "That will not happen again. I intend to marry this red-haired spit fire and no one is going to interfere. Especially ARKose."

CHAPTER 16

CAMDEN

THE FRAGRANT AROMA of curry and spicy red pepper filled the air, causing his eyes to water. Huddled close together, Shelby and Daniel whispered as he made his way to the table, a slight grin playing on his face.

"I'm not sure I want to know what you two are planning. You must be feeling better," he remarked, taking a seat next to Shelby.

"It can be summed up in one word: Diamox. Until Daniel was able to get me this medication, I wished I were dead. So yes, I'm feeling much better. As I was explaining to Daniel, if I am to be held here against my will I want to know why, isn't that correct Daniel?"

"I would use the term, guest, Shelby. As I explained to Shelby earlier today, she is our unexpected guest and because of the situation in Alaska, I had no other choice but to bring her here. As I told Shelby, you, Camden refused to get on the jet if I left your girlfriend at the mine." He stared at Shelby. "In a way, I was the one held hostage if I did not comply with his demands."

"And yet, you still brought both of us here, Daniel." He stated.

"Yes. That is true. You however, have a contract with ARKose to complete the processing of the rare earth element 87. And if you chose to stay, in Alaska, Peiling would do whatever it took to ruin your reputation and sue you for breach of contract." Daniel took a sip of his tea. "And no doubt, fire me on the spot for losing you. All because of her."

Shelby looked at Camden as he cocked his head with a slight nod.

There it was again. A shift in his demeanor.

"This whole situation could compromise the large contract Peiling is negotiating with China as we speak. You are not a guest but a paid contractor." Daniel stated with his voice raised an octave above normal. "Rather than that happen, I made a judgment call and brought Shelby with us. If we had been able to fly into Anchorage, she would not be here now. I believe that is called fate. I cannot control the weather, Camden."

"So why are we in Shigatse Daniel?" Shelby demanded. "And I need to talk with my parents. If I had access to the internet, I could contact them. When will that happen?"

Camden understood Shelby pushing on the man. Demanding answers.

"Since you are not listed as an employee you don't have access."

"Daniel, I still don't have access."

"You are not an employee, Camden. You can use any of the computers, including the two in your lab. Every click is monitored, but you have access to research whatever you need too on the internet." Another pause. "I. You."

Daniel was losing composure. His head was twitching and he could hear him, faintly mumble as if he was talking to himself.

"I what Daniel?"

"Shelby, I will look into the possibility of contacting your parents with the control center."

"What happens if I choose to walk out that door, with Shelby, and leave the compound? Is one of these guards going to shoot us in the back?" He stood up. "I did not agree to be held against my will and that, is what it feels like. You can talk to me Daniel or we are leaving."

What seemed like eternity was only a few seconds. He glanced at Shelby as they waited.

"We are out of here, Irish. Let's go."

"Wait." Daniel yelled as he stood up, pacing. He was running his hand through his hair and talking to himself. "I am sorry. I am under lots of pressure with Peiling. She will be furious when she finds out she is here and we lost…" He stood quiet, then spoke. "I was wrong to bring Shelby here, Camden. I was thinking of her safety and I was positive we would drop her off in Anchorage. I have handled this situation quite wrongly. I am not good with people issues such as this. We have a job to do and Peiling has a terrible temper."

Daniel had regained his composure. His voice was softer. He thought to himself.

"If you leave, Shelby will be in danger. We cannot risk our relationship, ARKose's relationship with China. She will be apprehended and it will not be good with the United States. I will make sure your parents are contacted. And yes, please use the internet but remember it is monitored due to security issues. There is much money and time invested in this project. Be sure of this, China is keeping an eye on us. Security of our work here is very important. Many would pay a lot of money to know what we are doing. Any breach can result in a dangerous situation for all of us."

"I understand that, Daniel. But know this, we will leave if threatened again."

"Yes. I understand. However, if you recall, Camden, your contract was not limited to francium nor did it specify only in Alaska. It did state that once the elements of choice, determined by ARKose, and at a quantity, according to ARKose, in Alaska, ARKose would have the discretion to relocate to another facility to process the remaining amount of francium, and include other elements as needed by ARKose. You were aware of this before you left for Anchorage, were you not?"

"Yes, Daniel I was aware. I however was not aware of when we would be relocating to a different country."

"I apologize for the last-minute notice to depart. Weather was predicted to get worse and to be fair, I was as surprised as you for such a quick departure." Daniel took a second before continuing. "However, to further answer your question as to why we are here, in Tibet, Shelby, China owns most of the rare earth elements on this planet. Peiling, at her discretion, found this compound with access to the tunnels. She had been working for months in acquiring a facility with access to mine the other elements that she is interested in. When this one became available, she signed the agreement but it had a stipulation for immediate payment. And that is why we had very little notice. And truthful, the timing was perfect as we were closing the mine in Alaska."

He studied Daniel's expression and then looked at Shelby. The man had an answer for all their questions.

"Daniel, to be clear, I am a paid contractor who also has other obligations…"

"Yes, you are but you sole sourced with this company. The duration of the contract is not to be less than 6 months and will not exceed 10 months with a clause to negotiate longer than 10 months. Those are the terms."

"So, if Shelby and I want to explore the city, we can do so?"

"Of course, with a guard and if it does not interfere with your work. Your priority is accomplishing the terms of the contract and therefore, what ARKose needs of you." Daniel leaned forward. "I apologize that you feel like a hostage, Shelby. I am also under great pressure by Peiling, to ensure this job is completed. I have not yet explained to her my, um, decision as to why you are here. To help both of us in this delicate situation, may I offer you a compromise?"

"I am listening."

"I propose a," Daniel stopped to think. "A field trip to the area that ARKose is sampling. It is a most interesting landscape of hot springs that we collect water samples for determining where we must sample for the few rare earth elements, that we are interested in. We could do that tomorrow."

"That would be an acceptable compromise."

"And to help me explain why you are here to Peiling, that is why I asked you to be our chemist in analyzing the rock and water samples. This job would have fallen on my shoulders as we could not find a geochemist this quickly. If you would like, I will draw up a contract. Yes. That is what I will do. That will work, what do Americans say, a win-win?"

"As long as ARKose is not doing anything illegal. Are they, Daniel?" She asked.

Daniel grew solemn as his head twitched side to side. "Well, yes," he laughed. "You being here is illegal Shelby. We have Camden's passport information which we required when Camden received the contract. But we did not list you on our jet's manifest. That is the other problem in having you leave the compound on your own. You came into this country illegally, which in China means, prison. That is another reason Peiling will be very upset at having you here considering she is negotiating a contract with China. You understand?"

He noticed a slight upturned smile on Daniel's face. Shelby is not only here to keep him in line, but if she leaves the compound she will be arrested. Daniel will make sure of that.

"It is understood that you know nothing of what our, ARKose's intention is, nor are you privileged to our activities here. Camden signed a non-disclosure agreement. But I will tell you this." He crossed his arms, and rubbed his chin.

"ARKose intends to make history by utilizing rare earth elements to provide sustainable long-term energy. Our intent, is to eventually replace fossil fuel development in the traditional, sense.

The mining of oil and coal. We are developing mining techniques that will eliminate slave labor in countries such as the DRC and Congo. China is open to this green mining concept. That is what you can be a part of. If you choose."

"I understand, Daniel. And when this project is over, how do you suggest I leave this country?"

"I will arrange your departure documents Shelby. You and Camden can leave together on the company jet. But until then do we have an understanding of your stay with us? Camden?"

Shelby looked at Camden. "Yes."

"I will fulfill my contract obligations and I will be grateful to you Daniel, to see to it that Shelby will get home safely."

"A change of scenery for a few hours would indeed be refreshing, Daniel. I've never been to Tibet or anywhere in Asia. It'd be nice to soak in some vitamin D and it is obvious Camden needs a break from that bat cave. His pallor is beginning to look more like a vampire." She quipped, a mischievous grin on her face.

"I concede my eyes are feeling the strain. Element 87 is stabilizing beautifully, though." He took a sip of his coffee. "Daniel, the equipment here for polarity reduction is leaps and bounds ahead of anything I've ever worked with. If we can harness that energy, we might just crack the energy crisis wide open. I swear." He took another sip of his coffee.

"Now, if Shing manages to get that drill under control, well, it will revolutionize mining." He tempered his enthusiasm; there was no need to oversell it. "Seriously, though, my concern lies with the area affected by the rock burst. Shing was exhausted when I stopped by this morning. However, I did notice, the vein is solid in one area. When we reviewed his notes, I suggested going around the vein. It would take a little longer but it will be more efficient."

Initially, Camden's visits to the laser room were fueled by genuine questions for Shing. Over time, these visits evolved into a routine, with the two men began departing together for dinner.

Observing Shing's routine, Camden noticed him retrieve a key from beneath a stack of folders. Diligently, Shing would stow a black notebook inside a safe beneath the work counter, locking it and replacing the key.

"We've been holed up in the imaging room all morning. The vein he hit is substantial. We've discussed your suggestion of rerouting that segment. It might be a longer drilling route, but it's safer. In the long run, the alternative path could prove more time-efficient. Peiling is eager for the chemical analysis of the rock cores. She wants the europium concentration identified and stabilized." Daniel stated. "And now Shelby can help with that."

"Europium? I did not think europium was a rare earth element."

"Yes, it is Shelby."

"I am familiar with europium. Can't we identify lanthanide and alkali metals through the sinter indicators?" Shelby queried, directing her gaze at Daniel. A flirtatious flutter of her eyelashes accompanied the question, a subtle test to show him her knowledge about lanthanide metals.

"Yes. We are looking at five lanthanide metals: cerium, praseodymium, neodymium, promethium, and europium. The term rare in describing earth elements is not entirely accurate. It is not due to their scarcity, but due to their intricate processing. Europium, however, is scarce. It's a neutron absorber." Daniel responded. "It's utilized in control rods for nuclear reactors, but it's also reactive—much like francium. We must shield it from atmospheric oxygen and moisture. In a world transitioning toward alternative energy sources, rare earth elements hold immense potential to meet that demand. The crux lies in containing the energy within the molecular structure." Daniel nodded. "Which is where Camden's skills come into play. And that is the reason for his substantial salary."

"I am not familiar with francium." Shelby lied.

"That is the element Camden was hired to stabilize in Alaska. We have more than enough francium." Daniel slipped. "I mean, we will have enough when Camden is finished with the stabilization process."

"I had processed 10 grams but somehow we lost 3 grams of elemental francium from Alaska to here."

"The process you developed did not work?" Daniel asked.

"No, it worked. Otherwise, all 10 grams would have burned itself out and probably left us as particles floating in the atmosphere, Daniel." He explained. "I discussed this with you when we arrived here. When I secured the francium just before we left the mine, there was 10 grams. When we arrived here, there was only 7 grams."

"Yes, yes. Of course, I remember. I cannot explain it. You must have made an error. Peiling will not be happy but we will have enough. We have the core samples. It will be enough."

Shelby looked at Camden as she furrowed her eyebrows as she thought to herself. *He is flustered.*

"Is that why you closed the mine in Alaska?" Shelby inquired.

"Peiling made the decision. It was safe to transport the rock with the element contained within rather than in elemental form. It was all in the timing. With this facility." Daniel asserted.

Shelby smiled, her gaze fixed on Daniel with her alluring green eyes. In return, he beamed back.

Ignoring Shelby's performance, he responded. "That should help Peiling's mood some when she arrives and finds she has a unexpected guest. And you are right, Daniel, maybe I did make a mistake in the amount of francium. I was in a hurry." He conceded. "By the time Shing gets the laser programmed, I will have element 87 isolated and stabilized for production. As for the element europium, a few tweaks with the stabilizer should do the trick after the process with francium is completed. I plan for the remaining francium to be in the processor tonight. It is a waiting game after tonight for the next 24 to 36 hours. So, a field trip to the hot springs tomorrow is perfect timing, Daniel."

Daniel agreed, suggesting they visit two of the hot springs and perhaps make a side trip to the nearby Palcho monastery near Gyantse. "I will arrange the departure for tomorrow morning after breakfast."

"Daniel, would it be possible for me to call my parents in Anchorage?"

"Yes, I will arrange for you to talk with your parents, Shelby." Daniel nodded as he stood up and left the cafetaria.

"You're treading on dangerous ground, Irish," he murmured. "That man is borderline psychotic."

"Yes," she responded undeterred. "I am not sure about psychotic, but definitely he is borderline sociopathic. That was very strange. You told me earlier in the week he was furious about the missing 3 grams. But just now, he acted genuinely, sincere that he knew nothing about it. Anyhow, we now understand he is a brilliant sociopath and you need to be more careful with your rocks. According to Daniel, the remaining francium was only in solid form, within the rock."

"Yes. According to Daniel."

"Did you find out about the other two locations?"

"Not yet. I am focusing on tweaking the francium. If I enter those locations in my computer, it will send an immediate flag to Daniel. I need to find out the locations discreetly."

During breakfast the next morning, Daniel allowed Shelby to make a call to her parents before they set out for the hot springs. Upon arriving at the control center, Shelby found Moo struggling with a problem related to satellite coverage. He explained the difficulties in reaching Anchorage to secure some equipment at the mine site. Shelby attempted several calls, but each one resulted in voicemail.

"That's odd. Could something be disrupting the phone service?"

Moo shook his head and shrugged his shoulders when Daniel arrived. He discussed the issue with Moo for several minutes in Chinese.

"Moo has been attempting to reach the mine supervisor for a couple of hours. He should be in the Anchorage office. Communication seems to be quite challenging from this location. Peiling is in Australia at another of our mine sites, and she could only reach us via fax. She mentioned similar issues with Anchorage." He told Shelby.

"Fax? Who uses a fax anymore?" Shelby asked. "Oh, yeah, I forgot. We are in Tibet." As they made their way to the administrative office, Daniel introduced Shelby to one of the clerical assistants.

"Do you know the fax number at your work place? Please write down what you want to relay. Um. I am positive you will find a reasonable excuse to tell them why you are not at work. Maybe a quick vacation for a week or two? Someone there, possibly can call your parents to let them know you are safe." Daniel stated. "Shall we proceed?"

Shelby nodded, concentrating on the Fax number for her office. A few minutes later they met Camden at the front entrance. She observed the driver of the black SUV; his robust, football-player physique. As he held the back door open for them, he displayed a chest harness and holster with what appeared to be a semi-automatic 9mm. He made no effort to conceal it from the passengers.

Daniel settled into the front seat, and she noticed that both men wore earbuds. A red emblem and dragon motif adorned the doors and license plate.

"Today, we'll be heading to one of the most productive hot springs for extracting our latest element, europium. The alkali metals lithium, rubidium, and cesium are also found here. There's a lake I'd like to visit as well, but it's quite a distance, around 9 hours of driving. Maybe next time." he stated. "I scouted the region and I believe there are other promising REE-rich hot springs. The findings from the research in southern and some parts of northern China, are exciting." Daniel spoke fast, in short bursts of information.

"Indeed, I recall parts of your conversation with Camden,"

Shelby affirmed. "By the way, what's the name of that large lake nearby?"

"Chabyer Chaka. 'Chaka' is Tibetan for salt lake. It's one of the three largest lithium salt lakes globally. It's quite astonishing that Tibet has more saltwater lakes than freshwater, despite its lack of proximity to an ocean. Chabyer Chaka is situated to the east, near Renduo village in the Angrencountry of Shigatse. The terrain is challenging with the altitude at almost 15,000 feet. It's a breathtaking place, with rocky four-wheel-drive roads winding through the mountains."

"This landscape is so captivating. The sky is nearly obscured by the mountains. Have you heard of Chabyer Chaka, Camden?" Shelby inquired.

"In research papers, mostly. It contains more borax than any other salt lake, and it's known to be abundant in various salts and minerals, including sodium, potassium, and lithium compounds. It would be a tantalizing prospect to explore the region for rare earth elements. But the area's remoteness, difficult access, and then the high altitude makes mining challenging."

Daniel nodded in agreement. "Absolutely. In the middle of Chabyer Chaka, there's a narrow stretch that divides the lake into northern and southern parts. The southern portion appears silvery white due to the salt, and it's dry. Meanwhile, the northern part contains water that's about 20 cm to 100 cm deep. Oh, and over there," he pointed. "In the western direction, you can see the towering snow-covered Ri'argeliang mountain, which stands at 6364 meters, or 21,000 feet."

Daniel gazed out the window for a brief second, then he continued. "Chabyer lies within the Gangdise Mountains, deep in the heart of the Tibetan Plateau. The road leading there is unpaved, demanding a 4x4 vehicle with high clearance. Due to these challenges, accessibility is limited to the summer months. Basic facilities such as electricity, medical assistance, hot water, and western-style toilets are non-existent. Traveling on the County Road means ascending to altitudes exceeding 16,000 feet, with a gradient of 12%. It stands as the highest-elevation road in the entire country."

"I am glad we are not going to be at that altitude," Shelby shuddered. "Tibet's autumn is nothing short of a fairy tale. The mountainsides look as though they are littered with gold. It reminds me of home, except that our dwarf alpine shrubs are brilliant red instead of gold. Wow. Golden plains at the end of a rainbow after a mist of rain." Shelby whispered. "The colors here are an absolute spectacle—blue, green, gold, red, all matching the vibrant hues of Tibetan flags. Is that where the flags 'colors came from?"

Daniel smiled, sharing in Shelby's enthusiasm. "Yes, autumn brings about the most exquisite scenery, with crisp, dry air. But it's also a reminder to stay well-hydrated. It's a unique experience—clear blue skies, cool brisk nights, and, naturally, intense ultraviolet rays. And in some places, you'll encounter strong winds."

"That explains the ruddy cheeks of the Tibetan people. Skin cancer risk must be high in this region. I have read that the air is thinner in the fall compared to summer, resulting in reduced oxygen levels."

"Look at that! Mount Everest offers a prime spot to witness the Jinshan sunshine." He interjected, pointing, while exchanging a knowing look with Shelby.

"This is incredible." She said.

"With lower altitudes relative to other Tibetan regions and abundant vegetation, this area is often referred to as the 'River South' of Tibet." Daniel said, then continued. "Given that Tibet hosts numerous Chaka lakes, the lush pastures around the salt lakes create a habitat for various rare animals and birds." Daniel gestured out of the window.

"Unfortunately, Asia grapples with water scarcity. Asia has less fresh water than any continent apart from Antarctica." He responded. "And water conflicts across Asia will increase with climate change and environmental degradation, leading to the depletion of nature's water storage and absorption capacity, perpetuating a cycle of recurrent flooding and droughts. The melting Himalayan snow that feeds Asia's major rivers is susceptible to accelerated effects."

"What about the Yarlong Tsangpo River in Tibet?" Shelby interjected, meeting silence.

Shelby grabbed Camden's hand, with a shake of her head.

"The imbalanced distribution of water resources within certain nations has given rise to ambitious concepts, all to nourish the arid regions in China's heartland. China's own issues with water scarcity and severe flooding are exacerbated by unsustainable intensive farming practices in its northern regions. They now focus towards the abundant water reserves held by the Tibetan plateau. China's river-damming endeavors, beyond hydropower generation, also involve redirecting water for irrigation and other applications. They are even considering vast interbasin and inter-river water-transfer initiatives." Daniel's avowed.

"These issues make you angry, Daniel? I can tell by the inflection of your voice." Shelby commented.

"Yes. China has invaded this land. They take and they take, what they don't own. It sickens me." He went quiet, before he began his narration.

"Tibet is one of the most geothermally active regions globally. We are collecting samples from several hot springs, spanning a transect from north of the suture site to the south, near the Yarlong River. Within a few hours' drive from our compound, we have three sampling sites—DA20N, SE15N, and KA13S—each with slight variations in bedrock composition and mineralogy. Notably, the DA20N hot spring is situated closest to the Gangdise arc."

"What is the Gangdise arc? Camden?"

"Basically, the arc signifies the age of a specific rock layer on the tectonic plates."

"It is all about the type and age of rock, then." Shelby responded.

"Our focus is on europium and cesium. Our primary attention are lanthanide elements which are quite abundant here in Tibet. And of course, the actinide elements or transition metals, like natural plutonium.

"Plutonium," Shelby nodded. "Yes, I suppose it would be prevalent here."

"While not considered a rare-earth element because it can be synthesized from uranium, we've detected it in our samples."

"The radioactive elements aren't so much rare, but their inherent instability causes natural decay over time, leading to lower quantities. Isn't that right, Camden?" Shelby asked.

"Um, yes. I am thinking of using a different technique to separate the lanthanides. One of the biggest challenges with elements that are radioactive—when atoms have extra neutrons or protons, the nucleus becomes energetically overloaded, rendering the atom unstable and causing it to emit radiation." He shrugged looking at Shelby. "In essence, it burns itself out. I have found a method to enhance stability by manipulating and slowing down the extra neutron or proton."

"I am confused," Shelby challenged. "I thought the reason for using these elements is for their extra energy? So, we can get away from fossil fuels."

"We do, but to use that extra energy surge, we put the element to sleep until we require it. Less dangerous." He explained. "Again, that is why I have no idea why we lost some processed francium during transportation from the Alaska mine to here." He shook his head and ran his hand through his shaggy hair. "Unless of course, I made a mistake in weights."

He rubbed his chin, shaking his head perplexed, he continued. "Nonetheless, the loss provided a test of its transportability. Peiling and Daniel were right. The raw rock held up very well and there were no unintentional explosions from the remaining, elemental 87."

Shelby responded. "That's science, right? It sometimes kicks your ass."

"You Americans have the most unusual slang."

"And Irish here likes to throw in Irish slang into the mix." Camden, chuckled. "With this new technique I am confident I can get the stability in the range of 98.9 to 100 percent."

CHAPTER 17

SAM

WINTER GRABBED HER hand dragging her friend away from her husband Jon as they walked to Winter's mint green Prius.

"You do remember I hate to shop." She laughed as she got into the passenger seat.

Winter raised her eyebrows and shook her head. "Let's hope we find everything. It has only been a week since the quake, and supplies are sporadic, requiring pained effort to find most items."

"Great. I just love that scenario."

As they turned onto the main road from the driveway, she noticed a black SUV appear behind them as Winter saw the vehicle in her rearview mirror and then nodded at Sam.

The two women talked about where to shop as she read the grocery list they had made. And then she went into a tirade about mining and why the hell didn't her best friend tell her about this new guy she was no doubt dating.

"She would not go caribou hunting with anyone, you know?" She exclaimed. "Shelby was very picky about that. She is all about giving thanks to the animal and respecting them for providing food, when she hunts. And yet she never told me his name or anything about this guy."

"Look for a parking spot, Sam."

"Holy crap," she said watching people pushing carts the size of a small car full of stuff. "I don't get it. People go to this place looking for a few items and they come out with fucking furniture and shit." She said trying to find a parking slot. "And somehow you save money?"

Winter giggled at her friends tirade on box stores. "Well at least Costco is open. Now to see if there is anything on the shelves."

"Ya do know I really fucking hate Costco. I never came here when I lived here."

"Yes, Sam you have mentioned that at least twice in the last 20 minutes. But who is counting."

She turned her head ever so slightly, appearing to look at Winter, confirming the black SUV was following as she noticed a military helicopter overhead.

"The air traffic is busy as ever. With hunting season and emergency services, the Alaska National Guard must be a frequent occurrence after the earthquake." She observed.

Three hours later, after stopping at a half dozen stores, they got out of the car near Earthquake Park, close to the North runway of the Anchorage International airport, to eat lunch.

"That was exhausting," she exhaled, biting into her sandwich and gazing west across the Inlet. "Our reward." She said as Winter squeezed her hand.

They sat on a weathered, worn picnic bench, its legs secured with a pile of small boulders, in the dust of snow.

The vista of the Alaska Range displayed stunning summits of jagged spires contrasting with the glacier-smoothed, rounded summit of Sleeping Lady, marking the end of the Talkeetna Mountain Range to the north and the beginning of the Alaska Range to the southwest. At the foot of Beluga Mountain, just north of

Sleeping Lady, lay a low-lying basin where the Susitna and Yentna rivers meandered their way to the Inlet, amid a mountainous terrain that had puzzled geologists for decades. But not the native people of Alaska.

"Do you remember the Sleeping Lady legend?" Her thoughts drifting to the words as she said out loud. "When the Sleeping Lady rises, our people will come together as one."

Winter nodded. "Until recently, Jackson said for years, geologists agreed the fault between Sleeping Lady and the Beluga Mountain front, was a normal northeast dipping fault. The original hypothesis by a geologist in the '70s said it was not a dipping fault but a thrust fault. With all the advanced technology, it was the expertise of a field scientist that had it right." Winter then added. "The irony. It always comes down to understanding the landscape, doesn't it?"

"Yes. Sleeping Lady is an example of that. A Roche moutonnée, which is a glacial feature resting on all that tectonic activity. Remind me why the fault type matters?"

"Thrust faults occur in weak areas of the Earth's crust, where one slab of rock compresses against another, sliding up and over it during an earthquake. Thrust faults have been the reason for some if not all, of the world's largest quakes. The 2011 Tohoku earthquake off the coast of Japan, which damaged the Fukushima nuclear power plant, was a thrust fault."

"Maybe our lady found out someone killed her beloved." She gazed across the narrow Cook Inlet. "Due west of where we are sitting is where the Coast Guard spotted the plane, or what was left of it. One wing lodged in a Sitka Spruce while the fuselage dangled, caught on one of the large branches, exposing the cockpit. The cockpit was full of sand and debris, nothing else. The other wing and the pilot's door had sheared off, disappearing into the waves of froth. They never found the bodies." She gasped. "And now we understand why."

Winter sighed. "With all that drilling at the Stoney Mine and then the activity with ARKose, maybe you're right. Maybe she got pissed when her sleep was interrupted by the reverberations of drill rigs. If only she could share the secret that angered her bowels of the earth where she lay. What spurned you, my sister, to shake the ground you lay on, without warning?"

She stared at Winter, her mouth dropped open. "Is that like poetry?"

"What?" Winter smirked before laughter engulfed the two women. "Oh my god, my stomach muscles ache. It has been a month since I have laughed." This time, they welcomed the tears that flowed from damp eyes.

"You think the guy following us got bored with the two emotional, weepy women?" She asked as they strolled back to the car. "You are the most brilliant, sneaky, badass woman that I know. I cannot wait for you to meet Shelby. I think I have a whole new respect for shopping."

"Well, from one badass woman to another, I look forward to meeting her. Although, I do feel as though I already know her after listening to your stories. But for now, according to my scanner, that guy in the black SUV is not within a quarter mile of us. So, I would say yes to your question. You ready?"

"Thanks, Winter for bringing me here. To this spot."

CHAPTER 18

JACKSON

JON AND JACKSON were standing in the front yard when they pulled into the driveway. They were more than happy to help with the groceries. Until, Jon walked up to his wife wrapping her into his arms, and kissed her, long and passionately.

Teasing, he yelled. "Enough. You got all night. Hungry people, and me, getting grumpy."

Sam laughed at her friend, being all too familiar with his ravenous appetite. And his grumpiness when in need of food.

Later that night, eight people gathered on the back deck with drinks and plates stacked with an assortment of food. Unlike a typical gathering of friends, the atmosphere was somber, and their voices muted with the sounds of violins, cello, and drumming. The dancing flames from the fire pit illuminated the surrounding forest in shades of red and gold. Two new members of this tight circle had joined them, Charles, the senior of the two FBI agents, and Ian, the younge rof the two.

"Thank you for being here. I am Samantha. Everyone calls me Sam. You probably, um, already know that."

"Nice to meet you in person, Sam." Charles nodded.

"Charles, you are Shelby's and Camden's boss?"

"Yes, I am. Shelby has told me a lot about you." With his easy manner, the muscular FBI agent with skin the color of molasses, answered. Sam caught a faint southern drawl as he spoke.

"Well, you know, she has never mentioned you to me," she teased. "That tells me how good my friend is at her job."

"She is at that."

"Considering, you have read our exchange of texts," she blushed. "which of course, I understand, but still. Well, you can imagine how shocked but relieved I was to hear she is an undercover FBI agent. I know she is alive."

"So do we, Sam." Ian, the younger agent, with copper blonde hair and a noticeable British accent, chimed in. "That is the life of an agent. I know it bothered her that she could not tell you, especially after the incident in French Guiana."

"Everyone, we are clear to talk but keep it down. Ian?"

"Thank you, Jackson. The license plate of the SUV that followed Winter and Sam today confirms it belongs to ARKose. All legitimate. However, the guy inside, not so much." Ian passed a photo of the driver.

"His name is Chul-Moo. Our records on him are spotty, but he used to be part of the Korean People's Army ground force, associated with the Pyongyang Defense Command. He appeared on the FBI and military radar three years ago while working in corporate security, but his employer wasn't identified. There are indications that he may have spent some time with a paramilitary unit in Pakistan, but it's not been confirmed yet." Ian waited.

"I cannot go into the details, but 9 months ago, a CEO of a large mining corporation that we had been tracking was assassinated while at a meeting in St. Petersburg Russia. He was part of a consortium of corporations, involved in the mining and selling of rare elements in the Central African Republic and Malawi. We believe Chul-Moo was the assassin."

"Malawi. Of course. Camden told me he was in Malawi."

"After the assassination, Chul-Moo went underground until today. Following you ladies."

Jon interjected. "Mik confirmed that the woman, Peiling, is North Korean but doesn't work for ARKose — she owns it."

"She's been a ghost until the FBI, with, uh, Mik's assistance, confirmed her fingerprints and DNA from that rock, at the mine site." Charles responded nodding at Jackson.

Jon continued. "Mik managed to piece together…"

Before Jon could finish, Winter gasped, "How did he find her prints? I thought the FBI and your team Jackson had nothing on her. This is incredible."

"We sent the print to Mik and," Ian said. "We don't know and…"

"We have learned it is best for us not to know." Jon added.

Winter's husband shook his head, took a long sip of his beer, and mumbled, "I knew it. A nerd duel. Man, I am so screwed."

"Peiling, like so many children, was born to a North Korean mother who is suspected of being abducted, taken into China and then sold to a Chinese man. It is suspected that Peiling, is the result of that union. She ended up abandoned on the streets." Jon stopped before continuing. "Many of these kids, that are half-North Korean, have been subjected to physical and psychological abuse. They don't get citizenship or basic rights to healthcare and education in China. Mik couldn't find any record of Peiling being repatriated back to North Korea or being granted Chinese citizenship."

Jon took out another piece of paper from a folder and passed it around.

"North Korean orphans and children can't be adopted, in most cases, by foreign agencies, but there are opportunities to provide them with food, shelter, and education. Someone found Peiling, in an orphanage, maybe."

Jon hesitated. "We don't know where she was found, but she was taken to the United States, as per the documents. A family in Virginia adopted her. Her adopted name is Wang Peiling, and she excelled in school. The last records Mik could find about her was her graduation from Brown University in physics at the age of 16, and her graduation from MIT where she earned a doctorate in nuclear fission from MIT."

"Shit." He said aloud, while thinking about the research assistant he knew at MIT. "I knew there was something about her, but I couldn't place her. Even this afternoon, I didn't make the connection," he muttered, shaking his head. "Let me guess, her thesis was analyzing rare and radioactive earth elements. Any chance Mik has a photo of her back then?"

Jon nodded as he gave Jackson an enlarged photo. The photo showed a younger Peiling with short black hair, standing among a crowd of graduates. The image was grainy and pixelated, but it was Peiling.

"I knew her. She was a research associate for one of my classes when I was pursuing my Master's in reactive elements from MIT." His voice fell quiet as he grasped the gravity of the situation. "This confirms it. Jacob wasn't the target. I was."

"No worries, bro. It all worked out. They took the bait." His twin said.

"They saw me with Camden in Anchorage. Peiling must have recognized me from MIT. If she remembered me, I would be a threat. She knew I was military. Where did she go after MIT?"

"He is still looking. She disappeared." Jon responded. "A ghost."

"Mik did some serious sleuthing after Camden took that picture of her without gloves," Charles added. "Mik also confirmed that Dr. Shing, Liu Shing is the CEO of a North Korean mining company called LSRE, Ltd. They promote themselves as leaders in green mining techniques. He patented several prototypes of the laser he is using now."

"In the last two years, LUNA, Inc. became one of the pioneers in that field under Jon's leadership." Sam interjected.

Jon nodded. "Mik and I are familiar with Dr. Shing but we never met. We thought it prudent to confirm him and his background. The

Chinese government has been pushing for green mining, with the focus on alternatives to cyanide for gold extraction and energy-saving technologies. They're using environmental and safety concerns, as a motivator to encourage mining companies to adopt these practices. Dr. Shing's patent on laser technology is a big win. And legitimizes ARKose when Peiling hired him. She has two leading experts, Shing and Camden. Where the hell is she getting her funding?"

"And that is why Camden refused to pull out." Jackson responded. "We don't know."

"The guy in the photo that Camden originally took with Peiling, is Yong-Sun. We know very little about him, except that he's connected to the North Korean government and appeared around the same time ARKose did," Charles the Senior FBI Agent said, passing the photo to Sam. "Mik is working some angles, but nothing yet. When you blow up the image," the FBI agent passed another photo to Sam, "he could be Peiling's twin. Interesting fact, Yong-Sun means 'powerful dragon' in Korean."

"Are we thinking North Korea is behind the earthquake in Alaska? Peiling, CEO of ARKose, specializing in REEs and nuclear fission is North Korean, or half. And then there is Liu Shing, CEO of a green mining company with connections to China, is North Korean. And now, Young-sun and Chul-Moo. All linked to North Korea." Sam summarized.

"What country does ARKose identify with?" Winter asked.

"Kent, my commander is working on it," Jackson responded.

"Even Mik has not found that out. Yet." Jon interjected.

Sam followed. "If the military base and Whittier were a target isn't that cause for war?" Sam asked. "Oh my god. Using rare earth elements as a weapon?"

"To accuse a leader of a foreign country we must have evidence, Sam. For the last year, ARKose has not committed any crime. After months of negotiations between Camden and ARKose, Camden finally signed the contract with ARKose to stabilize rare earth elements for them. Only recently, with Camden working at the mine site here, did he find out the element was francium." Charles paused. "We have a hundred plus of these small mining companies showing up around the world and by the time we get enough evidence on them, they either dissolve the company, are bought out by another, or disappear. Jackson, I assume you have had the same issue."

"Ditto," he answered. "My team was created because of those issues that Charles described. It is nearly impossible to track these guys much less catch them with enough evidence to prosecute. And every country has different laws. It took us 3 years to finally confiscate a small company in Malaysia, but the owner of that company disappeared before he even went to trial."

Jon's expression turned serious. "Mother nature didn't cause the destruction in the South Pacific, as we know from Camden's accounts of that trip. And the simultaneous earthquakes in Alaska. These were planned events using explosive elements, targeting vulnerable points in the earth's crust. And we have no direct evidence that ARKose is behind it."

"Speculation only." Jacob said.

He glanced at his brother and then at Sam. "We're dealing with something far bigger than we ever imagined."

"Why do you say that?" Sam shook her head.

"Someone or something with money is funding this operation. To find that quantity of and then stabilize element 87, and then the direct drilling using a sophisticated new technology type of drill?" He glanced at Winter. "Can you imagine? A war where the enemy is invisible."

"LSRE and Dr. Shing. His company specializes in robotic laser drilling for reactive elements." Sam chimed in. "Every natural disaster from a volcano eruption or an earthquake or a flood..."

"Could actually be caused by some fanatic with a grudge." Winter looked at Sam.

"Using climate change as a scapegoat for murdering millions of people."

"Exactly." Jon answered. "They've been developing a technique to drill deep below the Earth's crust with the ability to target specific areas. With sophisticated robots and lasers, there's no need for human labor." Jon paused. "It would take a small amount of element 87 in say, moist air or water directed at a weak area in the Earth's mantle, to cause a volcano to explode or…"

Jacob interrupted. "Or, cause an enormous mass of melting ice and mud to dislodge and fall 3,000 feet into a narrow fiord, causing a tsunami." Jacob added. "Or target a thrust fault and cause an earthquake in the largest city in Alaska."

"And all of this requires a lot of cash. The FBI and Jackson's team, has not been able to find that connection. This is why Camden and Shelby would not walk away." Ian said.

"JBER is the first line of defense against Russia and Asia." Charles stated. "But this is bigger. ARKose left the day before the earthquake. In a rush during a storm. Yes, we speculate they caused the earthquake but where is the evidence they caused it? All circumstantial."

"We believe ARKose has a facility in a place where a laser of such magnitude and precision can target weak or vulnerable spots, such as thrust faults, to cause explosive events." Ian, the junior agent responded. "There is much I am not able to say at this stage, but we do know ARKose was moving to another location. Camden mentioned this in a couple of discussions. ARKose, whatever they are planning, are not finished with Camden. We speculate there are other rare earth elements that need Camden's specialized skill."

Charles, the senior agent interrupted. "Shelby was never supposed to be an active player in the ARKose investigation."

"How long has Shelby been an undercover agent for the FBI?" Sam whispered out loud.

"Over Eight years. She is deep, Sam and only a few people in the FBI know her role." Charles answered. "She was unexpected at the ARKose mine site. The caribou hunting was her plan. We knew this was a risk but Shelby was willing to take it. The pilot was planning to be back at camp to pick Shelby up. There were indications that a storm was brewing. If the weather did hit, Shelby considered it to our advantage. It would provide her a cover story and give her more time to be there. She called it her Plan B. Shelby would stay at the camp until her pilot was cleared to come back but he would be the one to cancel the flight plan. Instead, someone from the mine, cancelled the flight stating bad weather at the mine site. When our pilot got the message that his flight plan had been cancelled, the FBI went into high alert."

"Maybe the weather got too bad there?" Sam said

"Yes, but the charter company or the pilot would cancel, not someone from the mine site."

Ian interjected. "If there was any indication that Camden was in danger, she was going to pull Camden. They both were coming back to Anchorage."

"And then the storm hit Anchorage and south western Alaska and the mine site. Our pilot barely made it back to Anchorage only because he is instrument rated. But he did not cancel".

"Who cancelled the flight?" Sam asked.

"We believe it was one of the security guards at the mine. It was not Shelby."

"Daniel." He said.

"Jackson, you mean the head geologist cancelled the flight?"

Jackson nodded. "Camden did not trust the guy. He said there was something off with him. It was Daniel. He made the decision. Either he was suspicious or…"

"He did not want Shelby to leave." Sam said. "You said she was deep. Could Daniel know she is FBI? Camden?"

"That would be almost impossible."

"Almost?" Sam asked.

"It's not probable, Sam," Ian hesitated. "And then we saw the text she sent you, Sam. That was a message to us plan B worked, but not exactly the way she intended."

"She would not be coming back with the FBI pilot." Sam said.

"Correct. Shelby and Camden would not be coming back to Anchorage. ARKose was making their move." Charles said.

"The bottom line is one of our own, an American, designed a technique to stabilize a dangerous, radioactive element and slow it down. He realized the potential of using francium as a weapon when he witnessed the explosion of Hunga Tonga. After knowing what it could do, even if francium was exposed to a droplet of water, it's potential explosion could have a dramatic impact."

"Camden would be the suspect. Not ARKose."

"Yes, Sam," Charles answered. "That was another reason he refused to back out. And why Shelby had a Plan B. Both needed to infiltrate ARKose."

"Didn't you say Camden was wearing a tracker?"

"Sam, the tracker went silent just before the earthquake struck." He rubbed his eyes.

"Shelby. She's not an expert in geology. If they find out she's FBI…"

"We do not suspect her cover is blown. Although she is not an expert in geology, her expertise is in geochemical engineering. And, she is posing as Camden's girlfriend. They took the bait." Ian remarked. "Daniel took the bait."

"Not realizing who that bait is or what she can do." Charles added.

"And the bait is Shelby." Sam reiterated.

Ian nodded yes. "ARKose will use her as leverage against Camden if he refuses to cooperate. The thing is, they don't know Shelby. She can hold her own. We will find them."

"Right now, we have the military, the FBI, and…" Charles, the senior agent was cut off.

"Us. You have us." Sam declared.

"Yes, that's clear. Apparently, it helps to have important people in high places," the senior agent said, looking at Jon. "Many of us are not happy with the terms Jackson presented us. However, I must admit, there is an advantage in having, um, assistance by non-federal agency people tasked to help in this unique situation." Charles nodded. "Your friend in the NSA spoke highly of the people behind the company, LUNA, Inc. Especially in this type of situation."

"Our expertise in this type of situation, is well earned." Jon responded, holding his beer in salute and then taking a sip. "And proven. We can do things, the government cannot."

"And we will bring our friends home." Sam confirmed.

"With that said, " he said. "While we are at the wake tomorrow, Jacob will be here working with the FBI and British intelligence."

"British intelligence?" Winter questioned.

"I am with MI6 on assignment with the FBI," Ian, the young copper haired Agent clarified. "We joined forces after Chul-Moo assassinated the CEO on British turf. Jackson's team will coordinate with his team, backed by U.S. military intelligence."

"Tomorrow will be a big day. Sam, you and Jon will be at Jacob's with Ian and Charles. Winter and I will join you for breakfast in the morning." Jackson stood up and yawned. "I also got a call from Enid and she will arrive just before the wake. She is getting settled in the officer's quarters at JBER."

CHAPTER 19

SHELBY

AN ACRID SULFUROUS scent caused her eyes to water which only got worse as she got out of the dust-covered SUV.

"Wow, that smell is strong." She coughed. "Wow. If I imagined what Mars looked like it would look like this."

Surrounding them was a desolate landscape of rock and desert pavement. A tapestry of yellow-gold prostrate vegetation contrasted against the scissored mountain tops of dark gray rock.

"At least we decreased in elevation. You, okay?" Camden stood next to her.

Trying to shield her eyes from the intense sun, she gazed upward towards the sound of screeching as she observed dozens of birds with massive outstretched wing riding the unseen currents in the blue-violet sky.

"Look at the size of those birds? Are they vultures?" She exclaimed. "Oh my god, Himalayan Vultures. The Tibetan sky burial birds." She turned in a circle, her gaze aimed skyward, as her flaming red hair whirled in the steamy air. Her rotation halted as she heard a faint clinking sound as she saw dark rounded shapes in the distance, moving.

"Yaks."

Twenty chocolate brown shaggy beasts, their stocky bodies the size of a small Volkswagen bus, were grazing on the dwarf grasses and forbs.

"Are they wearing bells?"

"Yes. Domestic yaks where bells around their necks so the shepherds can keep track of them."

Daniel explained as he stood beside her.

"The Qiang people of Tibet first domesticated wild yaks around four thousand years ago. These tamed creatures evolved from their wild counterparts and spread across the globe. They possess robust, well-built legs for scaling steep rocky terrains, along with larger lungs and hearts to endure high altitudes."

"You talk like a naturalist, Daniel.".

Blushing, Daniel responded. "I feel at home amongst animals. These animals have evolved physiologically, by having larger red blood cells thereby enhancing oxygen distribution within their bodies. Like camels, they sport a distinctive hump on their backs, housing a unique fat storage system that sustains their energy during prolonged food scarcity. These creatures are gentle by nature. Normally, quiet except for an occasional low grunt-like noise."

She noticed how unusually, calm Daniel was.

"They've adapted to the harsh Tibetan cold through their thick fur and a substantial layer of fat beneath their skin."

"An intriguing blend of traits. They seem like a cross between longhorns and muskoxen," Shelby remarked with a grin. "I could use a transfusion of that blood."

With Camden following, they strolled down the gentle slope amidst dense hummocks of prostrate shrubs, creating a cushion-like sensation underfoot. Brownish-gray rocks as sharp as slivers of ice, and white tufa marked the path to the hot spring. Eerie vapors materialized, swirling in the air alongside the strengthening sulfur-like odor.

She observed the vibrant orange and white rays cascading like molten wax from a bubbling white froth, captivated by the steam's billowing dance, dissolving into the air like ethereal white puffs. It reminded her of Yellowstone's hot springs, though here, the hues of orange were even more brilliant.

"It's like we've been transported to another planet, watching two aliens with these long tubes extending from their bodies," she mused. "Maybe the lack of oxygen finally got to me. I feel like I am in a deep dream state."

Camden raised an eyebrow at her. "You alright, Irish? Did you pack enough oxygen?"

"Just a joke, Camden. But seriously, look at this landscape and those two over there."

Daniel and Camden proceeded toward the two technicians who were collecting water and gas samples. Wrapped in thin silver suits, they were shielded from the hot water's intensity; the heat and the strong odor. Clear tubes and syringe-like copper canisters were their tools of choice. As she approached them, she heard snippets of the conversation.

"This peculiar hot spring is unveiling mysteries from deep within the earth's mantle, beneath the rocky exterior," one of the technicians explained to Camden. "This one is particularly odorous with obvious sinter formation."

"Carbon dioxide and helium gas are generating these bubbles, but it's the helium isotope that carries the key to its depth." Daniel remarked.

"Daniel, are you referring to the helium isotope ratios?" She asked.

"Yes, depending on where the ratio aligns, you can deduce if the hot spring's liquid emerges from such as the earth's mantle."

With a pause, she pulled a folder from her backpack and

skimmed through a spreadsheet. "Daniel, which sample is this?" She walked closer to him.

Glancing at his clipboard, Daniel replied. "SE15N."

"Europium dominates the chemical analysis for this site, and the helium ratio suggests the water originates from deep below, at least 75 kilometers into the mantle. The milky appearance of the hot spring confirms this." She glanced at the hot spring. "This particular spring boasts the highest europium concentration of all the sample sites. So far, anyway. These hot springs then, are significant indicators for the location and therefore, the mining of rare earths."

"Yes," Daniel answered. "But, the significance of rare earth elements extends beyond mining in Tibet. Here, rare earth elements in these hot springs hold the key into understanding plate tectonics."

"Plate tectonics." Her right eyebrow arched. "How so?"

"The location and manner in which REEs are discovered depend on surface geology and the tectonic plates beneath."

Camden, understanding Shelby's expertise in this field, smiled as she manipulated Daniel.

"There's been an ongoing debate among geologists about whether the collision of continental plates resembles the collision of oceanic plates. All rather boring, but important."

"In the past couple of decades, a group from Stanford undertook a groundbreaking endeavor. They mapped the boundary between the Indian and Asian continental plates beneath the Tibetan Plateau, using geochemical analysis from hot springs, much like what we at ARKose are engaged in now. Instead of relying on traditional seismological indicators, we are using helium gas isotopes." Daniel retorted.

"So, by sampling the water in these hot springs, you are also mapping the tectonic plates." She smiled. *Keep him talking Camden.*

"Yes. The researchers found two distinct signatures. One signature corresponds to gas originating from the hot mantle beneath the Asian plate, while the other represents the much colder Indian plate." Daniel squatted staring into the steam. Then continued in a monotone voice.

"Interestingly, the research reveals that the colder plate is detected in the southern region, beneath the Himalayas. However, farther north, India doesn't contact Tibet above—it's separated by a wedge of the hot mantle. This discovery contradicts the notion that the Indian plate lies flat beneath Tibet. That hypothesis can no longer be supported."

"Sounds fascinating, but what does that have to do with ARKose?" She inquired.

"It all boils down to earthquakes." Camden responded. "The Indian Plate plunges beneath the Asian Plate, giving rise to the largest structural feature—the Tibetan Plateau—and the creation of the Himalayas. This shift in geography alters the climate, causing significant flooding, not to mention some of the world's deadliest earthquakes. Isn't that correct, Daniel?"

"Yes. Geologists have conjectured that the subduction of oceanic crust drew the two continents together until they collided, closing the subduction zone and allowing the formation of mountains. This newfound evidence of the continental boundary beneath Tibet introduces the possibility that the continental crust might release fluids and undergo melting — similar to oceanic subduction."

"Basically, continental collision and oceanic subduction may not be distinct. Instead, they're geometrically alike." Camden chimed in.

Daniel affirmed. "As the Indian plate moves from the south, the thickest and sturdiest part of the plate dips beneath the Tibetan plateau, resulting in rifts in the Indian plate. We've identified those rifts in the same area where helium fluxes appear in the hot springs."

"So, why is this important?"

"Gems. Beautiful gems." Daniel remarked in a low voice. "Red crystals, the color of blood."

"Daniel? What do you mean gems?" Camden questioned staring at Shelby.

She squatted next to the man. He didn't move. "Daniel." She whispered as she touched his shoulder.

He looked at her or through her. His pupils were dilated. Then he smiled. A strange half opened smile, before he stood up. A few seconds later he continued talking.

"Where was I. Oh yes. Yes. I know." He closed his eyes, then continued. "Tibet is now acknowledged as a mineral-rich region. This is a challenge to explain using traditional tectonic plate models of continental collision. According to previous models, this shouldn't occur in a continental collision. But here we are. In Tibet, which boasts some of the world's most extensive and diverse mineral deposits in the world."

"Right. Diverse mineral deposits. And I suppose mining companies will be using this information as they move their mining focus to their next target."

"What is that?" Daniel demanded. "Shelby, what do you mean by target?"

"The ocean. Mining of the ocean."

"Gems, Daniel. I was not aware ARKose is interested in gems." Camden said.

"Gems? Don't be ridiculous. It's the location of active thrust faults that is of interest." The man moved away from the hot springs. "Skepticism is there, but ARKose believes Tibet holds a myriad of answers. Peiling is convinced that comprehending the Earth's mantle and the interplay of plates might unveil diverse minerals," Daniel paused. "And allow us to predict earthquakes before they strike."

"I have never connected the chemistry of hot springs to plate tectonics and earthquakes." She shrugged her shoulders looking at Camden.

Camden, shaking his head, ambled over to a sentinel of reddish-gray rock.

"Camden's fascination lies with the rocks and the mysteries they conceal."

"Yes. I believe so. Shall we proceed? We can stop at Gyantse for lunch on our way to the next hot spring." He said walking back to the SUV.

As they tackled the rough, pitted road to the next hot spring, she replayed the conversation between Camden and Daniel in her mind gazing at the scenery as they passed through the countryside. *This man is shifting. He has all the signs of personality disorder. We can use this.*

The dirt road weaved between golden fields of wheat and barley stretched against the backdrop of rounded, brownish-gray mountains—a striking contrast to the Alaskan landscape. Women, adorned in layers of vibrant clothing, stacked the dry grass onto wooden carts pulled by a solitary yak, decked in colorful fabric.

The scene conjured memories of Yupik women in a Western Alaskan village, dressed in their vivid blue and pink kuspuk, perched on dunes and weaving beach grass.

"Some things never change." She said. "The women are hard at work in the fields as groups of men sit around smoking pipes."

"Among the older male population, traditional wooden pipes are still common. And yes, women often hold the roles of laborers. Men are well, the thinkers, you could say. They smoke to clear their minds to think more clearly."

Camden chuckled. "Nice, Daniel."

"Yes, thinking without doing is so very important. Reminds me of our Congress at home."

Gyantse, an ancient village painted in shades of white and brown with accents of red and yellow, lay nestled within the contours of glacial-formed mountains. Steep valleys, swathed with dwarf grasses the color of soft pale green, cut into the loess-capped granite, like intricate spider webs. Flat-roofed buildings, constructed from dull slate mortar and gray bricks, seemed to rise organically from gray stones and sand.

"Wow, what is that building with the dome?"

"Shelby, that is the Kumbum. It means one hundred thousand holy images in Tibetan. The most famous Kumbum forms part of Palcho Monastery."

The bronze-tinted dome crowned with a petite spire, stood atop a multilayered structure on the horizon. It resembled a tiered wedding cake, each level adorned with a mosaic of reds, blues, and yellows, representing various Buddhist chapels.

Folded and warped, the arch-like rock thrusting through the earth's surface formed a perfect location for a fort. Carved into the rock, its white walls weathered by time, stood Gyantse Dzong, a sentinel over the town below.

"I read that the fort was Erected in 1390 to guard the southern approaches to the Tsangpo Valley and Lhasa with a wall spanning almost 2 miles encircling Gyantse, with its only entrance situated on the town's eastern side." Camden said. "Amazing."

Shelby knew Camden did not read about it. He was here.

"Here we are." Daniel announced. A bright yellow sign with red lettering, both in Chinese and Tibetan, proclaimed 'restaurant' on the narrow but empty road.

Upon opening the door, the fragrance of yak butter struck Camden, as a man with a cherubic face reminiscent of the Alaskan Yupik pilot, welcomed them. Daniel introduced everyone as the man smiled and nodded before retreating. Shortly after, a young girl in a long colorful, braided patchwork skirt approached, her smile radiating as she placed three blue cans on the small table. The restaurant was devoid of other patrons.

"Considering alcohol is limited, they serve this with the meal. It is called Chang. There's also sweet milk for after the meal." Daniel announced.

Having avoided Chang at the compound, drinking only black

tea, she found herself feeling much better and tried the beverage. She raised her can to offer a toast. "This is quite tasty. A delightful blend of sweet and sour, so refreshing on the taste buds. It is very similar to hard cider."

"Well, tiny sips, Shelby. We are still at a high elevation." Camden warned.

The young girl presented a platter adorned with six plump, doughy dumplings and three small bowls of creamy soup. Utensils were absent from the table.

The chatter grew quiet as the food was sampled.

"Vegetables are a rarity in Tibet. We have a local who brings vegetables to the compound, sourced from other parts of China and occasionally fruits from Indonesia. People eat what's available to cook which varies with the seasons; in winter, it's 'red food' or meat, while summer sees 'white food' or dairy."

After eating, they walked along a main street, where more people bustled about, with local restaurants teeming with tourists. Crossing the Monastery's entrance, she felt as though she'd journeyed back in time.

"The Palcho Monastery is distinctive and holds esteemed status in Tibetan Buddhism. It houses three sects—the Gelug, Sakyapa, and Kadampa. Its architecture is influenced from Han, Tibetan, and Nepali Buddhism. This ranks as one of the most vital Buddhist pilgrimage sites in Tibet." Daniel explained, leading them toward the Kumbum.

As he described the monastery, she relished the contrasting colors and musky, sensual smells.

"There is much to explore here."

A muted silence enveloped them with whispered conversations and rhythmic clicks of heels echoed across the aged stone floors. Within this tranquil expanse, she could feel the deeper meaning of this place—a spiritual connection between the Earth and the life it nurtures, cycling through different bodies. She picked up a brochure and read about the concept of karma, as it intertwines with a person's past actions, whether good or bad, and how those actions affect their future lives.

"What an enlightening explanation."

"Yes, Shelby, it is. Let's proceed to the monastery," Daniel suggested. "We will not need to ascend any more stairs."

While Daniel and Camden were engrossed in geological discussions, Shelby ambled behind, at a much slower pace. The plaza buzzed with people, with colorful prayer flags fluttering in the herbal, earthy scent between the monastery and the Kumbum. Her cheeks felt numb yet prickling, from the sun.

Lost in thought, she didn't notice a young boy staring up at her pointing his tiny index finger at her. With short, coal-colored hair his dark face held an expression of concern or perhaps astonishment. Bending down, she met his gaze as he handed her a picture of a Buddha, then reached to touch her hair. The boy's unease dissolved into a radiant smile as Shelby reciprocated, touching his small hands and then his hair. He responded with a grin and wide brown eyes.

Suddenly, a young woman dressed in layers of wool the colors of the rainbow scooped him up, uttering words she couldn't comprehend, though the tone felt familiar. The boy laughed while the woman bowed multiple times.

An older Asian gentleman, clad in simple wool pants, a white cotton shirt, and a colorful scarf around his neck, noticed the tall red-haired woman's unease. He moved quickly, with the grace of a crane, bowed and then conversed with the frantic woman. With a large grin on his brown smiling face, the man walked closer to the red-head.

"Her son has never seen fire atop a woman's head," he explained, grinning and pointing at her hair. "She's apologizing for her son's, um, curiosity."

She laughed and pointed to her hair before gently touching the child's hair, again.

"I see, he's given you a Buddha card. That's very special."

"You speak English very well. Do you live here?"

"Thank you. I reside in the United States now, but my parents still live here."

"Do you know what it means? This card?"

"Today marks the festival of Buddha Sakyamuni's Descent Day—a day when he descends from heaven. It's one of the four significant Tibetan Buddhist festivals that commemorate key events in Buddha's life. The others are Losar Festival, Saga Dawa Festival, and the Chokor Duchen Festival, as per our traditions."

Noticing the pen in the man's shirt pocket, she asked. "Could I borrow your pen?"

He handed her his pen. As she wrote on the card, she asked about the man's U.S. residence.

"I own a restaurant in Oregon, a small town near Portland," he replied with a smile. "And you? Where do you live?"

"I'm from Alaska. My name is Shelby, and I'm a biochemist." Shelby looked into the man's gentle eyes. "My life is in danger, and I need you to call the number on the card immediately. It belongs to my supervisor, and I can't stress enough how urgent this situation is. It's of national importance. Please read what I've written on the card to him. Timing is critical."

The man remained silent, taking the card and tucking it inside the jacket he carried. Shelby glanced away, then grabbed the man's hands. "There's a tall, white American man accompanied by a shorter Indian man walking toward us now. My friend and I need your help." She paused briefly, then whispered. "The short man is with a company called ARKose. They are holding us against our will in Shigatse."

A little lie but the situation demanded it.

"Is there an issue, Shelby?" Daniel demanded.

"No, not really. This gentleman helped me when a small child got excited about, well, my hair. He speaks broken English, Daniel.

I'm not sure I understood him correctly. Could you thank him for me?"

The gentleman began speaking in Tibetan while gesturing towards the young boy, who was being held by his mother as they walked across the plaza. The man was amused, pointing at Shelby.

"What did he say?"

"The child has never seen your color of hair before. The boy was quite concerned that you were on fire." Daniel chuckled.

"Oh my. Please convey my thanks to the gentleman. The boy was so excited. He was laughing and pointing at me. I was worried I might have done something. This nice man managed to calm the mother, who appeared quite upset with her son."

The man nodded, smiled, then walked away, his laughter lingering in the air. "Perhaps I should wear a hat the next time I venture out?"

Camden shook his head not saying a word, a grin on his face.

"This isn't funny," she scolded. "I could have sworn that little boy thought me a witch the way he looked at me with those big eyes. And on a day like today, which is some kind of festival celebrating Buddha's descent from heaven or something."

"Your hair is flaming red." Daniel pointed out. "Perhaps wearing a scarf before we enter the main hall of the monastery would be a wise idea?" He offered as Shelby walked away.

Ignoring them, she reached out to touch the gleaming copper prayer wheels lining the pathway to the monastery. "Please, Buddha Sakyamuni, help convey my message." She whispered, turning to smile at both Daniel and Camden, who walked close behind her.

It is getting warmer, windier, no snow, raining, it's changing. The Elders, long time ago, said it would be like this. Nupuat picurtuq nuna ciimertuq aqllat maqiluta.

—LILIAN ELVAAS

CHAPTER 20

SAM

JON SIPPED HIS coffee gazing at the snow-covered mountains beyond the wide, gray-blue waters of the Cook Inlet. She wrapped her arms around her husband's waist from behind. "This view. It is breathtaking." Jon responded.

"The short-pointed peak above the concave valley is Mount Spurr Volcano. Can you believe it? An active volcano just 80 miles due west of us." She paused. "And those two volcanos are Redoubt and Iliamna."

The morning sky was brilliant deep navy blue. A contrast with the white snow reflecting off the mountains, as stars were swallowed by the rare appearance of the sun slowing rising.

"Hard to believe all of this started just over there, beyond those mountains. Do you know Camden well?"

"No, not really. I enjoyed chatting with him at the conference where I met him. It is a small world." He took a sip of his coffee. "I look forward to chatting with him again. And seeing Shelby."

"Muffins have arrived." Winter yelled as she walked into Jacob's house.

Nibbling on a blueberry muffin, she watched her friends as

they prepared Jacob's home for a celebration of life. It was strange not seeing the twin in his own house.

This entire situation is nothing but strange.

Firewood was stacked near the fire pit and coolers full of beverages were covered in the fresh dusting of snow. Instead of flowers, cairns of rocks adorned the large backyard. Fairy lights sparkled on branches of spruce and birch trees, like ice cycles. And daylight waned; a signal that winter had arrived.

Enid, Camden's mom, a stunning woman with short platinum curly hair and bright blue eyes, was the first to arrive escorted into the home by Jackson.

"What an incredible view." Statuesque, dressed in a black pant-suit trimmed with a deep bronze belt, Jackson introduced Enid to the small group. As she was chatting with Enid, she heard her name called with that musical, Irish dialect. As she turned, she saw the small woman with short, auburn hair being escorted by a distinguished, silver bushy haired gentleman — Shelby's parents.

In her Irish tongue, she whispered, with a hand over heart. "Samee, my dear Samee. A-leanbh. Don't cry, Shelby is here."

She felt guilty for keeping the secret from Shelby's parents about their daughter. No matter how many times she told herself, this was a better option. *Would it be worse to tell her parents that Shelby is alive only to find out she was not alive? This is crazy. Sam, get a grip. You must be strong.*

More introductions were made as people streamed into the house for the next hour. Then Enid, receiving a slight nod from Jackson, carried a small bag onto the deck. As Jon put his arm around her waist, she noticed Enid held a multi-colored gong the size of a large dinner plate in one hand and, with the other hand, a velvety, red-tipped mallet. With a slight tap, a pulsating harmonic melody quieted the conversation. Jackson stood next to her as he spoke.

"Legend has it that a group of monks became captive of an evil spirit that confined them in caves and mountain hideouts, but they were released as soon as they heard the monastic gongs." Jackson swallowed. "Camden's mom, Enid."

"Thank you, Jackson and Winter for arranging a beautiful ceremony for those we love and remember. My son gave this gong to me." Enid swallowed. "After he returned from Nepal, one of his many climbing adventures. A monk, from a village he met, gave it to him. Camden said the sound reminds him of what it is to be free, of the vulture soaring through the wind. Today, we set Camden and Shelby and Jacob free." She nodded at Jackson as she slowly, tapped the gong, three times. Pausing briefly between each tap, allowing the vibration filter through the breeze.

"Let's raise our glasses to the sky. Stay free our friends, stay free." Jackson said.

The gathering continued with a series of toasts and moments of remembrance, as glasses clinked, and strained laughter filled the calm cool air.

The FBI agents blended into the crowd, of Jacob's co-workers and climber buddies as the afternoon grew dark and cool. Slowly, acquaintances said their condolences, leaving a few individuals lingering around the fire pit. And then she glanced across the Inlet to see the Sleeping Lady disappear into the Alaskan night.

"She is always keeping watch over us, Shel." She whispered. "We will find you. I will find you."

Feeling chilled, she walked inside to feel the warmth of the fire before stopping. Her eyes swelled with love observing two mothers, engrossed in conversation near the stone fireplace. The glow of the fire illuminated their melancholic expressions.

"Two grieving mothers," Winter remarked as she whispered in Sam's ear. "We will change that."

"And father," she nodded, spotting Shelby's dad with Jon and the British Agent, Ian. They were each holding a drink. "Today went well, I suppose. Thank god it's make believe. Where is the other agent?"

"Still with Jackson," Winter replied as they joined the two women in front of the wood stove. After exchanging contact information and tearful goodbyes, Shelby's mom gathered her husband and called it a night.

Cloaked in the darkness, a black SUV lingered on the quiet road next to the entrance of the Jackson's drive. A few minutes later, the SUV drove off following the last of the guests.

Jackson sat next to Winter on the couch, twirling her long, dark magenta streaked hair with his fingers, listening to Enid and Sam talk about Enid's time in Tibet.

"Jackson, I think it is a good time we talk about Camden and where he is." Enid said.

"You know he is alive."

"Yes, I do. A mother knows these things. And not to be to sentimental, Shelby's mom feels the same way about her daughter."

At that moment Charles and Ian both walked into the living room.

"A few minutes ago, one of our agents picked up a conversation between Chul Moo and another man. Chul Moo, in the same SUV that followed Sam and Winter, was monitoring this house. In that conversation, he confirmed that he had good news — that everyone of interest is dead and no longer a problem. Our agent is keeping Chul Moo under surveillance as he left after the last guest. However, we could not get a trace on what we suspect, is a burner phone. Yet." Ian said, nodding to Charles.

"Today, we received an envelope that was postmarked in Dillingham. It was mailed three days after the earthquake hit." Charles handed the envelope to Enid. "Do you recognize the hand writing, Enid?"

"No, that is not Camden's."

"Let me see?"

Enid handed the envelope to Sam.

Her hand shook as a tear flowed down her cheek. "That is

Shelby's. What was in the envelope? Where are they? Is she with Camden?"

Jon put his arms around his wife and kissed her cheek, as she grabbed his arm.

"Sorry."

"Inside was a piece of paper torn out of a notebook. There were three sets of numbers." Ian responded.

"We believe each set represents a latitude and a longitude." Charles handed the torn notebook paper to Enid.

Enid nodded her head. "This is Camden's scribble. I would recognize it anywhere."

Jackson leaned over as Enid handed him the notebook paper. "I concur. This is Camden's. Do we know the locations?"

"The first set of numbers is in China. To be exact, it is the lat and long of one of the largest dam's in the world. Three Gorges Dam."

"Jackson, could you show me?" Jon took a picture of the three sets of numbers with his phone. A few minutes later he received a call and left the room.

"Mik traced the call by Chul Moo. It was someplace near Lhasa, Tibet." Jon said as he walked back into the room.

"You said three locations. Where are the other two?" Enid asked.

"One is in Pakistan and the other is in Afghanistan."

"What? I don't understand. Why would Camden and Shelby be there?"

"Sam" Jackson cautioned.

"We don't think these are the location of our agents." Charles stated. "It is late. I suggest everyone try and get some sleep. Today was a success. Tomorrow, we will find where our agents…."

Ian noticed Sam's mannerisms as she stood up. "Yes, Sam, where Shelby is and Enid, where your son is. We are close."

"Jackson," Charles nodded for him and Ian to follow. "Your commander wants us at JBER at 8 am. We believe Camden and

Shelby are in China. If Three Gorges is a target, they will be close. My bet is Tibet. We are running scenarios and trajectories as we speak."

"Agree." Jackson watched the two FBI agents get in their vehicle and drive into the night before he came back into his house. "Jon, how about you and I head over to the house?

"Pantry?" Jon looked at Jackson, as he walked over to Sam and whispered in her ear. "LUNA's jet is at our disposal. I am giving notice to the pilot and crew to be ready to take off tomorrow."

"I imagine I am a rare individual who actually watched their own wake? " Jacob walked in. "I had no idea Amanda cared so deeply for me."

"Prospects happen. When you suddenly come to life?" Jacob grinned.

"Jon and I are working with Mik tonight. We are speculating that ARKose has a facility or a compound probably in Tibet. I am optimistic that between the FBI, my team, and Mik, we will have a location in the morning." Jackson looked at his twin. "Care to join us, bro?"

"I was looking forward to sleeping in my own bed tonight, but wouldn't miss it, bro."

Jackson repeated the plan for the next morning. "I don't think any of us will sleep tonight. Winter?"

"I will stay here tonight with Sam." She kissed him on the cheek. "We will see you guys in the morning at our house."

"Do I dare ask why they are going to a pantry?" Enid asked as men drove off.

"Jackson's bat cave or what we now call the secret spy room." Winter shrugged.

"It feels like a cave. A very tiny cave, especially when Jacob and Jackson consume most of the oxygen. And space."

Enid sat calmly, holding her tea cup in delicate hands as she crossed her legs. "It appears we have a good idea where our FBI agents are being held." She took a sip. "If my son is in Tibet, which is where I think he is after hearing the news we received, we now can make our first offensive move. A ceremony would be in order."

Winter smiled at Sam. "I cannot wait to meet Camden. If he is anything like his mom, Shelby has scored big time. I have heard stories about this guy for as long as I have known Jackson."

"We have the General and the mom."

"Tell us what you are thinking, Enid," Winter said.

"You can imagine as a woman officer married to an officer in the military, I was expected to conform according to certain protocols," Enid smiled as she held her pinky high as she gripped the mug. "Mind you, in our career as well as in our marriage, we, my husband and I, considered ourselves as equals. He understood the pressure I faced and he never faltered in his support." Enid paused. "After he died, I made the decision, after a talk with my son, to be the best and the brightest and the most successful of Generals. I accomplished that goal by maintaining empathy and humility. By listening to unspoken words. I am bringing my son and Shelby home. And to do that, we must work together."

"Oh my, I love this woman." Winter glowed. "We are with you. What do you need?"

"I received my doctorate from Columbia University in Tibetan Culture. After spending a few years at a variety of bases throughout Asia and the South Pacific I became fascinated with indigenous cultures. Especially the Tibetan language and their religious texts, and the tumultuous history between the Chinese and Tibetan relations. When Camden went to Nepal, and then, to Tibet," Enid chuckled. "He thought I didn't know about that little side trip. But a mother always knows." She smiled. "Anyway, I was so proud of him for making the decision to do what he wanted for his life, not what his parent's thought he should do or be. I never told him that."

"Did Jackson know Camden had been in Tibet?" Winter asked.

"I suspect he did. Camden was still in his undergraduate program went he went there to climb."

"You speak Tibetan?"

"Yes, Sam. Before I joined the military, I volunteered for a non-profit headquartered in Washington D.C. for Tibetan refugees while obtaining my doctorate at Columbia. I spent several months during a span of three years, primarily in Lhasa and Shigatse researching the local culture. But sometimes, I would travel hundreds of miles to remote villages. I was interested in their views not so much political but cultural difference and similarities, with their neighbors in Nepal and in China. Later, after I semi-retired as an instructor in Colorado, I focused on the relations of Tibet with China and the continued assimilation of the Tibetan people. I now volunteer for the same non-profit."

"When you said ceremony, Enid what were you referring to?" Sam asked.

"What better way to honor the memory of my son, than with a non-traditional Tibetan burial ceremony."

"With the vultures?" Winter asked. "The elders in my village would tell stories about death ceremonies. An elder, who no longer found themselves of value to their people would walk away usually in a storm at night, alone. It was our way to give back to the land."

"Fascinating, isn't it? How different cultures view the afterlife and respect their choice in death as much as their choices in life. But no, not a traditional burial ceremony since Camden is not Tibetan. We are going to Tibet to spread Camden's ashes in a country he loved." Enid paused. "With my connections, we will have access to several avenues of possibilities such as contacts within monasteries in both Shigatse and Lhasa. Once we confirm where Camden and Shelby are, I will make contact with one of our donors who has a home in Shigatse. You might say," she blushed. "He is a very sweet man."

"How would we do this since Camden is supposedly, you know, is cremated."

"All a guise to legitimize what we are doing there. If what Jackson suspects, I have a feeling we will be departing tomorrow and time is critical. However, once we find out where ARKose is, I will organize a traditional burial ceremony, only the body that will be buried, will be not a body."

"Like a dummy?" Winter gasped.

"Yes. We will stage a ceremony, fully equipped with a body. Now, this is all conjecture but if my intuition is correct, I believe Camden is in Shigatse or at least nearby. He and Shelby will need to be in a building that is secure, but not suspicious. Shigatse is a busy little city, with tourists and several major monasteries. The non-profit I volunteer with has several connections in the area."

"An undercover burial ceremony." Sam looked at Winter. "And to get to Tibet, we have Jon's jet. His pilot and crew are on standby for a departure tomorrow for Tibet."

"That means your husband, Jon, also suspects Camden and Shelby are in Shigatse." Enid contemplated.

"I don't want to bust anyone's bubble, but we are nothing more than private citizens," Winter stood up and paced. "How do you suggest we do all this considering this is a FBI operation?" Winter looked at Sam. "Jackson has put his career on the line already." Winter paused shaking her head quickly. "His military career, that is."

"Another crazy twist to this saga," she answered. "Damn girl, I can't believe you kept that a secret from me? Man. Jackson and Shelby."

"I know, Sam, but really it wasn't a big deal. I mean he went to USGS every day and his work at JBER was so undercover, I got used to it. He would work late into the night in the man cave. I assumed what he primarily did, was computer surveillance and tracking." Winter bit her lip. "This is the first time I have ever been exposed to the dangers of what he really does. Or what the bad guys can do."

"Leave the military and the FBI to me, ladies. Being a retired General has some perks. I plan to use every single star I have ever received to get my son home." Enid then explained her plan in detail as the women listened. "And we have use, according to Sam, of a private jet. And Jon, and LUNA have some close connections in high up places and within China."

Sam smiled with a nod. "Oh, he does in deed. I guess, really, one of the paybacks resulting from the French Guiana saga."

Enid nodded. "If the compound is in Shigatse, I will arrange with the local Monastery, a group of local artisans, to walk from the Monastery in traditional burial clothing, passing the suspected compound. We will have a child burial for ease of carrying the platform." Enid concentrated. "A distraction. Yes, we will have a distraction. Maybe we cannot find the trail to the cave or the burial site and we stop, deliberately in front of the security gate…"

"Maybe one of the people holding the body trips and falls. And everyone screams because the body of the child is going to fall?"

"I like that Sam." Winter nodded.

"Yes, and the guards see this and run to help the men carrying the body." Enid clasped her hands. "That would cause the guards to leave their post. Then Jackson and his team can infiltrate the compound."

"With me and Jon."

"Sam, that won't happen." Winter looked at her.

"Whoever is assigned to this, we propose a plan as a way for the FBI and the military to infiltrate. China will never allow US military into their country. Regardless of a threat to the dam. No," Enid shook head. "They will portray and suspect the US is the threat."

"Wait a minute. The US will not let China know?" She asked.

"No. The Chinese government would never allow military boots on the ground. We will be on Chinese soil and if the Chinese get wind of anything like this, well they will cry espionage the first chance they get. No, the FBI and the military will be under-cover. Jackson's team is special ops. A small contingency of soldiers. Whether or not they want civilians involved, well. We will see. If the Chinese find out there are two Americans in China, without documentation, it could be interpreted as a sign of war."

"War?" Winter asked.

"The result is always war."

"True, Sam. War is used as leverage, in most cases such as this. However, as private citizens, not associated with the government nor the military, if we have the proper documentation to enter the country, we should not attract any attention."

"I know my role will be helping Mik here," Winter stated. "You and Jon have been through this scenario before."

"French Guiana, I suspect?" Enid enquired.

"Well, another story for another time, but briefly I was kid-napped by a terrorist group in French Guiana where I was working with Jon." She took a breath. "A mining company had plans to impact the global monetary system by using a virus synthesized from a very dangerous plant. If they had gotten away with it, finan-cial markets all over the world could have been impacted."

"You at least got the cute guy when it was all done."

"I believe Camden mentioned this. The group had plans to kill everyone at the IMF conference in New York?"

"Yes. Mik and Jon met some very important people in National Security and Defense."

"When this is over, I look forward to hearing the full story." Enid declared.

"And that was the reason for Charles comment Jon having friends in high places." She remarked. "I believe we have our own undercover team. Now, all we need is the exact location of the ARKose compound."

"What if they are not in Tibet?" Winter asked.

"Well, we plan accordingly. We will know by tomorrow morning according to Jackson. If one of their targets is Three Gorges Dam, they are close."

"And if Pakistan and Afghanistan are also targets, a compound in Tibet would make sense."

"Yes, I agree Sam. Jackson told me a little about what Camden's role was with ARKose. My gut tells me it is Tibet."

Sam added. "Enid, Jon, Jackson and me are going to Tibet or China on the jet. Everyone needs to have their passports. Enid, maybe you can prepare a list of anything we need to bring specifically for Tibet, like Diamox."

"I will have a source for that in Tibet. I will check my travel bag. I always had a stash of that life-saving drug. With that, I am heading back to the base."

"And the FBI?" Winter looked at Enid.

"I suspect they are gearing up now. With Jackson's field team." Enid stood up.

"We have plenty of room here if you would like to stay?" Winter offered.

"Thank you, but I plan to be at Kent's office first thing in the morning."

"That would be Jackson's commander?" Sam looked at Winter.

"Yes," Winter answered as they walked Enid to the door. "Okay we will see you in the morning."

"And Sam? Be prepared to fly tomorrow. Bring everything you need for a cool environment." Enid winked as Winter escorted her to the door.

Winter looked at Sam as she said. "Ready?"

"More than. I'm glad I never unpacked. I need to borrow some winter clothing however?"

Chapter 21

Daniel

H OT SPRING, SAMPLE number DA20N appeared miniscule, boasting a diameter of less than six feet, than the other hot springs. Its' cloudy white bubbles were ensconced within siliceous sinters, painted in hues of green, white, and pink. Warped pillars of rock, a mosaic of grays and blacks, jutted from a landscape that was devoid of vegetation.

"Shelby, what are the elements from the analysis for this hot spring?" He demanded. When she read the chemical analysis to Daniel he was nearly jumping with joy at the abundance of dysprosium.

However, it was the subsequent elements in the analysis that caused her discomfort and unease.

"Oh my gosh," Shelby gasped as she walked away from the hot spring. "Plutonium and cesium concentrations are the highest at this location than at any of the other sample sites. Shouldn't we be geared up?"

"Our exposure is minimal at this distance. As you noticed on the previous site, the technicians always wear biohazard suits for this very reason."

"Why are you so happy Daniel? Aren't you worried about radiation poisoning?"

"Not at all." He answered.

"He is happy about the dysprosium. You are using it as an indicator of plutonium and cesium?" Camden asked.

"Yes. It is one of the most valuable elements for magnets and plutonium is one of the most valuable for many endeavors."

"I am confused. Why is ARKose interested in plutonium?"

Camden offered. "NASA's gearing up for a mission called Dragonfly to Titan, one of Saturn's moons, utilizing a plutonium-238 powered radioisotope thermoelectric generator. Plutonium's worth more as a technological asset these days than as a weapon."

Camden talked about NASA as if he even cared about the solar system. *You are such a foolish man, Camden.* He was laughing with joy at the unlimited prospects with the high concentration of the radioactive element. He tried to ignore the voice warming him. *Contain yourself. You will spoil everything with this recklessness.*

"Peiling will be excited about this sample site. It is getting late and we must be back at the compound before dark."

"It was helpful, Daniel to see the sample locations. I have a better understanding as to why you are interested in the chemical analysis from the hot springs to locate the rare earth elements you want to mine." Shelby said as they drove back to the ARKose compound. "The entire experience—the Buddhist culture, the intricate legends, the food. And the relationship between the rocks, minerals within these rocks, and the movement of plate tectonics of our earth." Shelby declared with a newfound determination. "Though the next time, I'll remember to bring a scarf."

"It is an interesting relationship. By studying the geology, we may be able to predict and to manipulate when and where earthquakes will occur."

"Manipulate earthquakes. That is an interesting choice of words, Daniel." Camden said as he squeezed Shelby's hand.

As she exited the SUV, Shelby looked upwards at the expanse of the deep violet sky. "The stars—they do resemble diamonds."

Daniel looked at the sky. "What's that you're referring to?"

"It's from a song by Rihanna called Diamonds."

A puzzled expression crossed Daniel's face at the reference to Rihanna so Shelby pointed to the sky. "You know, shine bright like a diamond —the stars up there."

Humming the melody, she clasped his arm. "Thank you, Daniel, for making today so wonderful. I now have a clearer understanding of the challenges and endeavors of ARKose as well as your role."

CHAPTER 22

SHELBY

A S DANIEL HELD the front door open for her, she caught faint, whisper of words.

"Oh, to be so innocent."

She smiled as she walked into the control room area, making note of the single security guard at the desk and said to herself.

Oh, Daniel, you poor man. If you only knew how wrong you are about me. Sam is going to crack up when I tell her you think of me as an innocent.

Following a light dinner, Camden noticed a slight wink from Shelby as she retreated to her room. From his peripheral vision, he noticed Daniel lurking in the shadows, watching her, as she walked up the stairs to her room.

It was much later when Camden slipped out of his room, venturing into Shelby's room.

Camden embraced Shelby as they settled onto her bathroom floor. "You know he watches you. I might not like the idea of having separate rooms, but I agree with you. It gives us more opportunity to be flexible."

"I know." She kissed him.

Camden found solace within the shelter of Shelby's embrace, nestled amidst a cocoon of blankets. Her voice, a mere whisper, tickled his ear. "You did what?" A hint of incredulity elevated his tone. "That guy might've been a plant, another ARKose guard."

"Shush, trust me, he wasn't. I was keeping tabs on a young English-speaking couple ahead of us as we left the Kumbum. I had them marked. The man, seated by the fountain, was engrossed in his cellphone and paid no attention to me until the kid started laughing and pointing. After I bent down to try and soothe the child, I lost sight of the couple. But then the mother started bowing and nodding her head as she tried to distract the young boy, away from me. When I stood up, not comprehending the situation, the man was there and in flawless English, he asked if I needed assistance. I seized the opportunity. He resides in Oregon, Camden. He's American." She recounted the rest of the encounter.

Camden brushed his hand through his hair. "Let's hope he can follow through."

"You deliberately brushed off my worries about plutonium and cesium at that last hot spring."

"Yes, and you're intentionally irking me by playing with Daniel."

"Yes. Wait, no. It's part of the plan."

A sly grin adorned Camden's face. "Daniel is an astute sociopath."

"Indeed, and he believes me to be an innocent. Me, a mere helpless woman, conflicted because of you."

Camden eyed her. "You should have been an actress."

"I am. As an undercover FBI agent. Except I get to carry a gun. Well, most of the time."

Camden leaned in to speak softly to Shelby. "If that message…" He was met with an ominous glare. "When the message arrives, we need to be prepared. Ready to fight or flee, Irish."

"He will call, Camden. You need to disarm that francium."

"Working on it. But to stop this using the element, we need Shing's help with the robot. It is time to have a talk with the man."

"Camden, what about the other radioactive elements? That is a lot of plutonium and cesium and europium."

"I am working on those as well. And the location of the other two sites. I circumvented the search parameters using technical jargon related to the stabilizing process. If it is flagged, it is easy to explain. Daniel has no idea that we are aware of the three target locations. It is tedious but so far, the two locations are in Central and or South Asia — Iraq, Afghanistan, Pakistan."

"Daniel is from Pakistan."

"And Three Gorges Dam is in China. What is the common thread?"

"All three countries are patriarchal. And all three with social injustice violations against women."

"We are in agreement that Peiling is not Chinese. Is she North Korean? Or both. What does she have against the Chinese?"

"That would make sense I suppose. We know Three Gorges is a target. That dam has always been one of controversy. Many North Korean women are abducted and taken to China. If she is both…" She gasped. "All three countries also have high violence against children. Not just women. Girls."

"I need the trajectories from here to potential targets. Shing. He will know."

"You told me about Nuwa and the flood."

"Three Gorges Dam will break and there will be a massive flood. Tens of thousands of people will die. Maybe millions if that dam is destroyed without no notice."

"And fire? What are the elements that would cause a fire. A volcano? Like in the South Pacific." She asked.

"Yeah, but a volcanic eruption would be slow and detected. I don't believe there are any volcanos that would cause burning or fire or…" Camden's eyes grew wide. "Radiation would burn. It would burn and kill everything. Cleansed by water and cleansed by fire the earth would be…"

"The Legend of Nüwa." She sighed. "Legends. Sam and I made an attempt when we were teenagers to snowmachine the body of Sleeping Lady."

"Say what? What is a snow machine?"

"Snow mobile. Alaskan name," she chuckled. "Sleeping Lady is Mount Susitna. We flew over her to get to the mine. I mentioned the legend after you told me about Nüwa. If you think about it, religious beliefs come from a story from the past that is believed by many people but cannot be proved to be true."

"And yet, when it comes to some religions, people forget that simple fact. They cannot be proved." Camden hesitated. "Shit. Afghanistan was one of the countries that was tapped by oil companies for oil exploration. There were hundreds of test shafts drilled in the 70's maybe even earlier. But with the increase in war and fanaticism, oil companies left."

"And I bet they did not cap those shafts with cement."

"And ARKose has enough radioactive elements, used with francium, not only to cause an earthquake but…"

"Those shafts would be perfect conduits for the release of radiation."

"Peiling and Daniel will prove the legend of Nüwa." Camden remarked.

CHAPTER 23

CAMDEN

IT WAS AFTER midnight when he stepped into the tunnel. He caught a faint glimmer of yellow light, and saw Daniel just as he entered the rocky alcove of the rock room. His lab. *What the hell is he doing in my lab at this hour.*

After a few minutes, with something in his arms, he walked back to the laser room. Quickly, with his eye on the retina scanner, he stepped into his lab but not before he put a pen between the door and the wall. And waited. It seemed an eternity until he heard Shing and Daniel approaching the rock room. *Keep walking, keep walking.*

As their voices faded and the lower section of the tunnel plunged into darkness once more, he retrieved the pen as the door sealed shut. In the confines of the rock room, he activated his computer and retrieved a folder about dysprosium. After a brief pause, he opened the door and walked toward the laser room, looked at the scanner, and strolled into Shing's domain.

"What are you planning, ARKose?" He murmured. Shing, a meticulous and disciplined geological engineer, lacked those same attributes in his housekeeping.

"Thanks, Dr. Shing," As he found the magnetic key attached to the underside of the desktop and unlocked the cabinet. He grabbed the black covered notebook and placed it on the desk. Carefully, he scanned the first few pages until he set his eyes on a page with a header. He recognized the two symbols: 重生

"You've got to be kidding me." He chastised himself, eyeing the calligraphy as he flipped through the pages. Some of the symbols were recognizable but not enough to interpret. To his relief, only the first few pages were in Chinese. Before going further, he skimmed back and forth, as he concentrated on the symbols. "There." He mumbled as he focused on the symbols: 女娲. "Yes. This is a copy of the legend of Nüwa. Why would Shing meticulously take the time to transcribe the legend?" Several of the symbols were circled. And then he turned the page.

"What the…" His gaze locked onto an image, recognizing the massive concrete structure—the Three Gorges Dam. He scrutinized the sketches and geological schematics but found Shing's notes indecipherable. His heart raced, and his mind went into overdrive. "This confirms Three Gorges is a target."

We had it all wrong. Alaska was never a target. But why the urgency to leave Alaska so quickly? "What is downstream of the dam? Think." His mind raced trying to remember the river. "A military base. Yes, there is a military installation." His mind wandered. "Someone of importance? At the dam or."

He examined the subsequent images taped to the pages, but they escaped his recognition—a series of grey-white cement structures surrounding a sprawling rectangular complex with multiple floors. A grand circular driveway, flanked by lush green grass on either side, which led to a fortified entrance. "This is a place of importance. The entire place is fenced with barbwire?" He squinted. "Yes. A guard house at the central area. All fenced in."

Dominating the scene was an ornate, oval-shaped building, crowned by a medieval tower that bore a flag aloft. He speculated, attempting to discern the colors adorning the flag. "Whose flag is this?" He whispered. *Horizontal stripes in red and green but is that blue or maybe black?*

Scribbled onto the page was a familiar set of coordinates, bereft of accompanying graphics, but adorned with notes in Shing's distinctive handwriting.

He flipped the page. At the top of the page in block letter there was one word in English. PAKISTAN. "The second target." As he identified the third set of coordinates, surrounded by an array of notes. In stark contrast to the previous page, this one exhibited a geological schematic, replete with arrows leading to notations. Amid dozens of calculations, his attention was captivated by a copy of a faded black-and-white photograph—an image of a slender, young boy with raven hair clutching the hand of a woman with dark skin and thick gray and black hair. The woman was dressed in pants and a jacket. In the background was a familiar structure with the curving arch over the water. The London Bridge.

Written along the margins with question marks and sweeping arrows were the symbols Fr and Pu. Further down the margin were more symbols that caught his attention. Eu and Cs.

Before shutting the notebook, he noticed a folded newspaper clipping tucked between a few pages towards the rear. Unfurling it, an overwhelming surge of anger coursed through him as he saw the headline of the Anchorage Daily Newspaper: 8.5 EARTHQUAKE AND TSUNAMI STRIKES SOUTHCENTRAL ALASKA.

The taped image below the headline was a single tower of the Hotel Captain Cook. The other two towers were gone.

"Shit." He realized the day of the earthquake was the day after they left the mine site and Alaska. "Fucking eh," he shook his head. "Now I know why we left so quickly and why Daniel did not leave Shelby behind. Anchorage and Whittier were a target."

He sat back in his chair. "Fuck."

He pounded on the desk and sprang out of his chair, running

his hands through his hair. As he did this, a folder fell off the edge of the desk.

"What the hell?"

He picked up a color photo. It was tattered and faded but it clearly showed a woman dressed in a kurta sprawled on the ground. One arm was stretched outward and the other over her head. One leg was curled and covered by her long dress but the other leg had a mangled bare foot, bone-white compared to the darkened clothes. A reddish-black stain contrasted against the lighter soil beneath her head and her leg. Rocks were scattered around her.

There was a crowd of mostly men, who had formed a semi-circle as if whoever took the photo was facing the woman. There was a familiar looking man in a sherwani standing over the body, holding a rock. He was all too familiar with this practice still allowed in many Middle Eastern countries. The woman had been killed by a public stoning.

He squinted, holding the photo closer to his eyes.

There, in the darkened background, behind the people, was a young figure, nearly hidden, peaking around a stone pillar. He could make out the whites of two large eyes.

Is that a child? A young boy.

"Why would Shing have this? You did your research, Dr. Shing."

He blinked his eyes and then focused on the child.

"Shit, could that be Daniel?"

And then the outer door swooshed open.

Without attempting to hide it, the notebook laid open on the table and next to it, the key. And then, Dr. Shing stepped into his office. His face was stone cold as he stared at his open notebook and then looked up at Camden.

"Shing, I've been waiting for you."

"And I see you found my notebook. You are quite astute Camden." He swallowed as he sat down, taking off his glasses. "Daniel required my presence in the control room. Peiling is arriving tomorrow, and our tasks are considerable."

The older man appeared exhausted, sporting raccoon-like bags under his eyes. He'd lost weight.

"We need to trust each other, Camden."

"Yes. We do, Shing." He replied. "I'm concerned about Peiling's intent in the use of element 87. Three grams of francium disappeared between the time I left Alaska and arriving here." He studied Shing's expression. "Daniel believes I made a mistake in my calculations. Do you believe I made an error, Dr. Shing?" He noticed a twitch in Shing's mouth.

"No, I do not believe you made an error." He stood up. "Come."

He followed Shing into a room as dry and cool as a cave as Shing settled at the keyboard. Three monitors flickered to life, casting a dim glow in the room. Through the substantial, thick glass window in front of Shing was solid bedrock.

He noticed a hole less than three centimeters in diameter drilled into the slate-gray rock—the cylindrical channel where the robot resided. Stepping closer to the window he saw the titanium robot, the size of a softball with its intense blue light reflecting off the rock.

The left monitor displayed a 3D schematic of the geological layers, revealing a channel within the rock bed, two miles away from a body of water. The middle monitor showed the robot, while the right monitor depicted a second robot channel beneath a substantial body of water.

"The channel is very close to that body of water, Shing. And those faults…" His face betrayed his concern. "Where is this?" Expecting to see the Yangtze River, instead it was an inlet, not a river or a reservoir of water.

"I didn't want to be part of this," Shing turned his chair to look up at Camden. "They killed my daughter and son-in-law. And now, they have my granddaughter Sunzi." He took his glasses off again, with his left hand, while rubbing his eyes. Slowly, he put his glasses back on and looked at Camden.

"I met Peiling at a conference. She was impressed with the laser technology my company developed and requested a meeting to discuss it. She's a brilliant scientist, but what I didn't know is that she's not Chinese – she's North Korean. Like me."

"You're North Korean?"

He nodded. "She laid out her plan to obtain the rarest and most elusive elements from deep within the Earth's core. I thought it was absurd. 'Impossible,' I said. She claimed to have found an unprecedented quantity of element 87. I thought she was delusional. I laughed it off and walked away, until she mentioned your name. Camden O'Connor. You. One of the leading scientists in working with rare earth elements was working at her mine in Alaska. And you were extracting francium. I didn't believe her until I saw you at the mine." He rested. "She pitched ARKose as the new 'ark' to revolutionize mining. The potential is boundless – new energy for space exploration, the eradication of fossil fuels, reduction in greenhouse gases, advancements in medical technology. I believed her."

His voice quivered. "We used the laser to cut two channels. One aimed north, targeting the area between the Denali Fault and the Castle Mountain Fault. The second went east, focusing on the Cook Inlet Fault."

Shing slumped in his chair. "Alaska was more than a test. Peiling armed two bots – one in the northern channel at the deformation zone and one in the eastern channel. She intended to cause two separate earthquakes — two different faults simultaneously." Shing fell silent, shaking his head. "I estimate she used only one gram. That means two grams is missing."

Three new images materialized on the screen. "You see the geological layers and schematics of the strata beneath the Three Gorges Dam. The rock channel is positioned less than 100 miles away from one of the world's largest reservoirs. The diagram on the left illustrates how she will arm the robot, with double the amount used in Alaska so approximately two grams of francium." Shing fell silent.

"You were deliberately delaying?"

Shing affirmed with a nod. "Until Daniel presented me with a video of my granddaughter with Peiling. She's just 7 years old. I can't let anything happen to her. But, I can't…"

"Peiling manipulated that to gain your cooperation."

Shing nodded again. "Yes, though I had no inkling that she would employ the francium to trigger earthquakes in Alaska. They timed the quake after the mine site was cleared and you were on the flight here with Daniel. I became aware of her scheme to demolish the dam when I arrived in Shigatse. Daniel grew incensed when he felt I wasn't exerting enough effort. He pressured me. I insisted on visiting my granddaughter and her parents."

With clenched fists, he pounded the desk, causing the monitors to tremble. Camden had never witnessed Shing lose control before.

"My daughter and son-in-law were killed in a car accident in Beijing. When Daniel informed me, I saw evil in his eyes. He said to complete the channel and then, once I obeyed, I would be able to go see my granddaughter. If I don't comply Peiling will kill my Sunzi." He wavered.

"Only I have control of the laser. If anyone else tries, the laser will detonate. I designed it that way to safeguard my technology. Peiling requires the detonation site to be 80 miles of the dam."

"Once the channel is complete, does Peiling have control over the robot?"

"Yes. My Sunzi." Shing was shaking his head. "I will not allow that dam to be destroyed." He grew quiet. "Millions of people will die."

"How do we deactivate the robot?"

"If we insert a virus into the software program. This is what I have been working on. There is no rock burst."

For the first time, he noticed a slight sneer on the man's face.

"Timing must be perfect. Otherwise, we will explode this entire area."

"Your granddaughter will be ok. We will stop Peiling and Daniel. Together. I have a plan."

Camden contemplated before saying to much.

"What about the cesium and plutonium, Shing?"

"My guess is both will be used with francium." He clicked the keyboard as more images appeared.

"Observe this." He brought up another schematic depicting layers of bedrock. "This is the southern shaft. Notice the 'Y'?" Shing enlarged the diagram. "Here's Pakistan and here's Afghanistan."

"There is a building there," he pointed to the notebook. "Who does it belong to?"

"I suspect a group of the Afghan Taliban. TTP possibly."

"Holy mother of," he got closer to the monitor. His face paled. "Daniel has the missing element 87."

"They will destroy the dam which will cause massive flooding and then they will cause not only earthquakes in those two volatile countries, but radiation. The goal is to cause chaos by turning those three countries against each other and against the free world. The US will be one of their greatest enemies. They will spread propaganda and lies across the dark web. It will be the next world war of the planet."

"Divide and conquer," Camden whispered. "The legend of the century. We have our work cut out for us, Shing. Good luck. I will be in my lab."

In a climate-controlled room, Camden unlocked a vault housing three lead casks. Inside each lead cask was a radioactive element, francium, cesium, and plutonium. In protective gear, he opened the cask with the stabilized francium. Exhaling he removed the silver element, transferring to the extractor. He locked the vault and settled at his computer. As the computer processed data from the extractor, Camden stared at his dented, tarnished lead coffee flask. A coffee flask that has never held any coffee or any liquid at all.

"Let's hope this works," Camden mumbled, as he sat back

down. "Let's see what you look like." Camden adjusted the electron microscope. The petri dish was alive with squirming, tubular creatures with fluid-filled sacs, glowing like luminescent diatoms of the sea.

Bacteria, despite their small size, make up the largest number and biomass among soil microorganisms. Endoliths — bacteria, fungi, lichens, algae, and amoebas, that reside within rocks, coral, or animal shells — are capable of surviving in hot and cold drylands where rocks provide thermal buffering, physical stability, and UV protection.

He only recently learned of the discovery by a group of researchers — a protein derived from the bacterium *Hansschlegelia quercus*, which they isolated from English alder buds. Because this protein exhibited the unique ability to distinguish between lighter and heavier lanthanides, He hypothesized that he could use the bacteria to diminish the explosive power of francium, cesium, and plutonium. He concentrated on the crucial final phase of the lanthanide element separation as he thought about Shelby and what she will do to Peiling after he tells her about the earthquakes in Alaska.

"Peiling believes she is Nüwa. Well, wait until she meets Queen Maeve. My Irish warrior." He chuckled remembering a legend Shelby revealed to him one night. It was about an Irish warrior of great strength, resilience, and at times, ruthlessness. *Even her name is intoxicating.*

Chapter 24

Jackson

AFTER AN EARLY morning arrival at JBER, the largest Air Force and Army military base in Anchorage, Winter, Jon and Sam followed Jackson into an uninspiring building typical of the 1940's World War II design. The only ornate feature on the dirty white, drop-lap wood siding was the double hung windows framed with six rows and six columns. Waiting for them as they entered was a member of Jackson's team. After an exchange of salutes, they proceeded to a sterile elevator that descended deep into the ground, concealing an undisclosed number of floors.

As they exited the elevator, another guard awaited them. "He's ready, sir," the guard said as he opened the door to a room filled with the beeping sounds of monitors and chatter between men and women dressed in camouflage military attire. A muscular man, his shiny bald head the color of deep russet brown, with many stripes and bars on his uniform nodded at Jackson. Standing next to his boss, was Enid.

"Commander." He saluted and then smiled. "Enid."

"I hope you slept well, Jackson. It appears it will be a very long day." She responded.

Sam heard Mik's voice among the chatter and noticed Jon standing in front of a monitor.

"Hey, boss-man," Mik nodded with a grin on his face. "Oh, that's right. You aren't my boss anymore, partner." He laughed as Sam walked over. "Hey there Sam."

"Hi Mik. Thank you for all you are doing to bring Shelby and Camden home."

"I love that red head, you know that. And I plan to give her a real hug this time when I see her."

"Listen up." Kent, Jackson's commander ordered. Within seconds, a series of monitors along the upper wall came alive. "As you all know, last night at 1900 hundred, a call was made from Chul-Moo, an assassin now employed by ARKose. Two federal agents located where that call went."

A satellite image of Lhasa appeared on one of the monitors.

"We traced the phone call to an area near Lhasa. It's isolated, but this region has the most active tectonic activity on the planet. The Tibetan Plateau."

"Mik." Kent declared. "All yours."

"The active Kepingtage fault, the frontal fault of the Kalpin thrust zone, is 137 miles long. Paleoseismology along the Kepingtage fault has ruptured alluvial fans and created several fault scarps at the foot of Kepingtage Mountain."

"Paleoseismology What does that mean, Jackson?" Sam furrowed her eyebrows.

"The study of old earthquakes, Sam." He rubbed his chin. "The basic assumption of Paleoseismology, is that if it happened in the past, it will happen in the future. There have been a series of earthquakes occurring on the west Kalpin thrust zone."

Mik interjected. "Triggered by the shallow slips during the 2020 Jiashi earthquake, something might have reactivated the basement fault."

"Can you explain that in layperson terms, please?" Sam looked at Jackson.

"In simpler terms, if element 87 were to be unleashed in this zone, in a coordinated combination of events, the result would be an apocalyptic scenario. If the target was hit, hundreds of thousands could be killed from the flood alone. Three Gorges Dam would be demolished within seconds."

The room fell quiet as everyone studied the images displayed on the monitors, understanding the potential devastation they were facing.

An image of a black SUV appeared on one of the monitors.

"We know the driver of the black SUV who made the call last night is the assassin, Chul-Moo. However, we have confirmed the man on the other end of that conversation is that of Yong-Sun." Mik interjected. "We have also confirmed the locations of the series of numbers that are reference locations. The first set of numbers refers to the latitude and the second set of numbers refers to longitude." Mik listed the numbers on the screen.

#1: Latitude: 30.8233° N, Longitude: 111.0037° E

#2: Latitude: 34. 5553° N, Longitude: 69.2075° E

#3: Latitude: 33.7380 ° N, Longitude: 73.0844° E

"In comparison, just picking a random point in Lhasa, the lat and long is 30.4731° N and 91.1011° E." Mik stated. "This information supports the vicinity of the phone call."

"If these are the locations of potential targets, we conclude that Alaska was more than just a test. It was accelerated. Unlike the test in the South Pacific, this one killed over 300 people. And impacted the primary transportation route for the rest of Alaska. The targets are not U.S. military installations which is what we originally suspected." Kent disclosed. "Mik."

"ARKose is ramping up. Ladies and gentlemen, I present to you the largest dam in the world — the Three Gorges Dam on the Yangtze River. If our suspicions hold true, this is the first target in using element 87 on the thrust fault system of the Tibetan Plateau. ARKose is planning to create an earthquake with a magnitude large enough to destroy the largest dam on the planet." Mik explained, taking a breath. "This dam spans two major fault lines—the Jiuwanxi and the Zigui–Badong faults. The reservoir extends 370 miles along the Yangtze River, upstream from the dam itself. When operating at full capacity, the reservoir covers a surface area of over 417 square miles."

At that moment, Charles the Senior FBI agent walked into the room, making eye contact with the commander.

"Charles, you have the floor."

"Early this morning, we discovered that the unknown North Korean Young-Sun is in fact, related to Peiling. He is her twin brother. As a boy of mixed blood, his life took a different path than his twin sister. Although it was not the most virtuous of paths. We asked Mik to use his, uh, to see what he could find on Young-Sun. Mik."

"Once I had a name, I did a deep dive on the brother and sister. As a young child, Peiling lived with her mother on the streets of China. There is nothing on her for a gap of three years or so until Peiling was found in an orphanage and illegally adopted by an American couple with connections to China." A pause as keys were heard clicking. "The father of the twins, raised the boy. Raised is probably not the correct word to describe the life this young boy had." Mik paused again. "Jon."

Jon continued the story. "Because the young boy was half North Korean, he was treated as a servant. They, the Chinese, did not acknowledge him, even though his father was an important man in the Chinese political circle. Who, by the way, was involved in a questionable and very profitable business. Yong-Sun was entertainment at his father's business parties as he grew older."

Mik added. "Without divulging my source, I managed to find a report with his DNA in a rather unusual location." Mik paused as an image appeared on one of the overhead monitors. "From the DNA, we found a match for his sister, Peiling."

Sam noticed Charles, the senior FBI agent shake his head and stared at Jon. In response, Jon raised an eyebrow and shook his head no. This time, no one asked where or how Mik got his information.

Charles interjected. "We suspect Peiling overheard a conversation between her adoptive parents and a gentleman from the Chinese Embassy, who frequently attended one of the many parties at her parent's home in the United States." He halted briefly. "When Peiling was at MIT, we have documents that confirm she was researching her past."

Mik took over. "From the dark web, I found information that Peiling did discover she had a twin brother. Once she graduated with her doctorate by the age of 22, she left the United States and her adoptive Chinese family. They never heard from her again."

The senior agent concluded. "Peiling found her brother, Yong-Sun, and together, they formed a plan of revenge. The target is not an individual. They are going after those responsible for kidnapping their mother and others within the child slave trade. We suspect, their focus is on cultures that treat women and children as slaves."

"We miscalculated the intention of ARKose. As everyone in this room understands, fanaticism can be as dangerous as power or greed. Peiling and Yong-Sun are holding the leaders of three countries responsible, punishing the country, regardless of the innocent lives lost." Kent nodded.

Enid spoke up. "The Chinese have, for millennia, manipulated waterways for flood control, irrigation, and navigation. But it goes beyond that. For China's imperial rulers, the ability to harness rivers saved lives and brought prosperity. But it also provided legitimacy to their reign. They consider natural disasters such as flooding a sign that the emperor has lost the mandate of heaven, by which he ruled." Enid crossed her arms as she looked at the image of Three Gorges Dam.

"Every Chinese leader since Sun Yat-sen, the founding father of modern China, dreamed of building a massive dam on the Yangtze, which historically, has wreaked havoc on its banks during flood season."

"Wait a minute," Sam took a breath. "Peiling will destroy Three Gorges Dam, a structure that uprooted more than a million local people who lived along the shores of the Yangtze River during its construction — people who relied on that very water for their livelihood all because of… unbelievable. " Sam took a breath.

Enid interjected. "Peiling and her brother would not destroy just the largest dam in the world — they would shatter the dignity of the imperial rulers' beliefs." Enid stated. "For nation shall rise against nation, and kingdom against kingdom: and there shall be earthquakes in diverse places, and there shall be famines and troubles. These are the beginnings of sorrows."

"Matthew 24." Mik stated. "King James Version, I think."

"Indeed, it is." Enid countered.

"Camden made a point to tell me that if we understood the legend, we would understand the intent. The reason behind ARKose." He noted. "What is the bible but a legend?"

"In the late 1970s, Deng Xiaoping, the new leader, brought up the idea again to build a great dam, but some of the most prominent hydrologists and environmentalists opposed it." Sam cut in.

"I remember this. They debated it throughout the next decade." Mik added.

"Displaced residents have complained about inadequate compensation and a lack of farmland and jobs after relocation. Farmers and migrant families were forced to abandon their fertile riverside flatlands to farm on the steep, highly erodible slopes." Sam commented. "Jackson, besides the thrust-faults under the dam, what is the geology?"

He nodded. "In addition to what Mik said about the thrust faults, the dam has had a serious geological impact. Chinese officials and experts admitted that the Three Gorges Dam increased the frequency of landslides. Geologists reported that the water in the reservoir saturates and erodes the base of the cliffs. The fluctuation in water levels changes the weight of the reservoir and increase the pressure on the slopes, destabilizing the shoreline."

"Not unlike Barry Arm Glacier and the landslide." Winter interjected.

"Which is why," Jon articulated, "scientists argue that the weight of the large reservoir and the permeation of water into the rocks underneath can trigger earthquakes in regions already under considerable tectonic stress."

"And the vulnerability of Three Gorges Dam is well documented," Charles said. "No one would be surprised if a massive earthquake destroyed Three Gorges."

"No one would even suspect that this would be an act of terrorism." Charles articulated.

Sam asked. "What about the other two series of numbers? If target one, is Three Gorges Dam."

"Target number 2 is in the region of Kabul, Afghanistan," Kent pointed at a map on the monitor. Target number 3 is near Islamabad, Pakistan. The intent of ARKose is to target countries with the highest rates of violence against women and children."

"We suspect both of these targets will be attacked simultaneously." Jon advised.

"Which is what they did here. They attacked Anchorage and Whittier." Sam countered.

Once again, silence filled the room as the gravity of the situation weighed on everyone.

The image of a small framed, dark-haired man appeared on the monitor.

"Camden provided this photo to me at my house. This man, Daniel, is the head geologist for ARKose, and he is from Pakistan. He was smuggled to London by his mother's Aunt when he was around 8 years old," he rubbed his chin with eyes focused. "This confirms what Daniel told Camden. And what Camden told me when he gave me this photo. Mik."

"From what I found, we suspect the mother was spotted without the boy and, when she refused to reveal his whereabouts, she was stoned to death, in a public meeting area."

Sam spoke up. "There were witnesses?"

"Yes," Mik answered. "I found this faded, black and white photo. Public stoning although not common, does happen especially to women."

"The boy was traumatized and did not speak for over a year. Apparently, he witnessed his mother's death." Jackson turned and looked at Charles, the senior FBI agent.

A heavy silence filled the room.

"And why Afghanistan?" Winter asked breaking the silence.

"We have not found a direct tie to Afghanistan. It's possible that it could be a diversion. Its proximity to Pakistan and the influence of the Afghan Taliban might play a role. Both Afghanistan and Pakistan have a history of mistreating women and children." Kent answered.

"All three cultures have a history of violence against women and girls," Sam uttered before continuing. "Not to mention, all three regions are prone to active and violent earthquakes and flooding. Pakistan has faced some of the most disastrous floods in history. While their carbon footprint is low, they are amongst the most affected by climate change — flash floods, due to deforestation and unplanned urbanization," Sam contemplated. "The first images Camden gave you show the TTP guy from Pakistan. Jackson, you suspected a role of the TTP initially because of Daniel."

"Yes, we now have a connection between Daniel and his father, a leader of the Tehreek-e-Taliban from Pakistan. In fact, the lat-long is in the area where the leader of the Afghan TTP is headquartered. Daniel is the link."

"The troubles that were mentioned in the bible." Enid repeated.

"And North Korea was also suspected and now we know Peiling and Yong-Sun are half North Korean. This is about revenge." Jon nodded.

"Three innocent children caught in the crossfire of cultural cruelty and political absurdities." Winter said solemnly.

"ARKose will do what they did here. They will hit both Afghanistan and Pakistan at the same time." Charles, the senior agent said.

CHAPTER 25

SAM

"MIK, TELL ME you are working on finding the money?" She asked.

"Sam, you know me all too well. I have feelers in the dark web and," Mik paused. "And other places while running several programs to find the financial link to ARKose. I will find the money."

While Mik and Jackson were discussing thrust faults, she noticed a sergeant enter the room. He whispered in the commanders ear as the commander then walked over to Charles. They both left the room. She leaned over to Winter and whispered. "Something is going on."

Winter looked at Sam as Kent rushed back into the room, accompanied by the elder FBI agent.

"We've received confirmation of a location, and we have visual contact." Kent announced with urgency. "Mr. Sonam, you are live. However, as explained, we can see you but you cannot see me. Security reasons." He nodded at the FBI agent, who took the lead.

"Mr. Sonam, would you recap the information you shared with me." The agent's tone was measured with intent.

An Asian gentleman appeared on the monitor, with silver streaks in his black hair. "Certainly. I was visiting my family in Gyantse. I reside in Oregon." He pronounced in clear English. "I happened to be at the Pacho Monastery's plaza when a woman approached me. She said her name was Shelby, and she was being held in a compound in Shigatse." Mr. Sonam continued, recounting his conversation with her, including a brief description of where she was being held. "I dialed this number as soon as I could."

Expressing gratitude, the agent assured Mr. Sonam that they were committed to bringing Shelby home.

"Thank you. The blessings of Buddha Sakyamuni watch over her. I am confident she will remain safe." The call ended.

"Are we certain it was our Shelby?" She inquired.

"Wolf 10. She signed the piece of paper she gave to Mr. Sonam. It's her, Charles, the senior agent affirmed. Camden is with her. I showed Mr. Sonam a picture of Shelby and Camden. He confirmed their identification. He also identified the man called Daniel or Dr. Biel" Charles paused. "Wolf is a codeword letting us know that we should exercise caution. We initiate deployment now and prep for reconnaissance. We'll hold off until Shelby can establish contact within the next 36 hours. It means the den is armed with ten."

She raised a pertinent question. "What if they can't establish contact?"

The elder FBI agent nodded. "In that case, we initiate contact and we bring them home."

"Sir, based on the description Shelby gave Mr. Sonam we have pinpointed the ARKose compound."

Kent affirmed by nodding his head. "On screen."

Charles continued. "Mr. Sonam showed me the piece of paper with Shelby's writing. Not only did she write where she and Camden were located with my phone number, she also wrote three symbols PU, CE, PR."

A satellite image materialized, revealing a small city nestled on a broad plateau at the base of a mountain. Commanding attention was a massive white structure, resembling a fortress, integrated into the mountainside. Adjacent to this imposing formation lay an intriguing beehive-shaped building crowned with a gilded dome, situated beside an expansive open plaza. Weathered prayer flags fluttered gently, encircling the entire complex with a protective wall.

"Shigatse." Jon voiced with recognition.

"You have been there before?" She asked her husband.

"Yes. I have been to the fort and the Monastery," he said as he pressed his phone to his ear, smiling at Sam. "Enid, we are going to Shigatse." And then he walked out of the room.

The satellite's focus journeyed through the city's outskirts before zeroing in on a particular locale. The image sharpened on a two-story gray edifice boasting a rooftop garden, ensconced within a robust stone perimeter. A formidable gate crossed the entrance of the small drive. Overlooking this structure, a sleek expanse of rock soared hundreds of feet into the sky. Almost as if a portion of the mountain had been cleaved away, this stone wall formed the compound's rear facade. The remaining half of the mountain sloped precipitously, flanked by narrow ravines on either side. A spacious open plaza connected the building to the rock.

"Enhance the view." Kent directed. A hidden but perceptible feature emerged: a shadow traversing the boundary between the plaza and the rock. "Again, angle it 45 degrees." This was no mere shadow, but rather an entrance carved into the rock slab.

"This building looks like any other of the numerous lodges found in Shigatse without Mr. Sonam's description. Except for that tunnel." Kent observed.

Jon walked back into the room. "Kent, Charles. We have been working on trajectories but with the information about Shigatse, Mik using AI came up with some interesting data on this. Can we interrupt?"

"Floor is yours."

"Mik." Jon asked.

Mik presented a schematic. "Based on Camden's description of the channel parameters, after the test was conducted in the South Pacific, we enhanced the ultra-cool ground penetrating radar system developed by LUNA, which we are adapting once we found out about the three targets." Mik punched some keys and another image appeared on the monitor. "We guesstimated a location near Lhasa but we have confirmed where the ARKose compound is. With some tweaks, this is the trajectory of the channel."

The image illustrated layers of bedrock, with a highlighted channel running from the ARKose compound to a complex fault zone intersecting beneath Afghanistan and Pakistan.

"This is the estimated channel pathway."

"Mik, what are those straight vertical lines? At first glance, they seem random, but upon considering their positions within the geological formation, they appear deliberate. Some align with the channel originating from the surface." Ian inquired.

Jon chimed in. "Those are test wells drilled around sixty years ago for oil exploration. In fact," Jon turned to Mik, as another image emerged. "There are a dozen of these shafts spread across the region. None of them have been sealed."

"Crap." Ian responded, comprehending the implications of Jon's statement.

Kent interjected. "Their plan involves utilizing the elements to trigger an earthquake while releasing…"

"Radiation from plutonium, cesium, and promethium through those shafts, utilizing them as conduits." Charles, stated who had remained silent through most of this discussion,

"Indeed. That's our hypothesis. Given Daniel's statement, we need to be prepared for the possibility that ARKose possesses more than just two radioactive elements." Jon added.

"Plutonium, promethium, and francium - element 87, which initiated this ordeal," Jackson said.

"But it's not just the location," Jon added. "It's also the timing. We are reaching a point where the convergence of tectonic forces, combined with climate change, could lead to catastrophic events in these areas. ARKose understands that."

Only the sound of clicks on a keyboard and the buzzing of the monitors could be heard as the tension in the room grew.

"Does ARKose, a small fairly unknown company have the financial savvy to do all of this?" Sam asked.

"We do not believe they do, financially. Technically yes but there is someone or some group that is funding this operation." Kent nodded.

"And that has been the dilemma." Charles stated. "We need a name or an organization that is funding this operation. It is why Shelby and Camden refused to quit. Until we find who is supplying the cash, ARKose will only be replaced by another fanatic group."

"Two sociopathic scientists with major daddy issues." She responded.

"Exactly, Sam," Jackson added. "Peiling and Daniel."

"But who has the capacity to fund this?" Enid asked. "And the determination. We have the resources of the military and the FBI and yet we still do not have an answer. They are deep and they are big. What about that consortium? There must be a link between Chul-Moo and ARKose."

Kent was solemn. "The implications could be disastrous in multiple dimensions. The US would face allegations of espionage, and if our warnings are brushed aside, and this disaster unfolds, the US could even be accused of orchestrating Three Gorges collapse. To salvage their reputation, the President might even resort to…"

"War." Jon interjected, the gravity of the situation hanging heavy in the air.

Turning to Jackson, Kent sought his opinion. Jackson's gaze shifted between the Enid and then Jon, as he reentered the control room. Jon took the cue.

"Our company jet is primed and ready for Tibet," Jon declared. "Last night, we formulated a strategy for an on-ground presence in Lhasa. Instead, we'll be touching down at Shigatse Airport, where Ian will have a vehicle waiting. As we now know, Ian and Jackson's team flew last night to Tibet." Jon nodded at Jackson. "My jet and crew are standing by."

"Kent, we won't interfere directly, but we can orchestrate a diversion or at the very least create a distraction to support your recon and rescue. Your authority is military; ours isn't. You're bound by political channels. We are not," Enid added. "And that feels empowering right now as strange as that seems." She paused looking at Sam and Winter before continuing.

"I have connections in Tibet and I speak fluent Tibetan."

Jackson addressed Kent with clarity. "Jacob and Winter will stay in Anchorage. And Mik will be the connection between the teams." Jackson said as Jon nodded. "They are at your disposal, Sir."

"I'll manage communications from Anchorage, and deal with the Hill," Charles the senior agent instructed. "Ian and his team will initiate the recon in Shigatse. There is a secure location that we have used in the past. We now possess the necessary authority." He nodded at Jon.

"Diplomatic support for entry is in place. This isn't the first time my crew has landed in Tibet." Jon contributed. "The region is rich in rare earth elements, and LUNA, Inc. is well known there. We've cultivated some friendly ties with China's political powers."

"However, this excursion marks a tribute to my son Camden O'Connor, an esteemed member of the Nepalese and Tibetan climbing community, and a well-regarded figure in the mining sector." Enid advocated. "We devised a distraction, and fortuitously, we all met at the memorial service. Jon is providing both his expertise and his jet to help me honor my son's memory in a land he cherished." Enid smiled. "A perfect cover."

She smiled at Enid and exchanging a nod with her husband. "Confronting fanatical terrorists isn't foreign to us."

"Jackson." Kent nodded firmly. " No one will operate independently, do you understand?" Kent then walked over to Enid. "Our goal is to bring your son and Shelby home, General."

"And prevent an environmental and political crisis." Charles added.

"Jackson, with me." Kent instructed.

"Yes, sir." Jackson acknowledged. "I'll catch up with you at the plane. I'm sure I can hitch a ride." He hugged Winter, and trailed after his commanding officer.

Thirty minutes elapsed, and as the sun dipped below the horizon in the land of the midnight sun, Winter watched Jackson join the others on LUNA, Inc.'s jet. They remained there until the aircraft vanished into the shroud of clouds, leaving the world below to settle into darkness.

CHAPTER 26

SHELBY

ON THE UPPER terrace, she breathed the fresh cool air, her face towards the night sky when Camden walked up behind her.

"It's after midnight."

"I couldn't sleep. What did you find out from Shing?"

"Irish, I need to tell you something but please stay calm. You must promise me."

She nodded as Camden grabbed her hand and whispered in her ear.

"What? There was an earthquake?" She looked into Camden's eyes. "I am fine. Tell me." He told her everything he discovered in Shing's notebook.

"Alright, I'm composed. I am thinking about my parents."

"I know."

"This explains why Daniel never informed you about the mine's closure, and why ARKose was closing the mine on such short notice. My parents will assume I'm dead. Shit," she rubbed her hands through her hair. "How many lives were lost in the quake?"

"Let's not dwell on that, Irish." He rubbed her back. "Let's hope that guy you met in the square got your message to Charles. He will be in contact with your folks."

"Peiling's arriving today. We assume our Tibetan friend made contact and the FBI and Jackson's team know where we are. I need to find out where the money is coming from Camden." The spark of Irish determination ignited in her forest-green eyes.

"According to Shing's notes, the laser has not reached the launch site for the detonation. There's sufficient francium, but…" Camden's voice trailed off.

"What's wrong?" Shelby's concern grew. "Camden."

"The francium didn't destabilize. One gram was used for the earthquakes in Alaska. Two grams are missing. We think Daniel will use the remaining francium on the two targets, Afghanistan and Pakistan."

"What about the plutonium?"

"Shing said they will be used with the francium, but not on the dam."

"Afghanistan and Pakistan. Fire."

"They're repeating history. That's what Peiling mentioned the first day she arrived at the mine. The sociopath that she is, she will personally arm the robot with the elements. In her eyes, she's the savior of her people, like Nüwa."

"Whose her people? North Korea? Does she have any connection with North Korea? Other than being half North Korean? She is willing to kill innocents."

"Yes. She is. With Pakistan and Afghanistan next. Daniel's people." He paused. "First the flood for purification, then the fire to cleanse the sins of humanity. Peiling will destroy the dam but Daniel? He will arm the bot to destroy in those two countries. But I wonder. Do you think Peiling will relinquish her power and control to Daniel?"

"No. I can use that. I will handle Daniel. You need to disable that robot. Is there any way we can access the control room?"

"Shing is already doing that. He is creating a virus that will intentionally blow up the robot far enough from us and not close enough to destroy the dam. Timing is critical. I am starving after a late night. Hell, forget sleep. Sun will be coming up. It's almost dawn. Shower and then breakfast."

"I will join you for a shower." She snuggled.

After a refreshing, long shower, they started down the hallway to the mess hall.

"Give me a minute," she smiled. "I am going to try something first. Then I will meet you for breakfast."

She turned her head slightly, tilted her head as he noticed a subtle wink as he stopped, noticing the dawn was breaking as she walked out onto the terrace. He watched her raise her hands to greet the morning sun. Her fiery red hair blazed as the first rays of light appeared, but it was the deliberate dance of her graceful fingers through the crisp air he noticed.

"Tai chi? That woman never ceases to surprise me." He sighed as he walked down the stairs to the mess hall.

As Camden finished breakfast, she walked into the dining area. Slightly touching his hand, she beamed focusing on coffee and food when Daniel walked over to her.

"What do you have planned this morning?" She asked Daniel.

"You look a little flushed. Are you alright?"

"I am. I did Tai chi on the terrace." She touched his hand. "Considering I am your guest under constraint, you are considerate, Daniel." She hesitated. "I must admit, I'm anxious to meet Peiling considering she would prefer me dead than to be here." She took her tray and replied. "Feel free to join us."

Daniel sat down next to Shelby and Camden.

"The next two days are crucial. History is in the making, Camden. ARKose will be recognized worldwide, not just as a leader in mining technology, but as a savior of humanity."

Her stomach lurched as she tried to swallow her eggs.

"History? How so?" Camden asked.

"The first for a laser guided robot to channel through rock without corrupting the environment."

"I suppose. I need to get to the rock room. Later."

She barely acknowledged Camden's departure. "Daniel, I work for a large oil company with layers of money coming in. How is ARKose funding such a massive project? Unless Peiling is rich or has a sugar daddy."

Daniel glared at her. "Sugar daddy? I am not familiar with this term. Peiling's father abandoned her at a young age. She does however, have many investors who are interested, including some from the United States."

"Really. Who?" She fluttered her eyelashes and focused on Daniel.

"I don't know the names of her investors. However," he concentrated. "there is someone on a committee called this city."

"City? Do you know the state this senator represents?"

"Oh, no, I am not sure he is a senator. I don't know these things. Peiling happened to mention he was high up and in charge of this city. Through him he has provided much funds for this operation."

She watched the man go from confident to nervous. She speculated he was not allowed to divulge anything about ARKose other than in geological terms.

"Shelby, I have many things to take care of before Peiling arrives."

She watched the man as he quickly left the room, leaving his tray on the table.

"I got to you, Daniel. This senator is important." She mumbled.

As she was refilling her coffee mug, she noticed a Tibetan man get up from his table. His plate, was filled with a selection of every fruit that was offered.

"You like fruit?" She asked the man as he was getting coffee.

"Yes, I sample every fruit I deliver." He smiled.

She looked around the room, keeping an eye on the door. "My name is Shelby," she whispered. "Are you a local here in Shigatse?"

"Yes, my name is Tenzin. I live on my farm. Nor far away." He said. "I am born here. Third generation farmer and sherpa."

"Sherpa? My friend is a mountain climber. He climbed Everest and then traveled this region. Years ago."

"Ahh. What is his name?" He asked.

"It was years ago." she answered.

"I never forget a name of those I have climbed with on the mountain." He said as he nodded for her to follow him to his table.

Her mind was racing. It worked once, why not again. "His name is Camden. Camden O'Connor.

The man stared at her. "Camden. Camden from Colorado in the United States. He was studying geology. I was his sherpa. His first climb up the mountain." He shook his head. "The last time I saw him was fifteen years ago. It was his second climb."

Shelby stood speechless. "We need your help Tenzin. Camden is here."

As she sat down, she spilled her coffee, splashing some on the table where Tenzin sat. "I am so clumsy." She got up and grabbed a handful of napkins. As she wiped the coffee off the table and the floor, she slipped a pen out of her pocket and wrote a number and a name on the napkin. "Here," she took a clean napkin and dabbed splattered coffee on his sleeve. "I am so sorry." She whispered. "Please, call this number. He is a friend of Camden's. It is urgent." She put her finger to her mouth.

"There. Maybe I don't need any more caffeine." She smiled. "When will you be back?"

"I am scheduled to bring fresh produce the same day the owner arrives here. She likes her produce fresh."

"Today."

He nodded. "I have not been given the time yet."

She stood up and leaning close, whispered. "I work with Camden. This is very important. Life and death important. We are not safe here. Camden or me will be here when you come back."

She walked away quickly as she went back to the terrace. *Tenzin is our link.*

CHAPTER 27

SAM

A S THEY LEFT the Shigatse Airport, she watched her friends in admiration. Jackson clicked on a keyboard as Jon listened to Mik through his earpiece. Enid conversed on the phone with a contact in Shigatse, connected to the non-profit organization devoted to supporting Tibetan culture.

"Pull over." Jon commanded, pointing to a turnout off the highway. "Jackson, you should be getting a live satellite feed from Ian. Mik you are on speaker."

"Commander, are you listening?"

"Yes."

"Sam, I got something for you to watch. Winter recalled a form of communication between you and Shelby – I must say, it is helpful being here in Anchorage. Winter is crazy good at this," Mik said. "She mentioned it was extremely valuable on double dates. Anyway, after she saw this satellite link, she said you would understand."

"Well, using our fingers to communicate had unique advantages. We used it like a secret language. It was very helpful during dates and Tai chi practice."

"Wow. This is fucking old school. A different version of morse code or something." Jackson said. "Look at this Sam."

As she was watching the video link, she whispered. "Shelby would sign to distract me during Tai chi. To slow me down. Winter remembered this? She is awesome."

They watched in silence as Jackson displayed the satellite feed showing Shelby on the terrace. "Son of a bitch." She murmured. "She knew I would be involved."

"Winter told me she had never met Shelby but she remembered the stories you shared about the two of you. Even continents apart, you and Shelby remained close." Jackson mentioned.

"Shelby used to drag me to Tai chi. Every time I attempted White Stork Spread Wings, I was convinced I'd tip over if I went any slower. 'You are like a hummingbird on crack. Calm your mind." She mimicked what Shelby would say to her.

Jon squeezed her arm.

"She always told me that one day, I would thank her. I gave her so much shit. I would do these spins and kicks and make up stupid names like chop the guy's head off with fist. And Shel would shake her head in total dismay and then we would start laughing." She swallowed. "Can you zoom in closer to her hands, Mik?"

As Shelby's fingers moved, Sam jotted down what they were revealing.

"Mik, how would Shelby know to do this?" Jon asked.

"She assumed her message from the Tibet dude would be delivered. She is taking advantage of that assumption. I remember when the satellite was over the compound, there was a small terrace on the second floor. She used that. Shelby knew if she could get a message to us, the satellite would pick it up. The terrace gave her access to the sky."

"She has been an FBI agent along time. She knows our strategy and our process. She took advantage it." Ian indicated. "She knew the FBI would take control of a satellite to locate the compound.

This no doubt, was the safest way for her to communicate to us. She was betting someone would recognize her hands. And Winter did. It is genius."

"And she knew, Sam would be able to interpret it." Jon offered.

"I'm a bit rusty, but here goes." She looked at her notes. "The first set is easy. Peiling is arriving today. Then the question mark. Shelby thinks there's a reason for her arrival. Something's up."

Ian interrupted. "The airport. Did anyone notice another private jet? Anything?" Everyone shook their heads no.

"Negative, Ian." Jackson said.

"Keep your eyes open. What's next?" Ian asked.

"'The second set confirms the three locations or according to Shelby, 3 targets." She paused. "The next set, she is confirming that the dam is a target? I think."

Jon looked at Sam's notes. "The first target is Three Gorges Dam using francium. We now have confirmation of their plan to destroy the dam."

She continued. "After that, dog CePL followed by package CePL. Not sure."

Jackson chimed in. "'Dog' refers to Afghanistan. CePL stands for cesium and plutonium. They're extracting cesium and plutonium. And Package must mean Pakistan."

Jon added. "Shelby found out about the two earthquakes in Alaska," he continued. "Tibet is rich in silicates – sinters. With the numerous hot springs here, I bet ARKose has been monitoring and sampling the waters to pinpoint a trajectory for a target location. Given the extensive research on plate tectonics and rare earth elements, let's assume they plan to use francium to trigger the plates. She is confirming what we understand about ARKose causing a direct hit on two different plate locations."

"Kent, we have confirmation that ARKose will use plutonium and cesium for Afghanistan. And francium for destroying the dam."

"And Pakistan. Two hits, like they did in Alaska." Mik added. "We have solid confirmation."

"Confirmed, Jackson," Kent declared. "The Director has been informed and is on his way to the White House. I will be joining him. You have it from here Jackson. We are keeping to the plan. I will keep you in the loop. It is now up to the President to work with China. He wants me and Charles in that discussion. When we have a decision as to how he wants to handle this, I will let you know."

"Hey guys, I have the rest of Shelby's message." Sam interjected. "Her next words are a bit confusing about a fruit delivery which is scheduled for today." She bit her lip. "I think."

"In Tibet, produce and fruit are limited, even more so in the winter. I think she's telling us that they receive produce at the compound, and it's scheduled for delivery today." Enid remarked. "If we find out the produce delivery schedule, and who delivers, it allows us a possible way into the compound. They will be delivering from the airport by freight. We need to find out when that flight is expected to land."

"We will use the produce delivery to make contact with Shelby or Camden. We will see you guys in a few." Ian said.

"Mik, work with Ian and find out who and when to expect the produce delivery." Jon said. "I'm guessing the schedule changes."

As Jackson turned to look at Sam in the back seat, he noticed a vehicle coming from the direction of the airport. "Ian, we have a black SUV coming from the airport. It just passed us. The SUV has red and gold symbols on the doors."

"We got it on the satellite." Ian yelled.

She watched as her friends sprang into action to rescue those they cared for and for the countless others they didn't know. Feeling a bit light-headed with a slight headache and her tongue swelling, she took a Diamox followed by water. Jon squeezed her hand when he noticed her taking the pill. She was rewarded with a set of dimples, still visible beneath a few days' growth of dark sandy stubble, with a sprinkle of grays.

They drove a few blocks, taking a left and then a right, circling back to a main street. The driver slipped the vehicle into reverse, backing into what seemed like a narrow dead-end alley. Within seconds, the rock wall split open down the middle, allowing the SUV to squeeze between the halves. The rock gate closed in front of them with the assistance of two men as the SUV came to a stop. Ian stepped out of the stone building, exchanging handshakes, and nodding silently. No formal introductions were made as Ian guided them into the side of a slate-black stone building. The narrow door, imperceptible in the recessed alcove, blended seamlessly with the texture and color of the stone.

She was awestruck by the transition from ancient civilization to modern technology as she stepped across the threshold from the alley into the stone structure. The room, situated ten feet below the landing, was the size of a Starbucks. It was filled with half a dozen monitors, their screens alive with the hum and buzz of computers, accompanied by the rhythmic clicking of keyboards.

Solid rock blocks formed the walls of the room, providing a stark contrast to the advanced equipment within. An open loft, about 20 feet above, was visible through the grated metal floor lining the perimeter of the loft. Rectangular windows, were placed cleverly into the front and side of the building, situated just two feet above the grated floor. On the back wall, a set of stairs ascended from the main floor to the ceiling, allowing access to the grid walkway.

"We're monitoring satellite feeds from both the airport and the compound," one of the British-accented agents informed them. "Six operatives are stationed around the compound entrance, but the rear of the compound is built into the mountain."

On one of the monitors, a blonde figure dressed in black stepped out of an SUV. Jon watched Sam get close to the monitor.

"Peiling," She said. "And her brother."

Turning to Mik on one of the monitors, Ian inquired, "Any updates on the delivery?"

Mik responded. "The delivery service operates locally, covering the surrounding area—except the compound—on its usual route. Typically, they make two deliveries a week, each on different days and times. A cargo plane is scheduled to receive the van at Shigatse Airport in less than 2 hours. We have one glitch—the same person makes the delivery." Mik queued up two images.

One monitor displayed a dusty blue delivery van with red apples painted on its side, parked in front of a modest, weathered stone house. The next image showed the same van with an older man standing beside it, a wide grin on his face. The man's face was magnified.

"This is Tenzin, a local," Mik explained. "His family has been farming the Chengtang Valley for generations.

"Who do we got? We need his doppelganger." Ian stated.

"No need. We've got our guy." Jackson affirmed as he got off the phone. "That was Tenzin. He had a nice conversation with Shelby. He is in."

CHAPTER 28

PEILING

IN THE EAST tunnel, Shelby huddled under the vented hood. It would appear she was completing the analysis of the last set of elements that Camden had provided her for the spectrometer as Daniel, Peiling, and Yong-Sun entered the lab.

"Shelby, how's the analysis progressing?" Daniel inquired.

"The final elements from hot spring KA13S are processing. The vein is rich. I will have a final report in a few hours."

"Good, good. This is Peiling and Yong-Sun," Daniel smiled.

"Shelby, to be clear. I am not happy that Daniel brought you here. I would have left you at the camp to fend for yourself. You were not our responsibility. Although, if I had known, I would have left Daniel to keep you company as you both starved in the cold. But him I need. You I don't." She stared at Shelby. "Daniel has spoken well of you. For now, do not disappoint me as I will not give you a second chance. Do you understand?"

"Yes. Perfectly. It was not my choice to come here. My arrangement with Daniel is to help and then I will be allowed to leave."

She looked at the red-head and thought to herself. *You will leave that is true. In the fire after we are done using you.*

"Shelby, what's the estimated concentration of promethium?" Daniel inquired.

"I anticipate it's around 75 to 83% of the water content in the last two hot springs. Shing's robot extracted the last remaining of the rock core samples where sample site KA13S is located. I'm sampling both core rock specimens and water samples. Camden's hypothesis is that the layer beneath KA13S contains the highest concentration of promethium he's ever encountered." Shelby looked back at her analysis and added. "My estimate from the analysis is the promethium concentration in the samples of rock could be as high as 0.900. I cannot confirm that until the analysis is complete. His worry is the contamination from other elements during his refining of the stabilization process. So far, my data concludes the contamination will be less than one percent."

"When?" Peiling asked.

"Early tomorrow morning. Shing will be very busy I imagine, extracting the rock here. The quantity of rare earths is beyond belief. Not unlike the quantity of francium Daniel found in Alaska. I don't know how he does this?" Shelby smiled. I plan to be here in the lab by 4 am."

"One of the few radioactive lanthanides," Daniel added, a smile on his face as he looked at Peiling. "Good news."

"Yes. With that amount of promethium, we should have nearly 15 grams of stabilized element from those rock cores. It will change the balance of power. The amount of radioactive elements will be staggering. Francium?" She stared at Daniel.

"Over 10 grams."

"What do you mean change the balance of power? I thought China controls 80% of the rare earth elements on the planet. As a Chinese company..." Shelby asked.

"ARKose is not a Chinese corporation." Yong-Sun asserted firmly.

"I apologize. I assumed ARKose was a Chinese corporation. Considering ARKose is at the forefront of mining the rarest elements and we are in China." Shelby conceded, bowing her head. "And the expense must be, wow, I don't know in the millions."

"We have many investors in our project. ARKose may be small, but we wield significant power," she replied. "Countries will be begging us to," she cocked her head. "help them. We will have, much power. Daniel, we are done here. Make sure you bring me the final report." Daniel nodded, as they left leaving Shelby alone in the lab.

"You know what to do tomorrow after we destroy the dam, Young-Sun." She turned to Daniel. "Did you say something, Daniel?"

"No." He quivered, looking at the ground.

As they walked up the slight incline of the tunnel to the juncture of the second tunnel she grinned.

"When Camden is finished stabilizing the remaining radioactive elements, he too is no longer necessary. Once we destroy the dam and then the remaining targets," she glared at Daniel then spoke directly to Yong-Sun. "Incapacitate them in Shing's laser room. Along with Shing. They will all burn when we detonate the compound." She started to walk down the second tunnel. "And make sure they are conscious. I want them to watch everything and to know they played a key role in killing."

CHAPTER 29

JACKSON

"JACKSON, THAT'S TOO risky. He's a farmer. We're uncertain about his ties to Peiling and ARKose," Ian cautioned. "That van is considered new for here. He's being well compensated for his deliveries."

"Mik?" Jon asked.

"Already on it."

Jon turned to Jackson. "What are you thinking, Jackson?"

"He knows Camden. He is in debt to him. The cargo plane arrives this afternoon. We send an agent dressed in an airport uniform to help him unload at the airport. That agent gives Tenzin two sets of communication devices. Tenzin told Shelby he lets the cook know when he is arriving at the compound. Tenzin met Shelby once he can do it again. Or Camden. She knows Tenzin will be making a delivery the day Peiling arrives. And that is today. Peiling is here. We do this."

Ian nodded at the young Tibetan agent waiting. "Go. You know what to do."

Mik interjected. "He appears clean. I couldn't find any connection between him and Peiling or anyone associated with ARKose.

His delivery business is legitimate. He bought the van six years ago." Mik's voice lowered as he continued. "When he delivers to the compound, he has no other deliveries." A few minutes later, Mik yelled. "Got it. The money came from a bank in London. The account belongs to a businessman. Yes, makes sense." Mik whispered. "He was the climber with Tenzin's son."

"That is the debt I mentioned. Tenzin's son died in a climbing accident. Camden carried him to base camp and brought him home to his family. That rich business man refused to go back to base camp when the weather turned deadly."

Sam inquired, "Jackson, what happened to the rich climber?"

"He survived. He was Chinese and split his time between London and Hong Kong," "That year was deadly for climbers. It is guilt money."

"What is the ETA of the cargo plane?" Ian inquired.

"It will touch down in 90 minutes at the Shigatse Airport."

"Go." Ian looked at the young agent. He was now dressed in work coverall's with an airport logo. He was the person Ian had planned to make the delivery.

"Guys, we're doing this the old-fashioned way. Turning to the monitor, his intensity remained. "Alpha, I want everyone in place. Any message from Kent or Charles?"

"No sir. All Quiet."

"Dammit. We proceed. We have one shot at this."

"Our agent will give the communication devices to Tenzin. He will explain to Tenzin what his role is in this plan. Jackson." Ian nodded.

"Tenzin's entry routine is consistent. Always through the front entrance, presenting his ID. They perform a thorough search including a scan of his van for any electronics. We are ready for that. He's not allowed to carry a cellphone once he leaves his van. Once the vehicle is cleared, he heads to the side of the building where the kitchen entry is." He focused on a wall monitor showing a hand drawn blueprint of the compound that was uploaded from his phone.

"Produce doesn't get touched until Tenzin unloads it in the kitchen. Only then does he let the cook inspect it. After all the produce is offloaded, they offer him a meal. The cafeteria's marked here." He pointed to the designated spot on the map.

"Tenzin will take his meal and sit in the cafeteria. When he spots Camden or Shelby, he is to approach cautiously without recognition and pass on the package. Once the delivery is made, he is to follow his normal protocol for leaving."

"What if Camden or Shelby don't show? Then what?" Sam asked.

"We wait to hear from our FBI agents." Ian responded. "And then we implement our rescue plan."

"Diversion team. Enid?"

She nodded at Jackson. "In place. They are waiting for me to contact them."

"Tenzin's finished loading the van. He's in motion. Any activity above us?" Ian asked.

"Nothing, sir. The terrace has been quiet since we received Shelby's message."

"Any news from the House, Kent?" Ian asked.

"Not a peep. General, any insights from your end?"

"This process takes time. If the President decides to tell the Chinese they will accuse the US of espionage. They'll assert the dam is secure against any potential terrorist threats. Unless we furnish irrefutable evidence to support our claims, it'll come across as the US spying on them."

Kent added. "It's a delicate balance between life and honor for them. In China, the two are held in equal regard."

"Tenzin's on the move, sir," came the timely update.

"Kent, keep your eyes on him." Ian directed.

The tension in the room was intense and growing with each

passing second, palpable while Tenzin was waiting at the front gate. Until the metal gate opened, the room was suspended in silence. Then slowly, Tenzin maneuvered the van through the gate and drove around to the side of the compound, just as the outdoor kitchen door swung open. Stepping out of the van, Tenzin bowed, greeting a robust man clad in white.

For the next hour, an unusual hush continued within the room. Sam's keen observation didn't miss the absence of Jon.

Mik's chatter broke the silence.

"I ran some scenario's. The floodwaters could reach Yichang village—sitting about 150 feet above sea level—within 4 to 5 hours post-break, submerging the entire city. The dam's reservoir can hold a staggering 39.3 billion cubic meters. China needs to initiate controlled releases of that water right away," Mik asserted. "If ARKose's plan materializes unchecked, it would be an invisible war."

He appended. "If China doesn't react now, the middle and lower reaches of the Yangtze River could witness flooding ten times the scale of 1998. Wuhan, Jiujang City, and Nanjing—submerged within hours. The Yangtze River Valley, the lifeline for water, fertile land, crops, cotton, freshwater fish, and a population of 350 million, would be lost."

"And you, Kent," Enid spoke, "understand better than most the far-reaching consequences for China's military and its defense capabilities."

"The lower stretches of the Three Gorges region have historically been a battlefield, and now it's the nucleus of China's military operations—a strategic epicenter."

"The tidal wave from such a dam breach would obliterate countless cities and decimate China's military defensive capabilities." He declared with his arms crossed, one hand rubbing his chin.

"And yet, we require concrete evidence that unequivocally implicates ARKose as the adversary, not the United States. No matter the outcome, we have FBI and special military operations personnel in China in violation of their laws." Kent affirmed.

"From a technical standpoint, that's correct. However, LUNA, Inc. was granted permission by the Chinese authorities. Our presence here is not military or FBI. Additionally, China was aware of ARKose's activities, including their rare earth element mining. ARKose's operations didn't go unnoticed," Jon offered. "We're navigating through a complex web. If shit hits the fan, we have a retired general, a military man who is AWOL, a witty environmental scientist with a black belt, and a mining expert. We are well versed in handling fanatics."

"And me, the computer genius who hates to lose." Mik appended.

"We have full documentation approved by the Chinese government to be here." Jon acknowledged. "We will do what is needed to prevent an environmental crisis and prevent a world war."

"Yes, we will." Enid assured.

CHAPTER 30

CAMDEN

A S HE WAITED for the last two elements to be processed in the vault, the door to the rock room swished open. Daniel entered, followed by Peiling and Yong-Sun.

"Camden. Status of the radioactive elements."

"Hello Peiling," he acknowledged, moving closer to a thick glass enclosure, as he dimmed the lights, and lifted the cover. A deep blue light, resembling the bioluminescence of the sea, filled the small solid steel vaults.

"The final two radioactive elements are in their last step of stabilization."

"Cesium and promethium," Peiling murmured, a smile on her face. "What about plutonium?"

"The three are being processed at the same time. To quote you Peiling from our initial meeting at the ARKose mine in Alaska, we're reshaping the mining landscape. We're making history." He declared, locking eyes with Peiling. *If that protein does what I hope it will do, they will never know why their plan failed.*

He continued. "The results are, I must say, spectacular. Without the equipment we have here, particularly the X-ray crystallography,

I would not have been able to process these elements so swiftly. The protein extract from the bacteria from the alder mycorrhizae did exactly what the research said it would do. Daniel's foresight in setting up this facility has proven brilliant."

"When will the elements be ready?" Peiling asked.

"I estimate at the earliest 6-ish, maybe 6:30 am. It is a delicate process which is why I need to relax. I will be back here about 5 am. By 7:00 am we will have four of the rarest, natural radioactive elements on earth at our, or I should say, your disposal, Peiling. Francium, cesium, plutonium and promethium. A beginning to the end of our dependency on fossil fuels." He grabbed his dented mug. "Anyone care to join me?"

Almost as if on cue, Shing approached as they made their way into the shadowed tunnel. Peiling glanced at Yong-Sun, who nodded in agreement.

"You go ahead, Peiling. I'll wait for my friend Shing," Yong-Sun started walking down the tunnel toward Shing. "We will meet you in the cafeteria."

He walked with Peiling in silence from the tunnel to the cafeteria and noticed Shelby sitting at a table studying a notebook.

"Please join me." Shelby offered.

"I am starving. Food, shower, nap." He looked at Shelby.

"I estimated as such."

"I want to check the laser's status," Peiling responded. "Daniel, with me. We will meet at 7 am in Shing's lab." Peiling turned around and looked at Shelby.

"Shelby, I want you with us. Camden can escort you. As a reward, you can witness what we have achieved."

"Shelby doesn't need to be there." Daniel interjected.

"Of course, she will be there, Daniel."

"I'll be there."

"What was all that about? I never thought I'd say this, but I'm with Daniel."

"It's better to have me there than not. I can handle myself," she whispered. "Tenzin says hello."

Camden did not say a word.

"Shall we go to your room or mine?"

"I'm all ears," he replied as they walked through Camden's room to the adjoining bathroom.

"I lied. I have the results of a couple of the concentrations. The promethium is at 88%, and cesium is at 22% in the latest batch of samples. That suggests," Shelby paused, leaving her statement hanging.

"It confirms that the most sensitive area of the Tibetan Plateau is located beneath KA13S. That's where the tectonic plates are most active. I've never seen such high amounts before. Are you certain? Never mind, of course, you are."

"And plutonium. I didn't mention that."

Once they settled in their usual spot on the bathroom floor, Shelby whispered.

"I met Tenzin today, twice, in the cafeteria. He made contact with Jackson who is here with his team. Ian has a team here in Shigatse." She smiled. "Tenzin gave me the communication devices and trackers. They want to know where we are when they raid this place."

"Tenzin? How did he get involved in all of this?"

"He delivers fruit and produce. Peiling made it clear to him that he was to deliver fresh produce on her arrival. When she visits, he removes the older produce for composting at his farm. I gave him Jackson's number." She said. "I know. Crazy. The FBI is leading the operation, with the military in the shadows, except Jackson of course. And with Sam's help, they understood my message. She is here."

"The Tai chi," he stopped. "I have heard it all. Sam is here too?

"Yes, Sam, Jon her husband, who you have met, and your mom."

"What? The General is here?"

"Say hello, Camden."

"Good to hear your voice, my friend." Jackson replied and filled him in on their plan.

"I will place the third listening device in in the laser room. The robot will be armed with the elements and that is where Peiling will trigger the detonation. Shing is the sole individual who can operate the laser, but Daniel and Peiling—they're capable of controlling the robot." He looked at Shelby as he spoke with Jackson and Ian.

"Yes, Camden," Ian responded. "Got it. Listen up. The robot responds to voice commands and keyboard inputs. Top priority. We need access to that computer. Mik?"

"Camden, I need details about the computer system." Mik inquired.

"You got it. We believe Peiling is intending to detonate the targets tomorrow morning." he responded. "Lucky for me, I am one step ahead of you. As a backup, in case anything happens to him, Shing provided me access to his computer for the robot. However, his computer still requires the server at the compound."

"Which means we will need to break their firewall." Mik replied. "Give me what you got, Camden."

CHAPTER 31

SAM

"MIK, GET CONTROL of that robot," Ian demanded. "Do your magic, Mik. I don't care how you do it. Hell, we are all ghosts right now. None of us are here legally except," he looked at Sam. "Except you three."

"There has to be a virtual backdoor, Mik." She asked.

"Working on it, Sam."

"Enid, one more time. What is your diversion plan?" Ian asked.

"Jon, Sam and I will don traditional Tibetan clothing where we will be part of a burial ceremony for a small child a quarter mile from the compound. Leading the ceremony is a monk, a friend of mine who works at the Monastery. The local dress is bulky and will hide our armor and clothing. Sam and I will be cleaning staff and Jon will be part of the kitchen staff, if we are confronted. The cook, a friend of Tenzin's understands his role. I will be the only one carrying a weapon."

"Ma'am?" Ian asked. "Jackson."

"I already had this conversation with the general, Ian." Jackson smirked.

Enid nodded. "There will be a disturbance just outside the

236

compound. My friend will start looking for the trail to the burial cave. There will be confusion and two of the women will be screaming and crying. The plan is to lure the two guards from the guard house at which time, the three of us will enter once the security system is blocked."

"The timing is critical for that to happen, Ian. Mik is going to be busy with the computer system." Jackson stated.

"It will be ready on your signal, Enid."

"We will enter through the kitchen door that Tenzin outlined for us."

"I am not happy about bringing in unknowns." Ian said.

"The cook likes Shelby but being Tibetan, he dislikes Peiling and Young-Sun. He will not be a problem." Jackson responded. "The diversion will allow two members of my team, dressed in identical uniforms as the guards, to take down and remove the two guards. Once we get an all clear from Enid inside the compound," Jackson nodded at Enid. "Then my team will take over the control room. When they have cleared the control room area, I will enter with the rest of my team. We want this quiet and efficient. We must not allow any communication between Peiling and her guards. If they suspect anything they will not hesitate to kill Shelby or Camden."

"We will be ready at your signal, Jackson." Ian paused. "Right now, Jackson, I want you and your team to take a break. Get some food and if possible, sneak in a cat nap. There are cots upstairs. Food in the back. Agent," Ian pointed to a young Asian man sitting to the right of him. "Monitor Shelby and Camden. Record every word they say."

"Do we have word from Kent or Charles?"

"Not yet, Sam," Ian shook his head. "We have less than 2 hours until dawn. Peiling will not be able to do anything until Camden finishes stabilizing the remaining elements," he paused. "Camden alluded to some of the francium missing. That bothers me. Don't second guess. Our goal is to prevent the explosion of the dam and get our people out safely." Ian rubbed his face, looking at Jackson.

"Camden, get some rest."

"Ian, Peiling is keeping me and Shelby close. She wants an audience. She wants us to watch as he she kills millions of people. She will be Nuwa," he waited. "I am betting Daniel's redemption will be the last two targets. Taking a break. See you guys soon, Jackson."

"Stay safe, Camden." He answered.

"Why don't we go now?" She asked, pacing.

"Legally, ARKose has not committed a crime. Or at least, not one the FBI can prosecute for." Ian responded. "Camden was correct. If we don't do this right, they will go underground and they will not stop until the end goal is complete."

"The earthquake in Alaska? Isn't that proof enough?"

"There is no proof, Sam. They will put it on Camden or Shing," Jackson put his arms on her shoulders. "If we go in too early here, China will come after the United States for espionage. If we are too late. Well, there are no contingencies."

Ian spoke. "Get some rest, Jackson."

The room was eerily quiet as Jon held her hand as they walked into the kitchen. "I don't like the waiting. I feel like we should be doing something. They are so close. Shelby is so close." She wrapped her arms around Jon's waist.

"She has never had any patience." Jackson looked at Jon as he headed to the small refrigerator.

"For our plan to work, we must be patient. The burial ceremony begins at dawn so timing is critical to access the compound gate. It is the reason you civilians are here. I want everyone to calm your minds and relax your body. You need to eat and to hydrate and be ready for action. If this thing goes down before dawn, we will need to adjust our plan. And Sam, there is the possibility that Ian will need military assistance. That means, Kent will be taking over this mission," he reiterated. "Right, now, my ops team, as Ian said, are ghosts. We are not here. You will stand down and come back here. Am I clear on that?"

"But what about…"

"Sam, I will repeat. You will stand down and abort on my order." Jackson stared at her.

"Yes, sir."

"We understand." Enid pronounced, as Jon nodded yes. The three of them knew their role.

Under a starlit sky, Jackson's team got into an unidentified van and drove off.

Chapter 32

Shelby

Shortly after 0500 one of the agents shouted, "We have two tracers moving together."

"Quiet." Ian shouted. "Put them on speaker. Now."

In that instant, they heard Camden's voice. "Do you read me?"

"We got you, Camden."

"Shelby and I are walking down the solid rock tunnel. There is one egress. The tunnel is 2200 feet long from the compound and descends downward. You may lose contact with me." Then they heard Camden's voice in a whisper.

"We are outside the rock room, my lab. All is quiet further down the tunnel. No activity. The door is steel and opens using a retinal reader. Peiling, Daniel, Shing and myself have access."

A quiet shoosh sound could be heard over the listening device in the control room.

"I have added a bacterium to the last batch of francium, cesium, promethium, and the processed plutonium. There will be a reaction when the elements react with moisture but it will be extinguished quickly."

"Anything on the robot?" Ian asked

240

"I have never seen such a series of fire walls and blocks. At every turn, Winter and I have found a block. And when that happens, another wall is created. There is a trip wire randomly inserted which can alert ARKose that someone is breaking in."

"Shelby, this is Winter. Can you log into a computer there in the lab? Once you are in, I can create a virtual door into Shing's computer."

"I am doing it now." She responded. "I am logged in."

The clock ticked. Silence. Twenty minutes later Winter responded.

"We are in the system."

Whispering between Winter and Mik was overhead with clicks on keyboards.

"We are leaving the rock room to check on Shing and we're leaving the elements in Camden's vault. Increasing stall time."

"I am almost in Shing's computer." Mik said.

Camden murmured. "We are near the laser room where Shing, Peiling, Daniel, and Yong-Sun are waiting. There are two armed guards outside the door. Note that Shing is not a willing participant. Shing is being held under duress. Peiling has his granddaughter at an unknown location. If he fails, she will kill her. Shing has inserted a virus to disrupt the robot but," he hesitated. "It would be preferred if you have control. This combination of elements will be a—"

And then the ground shook violently, knocking Camden and Shelby to the rocky floor, as the tunnel went pitch black. Instinctively, Camden shielded Shelby as he covered her body with his. As violent as the shaking began, it ceased.

"Shel, are you okay?"

"I'm fine. And you?"

"Yes." He grabbed her arm and helped her off the cold rock.

Daniel emerged from the laser room, covered in blood and shouting at the armed guards.

"He's in here, quickly!"

The tunnel lights flickered as two more guards could be heard as a series of clacking sounds echoed through the tunnel from their boots.

"What the hell happened, Daniel?" Camden demanded.

"Could they have detected the communication devices?" She whispered.

Camden shook his head. Then he brushed past Daniel as he followed the two guards into the room.

Daniel nodded as the two of the guards arrived with weapons raised. "Guard the door."

She eyed the guards as she entered the room and saw Shing on the floor with Camden leaning over him. He appeared to be unconscious, as a dark stain spread beneath him. Camden stood up and in one swift movement, his hands were around Yong-Sun's neck.

Reacting swiftly, she stepped between the two men. "Camden, calm down. We don't know what happened," she implored, grabbing his forearm. "What happened?" she asked calmly, kneeling beside Shing's still body while a guard retrieved a compress from the medical bag and applied it to his head wound.

"Yong-Sun did nothing." Daniel responded. "Shing was standing as he was directing the robot through voice command. And then there was an explosion and everything went dark. When the lights came back on, we found him on the floor."

Camden stood behind Peiling. "Peiling, did you trigger the robot to explode? That was an earthquake."

Peiling's fingers clicked keys as she tried to regain control of the robot. "Voice command isn't working. Dammit, what did he do!" She exclaimed, mixing English with North Korean. Her eyes remained fixed on the keyboard as her monotone voice responded.

"Peiling answer me?"

"I do not bow to you, Camden." Peiling hissed. "But the answer to your question is yes. The robot was armed with francium and promethium, that you processed. And the greedy Dr. Shing, so eager to get his patent tested, devised a method to deliver those elements, for me." She turned in her chair. "There was an explosion in the channel and we lost the monitor. I don't know what happened. It detonated too soon. He did it! He caused it. Stupid man." Anger was eroding her composure.

Camden glanced at Shelby. "Why was the robot armed with francium and promethium, Peiling?" No answer.

"You aren't that clever, Camden. Chul-Moo saw you with your college buddy in Anchorage. We thought we dealt with him. Apologies about his twin." She laughed. "Collateral damage. Twins can be useful, sometimes, can't they?" She glared at Yong-Sun.

"What did you say?" Rage was in his voice as he moved towards her. "What did you do to Jacob?"

With two armed guards outside the door and with the two inside, Camden knew he was outnumbered. His chances were somewhat improved with Shelby. His secret weapon.

"I did nothing to Jacob. It was his misfortune to be in the wrong place when the tsunami in Prince William Sound struck Whittier."

She needed to protect their cover. "Camden." She said making eye contact with him. "You need to assist Peiling." She was stalling for time. "I will take care of Dr. Shing."

"Peiling what the hell did you do?" He looked at the fluttering lights of the monitor.

"What did I do? He did this." She spat at Shing. "You make me sick with your morality, Camden. I am purifying the evil of those who corrupt this earth with their moral indignation and patriarchal supremacy."

"Why was the robot armed with my elements? You should have waited. You caused this, not Shing. I could have prevented this."

"Get him out of here." Yong-Sun's patience was waning as he yelled at the two guards.

Camden turned ready for a fight when he realized Yong-Sun

was referring to Shing as he noticed Shelby leaning close to one of the guards as he crouched next to the lifeless body.

Trying to move out of the way, she inadvertently tripped on the guard's jacket, causing her to stumble against the guard. After apologizing, she stepped closer to the door, while the two guards carried the man out.

"Your elements," Peiling said with a laugh. "You must have hit your head, Camden. I hired you for your expertise to stabilize rare earth elements. We're cleansing the earth of parasites. These are my elements."

Yong-Sun said something in North Korean, sparking a heated argument between the siblings, slamming his fist on the table.

"Quiet." she yelled, springing up from her chair. "I will blow up Three Gorges Dam. He did something to the controls. The robot was programmed to my voice."

"Are you crazy! That dam sits on two active thrust faults. The entire Tibetan Plateau will be impacted. Millions of people could be killed. I wasn't hired to blow up a dam."

"Oh, but you were. You believe all of this was for saving the earth? To solve our dependence on fossil fuels? Corporate greed will never allow that to happen. You and her," she glared at Shelby. "Will witness what you helped create. The earthquakes in Alaska are a testament to your legacy Camden."

"You used the francium to target thrust faults in Alaska. Why?"

"That is an arrogant question. The melting of the glaciers. The disappearance of the permafrost. Oil companies are lining up like horses at the starting gate to rape and pillage the Northwest Passage. Your congress is already passing bills to allow mining of the Beaufort Sea and the transport of oil to the Atlantic Ocean. You don't even know who funds this project?" Peiling laughed. "The gluttony of the United States. You want to know who pays for this? A Senator from Alaska. He was a shareholder of the Stoney Mine. Yes, don't look so smug, Shelby. He is among many like him."

"You lie, Peiling." She answered.

"The Senator is chairman of the CITI. Oh, Shelby, I see a flicker in those green eyes. You know who I am referring to. He is a powerful man, this Senator from Alaska. Americans. So gullible. So ignorant. They hide behind their big trucks and their big houses. Their children dressed in designer clothes and private schools. Spoiled brats. Have you heard of the Cyber, Information Technologies, and Innovation Subcommittee, Camden? Well, there are a handful of political ego's, who supported our cause. You see, they want control of everything. Rare earths. Oil. Who lives and who dies? The apocalypse is what they intend. A world war. And money. Lots, and lots of money." She slammed her fingers on the keyboard. "I am Nüwa. They will not control me and that is there flaw in all of this."

Regaining her composure promptly, she said, "It's time to prove yourself, Camden. Daniel, escort him to the rock room and retrieve the elements. I need to focus. Focus. I will regain control of the computer. Take the guards. Yong-Sun will look after Shelby. Don't worry, Shelby, you're safe for now. Isn't that right, Daniel?" Camden glanced at Shelby before leaving with Daniel. He saw the fire in her eyes.

CHAPTER 33

JACKSON

THE AIR WAS crisp, as dawn light blended into the night sky, painting a canvas of purple and yellow hues. He sat with his alpha team in the van monitoring the communication as they drove to their drop off location.

"Status." He demanded.

Ian responded. "Jackson, Peiling armed a robot. There was an explosion inside the tunnel. We believe Shing sabotaged the robot."

"The computer?"

"Mik has control." Ian responded as static filled the comm. "Jackson, we have the proof that ARKose attempted to destroy Three Gorges. Kent is with the President. Proceed as planned."

"And the earthquake?"

"Magnitude 4.5. Limited to the region of Shigatse and Tagqu. No damage being reported. Three Gorges Dam was not affected. The explosion was in the shaft but far enough from the dam to cause anything but some shaking."

"Go," Jackson looked at Sam. "I will see you inside."

Enid, Jon, and Sam, donning the traditional bulky Tibetan attire with colorful sashes and thick leather belts, joined a small gathering of local Tibetans led by two monks in crimson robes. Chanting echoed in the dawn light as the small group gathered near the compound's guardhouse. What appeared to be a small bundle on top of the litter. It was wrapped in white cloth, with two shoulder poles balanced on the shoulders of four men. A woman walking next to the litter, wailed as her hand laid upon the white bundle.

Enid nodded her head, whispering into the comms. "Distraction implemented."

One of the monk's walked to the side of the dirt road, turning his head and pointing. Murmurs spread among the group as they searched for the trail leading to the cliff that would serve as the final resting place.

"We are in front of the guard station." Enid whispered.

A guard emerged from behind the compound gate, yelling at the crowd to disperse. Another woman began to weep, as a man tried to comfort her.

Sam watched as the monk walked over to the guard. He was pointing and nodding his head as the guard shook his head no. Now the second guard was yelling. As the murmurs grew louder, a passersby halted to observe the scene.

"This is better than expected. Be ready." Enid whispered as the scene unfolded.

Gradually, a crowd gathered causing such a disturbance that the narrow dirt road became congested. A forceful sharp honk from an impatient driver startled a yak harnessed to a wooden cart. As the young shepherd, attempting to calm the agitated creature, realized his efforts were in vain. With a single swing of the yak's massive head, the head caused one of the men to stumble, losing his grip on the litter, as it slowly slid off his shoulder.

Amid the unfolding chaos, members in the group screamed in alarm, fearing the small body would plummet to the ground. An exchange of glances between the guards prompted them to rush forward to assist the four men, each seizing the sling to prevent the white bundle from falling onto the dusty road.

Enid nodded her head at Sam and Jon. "We have an unexpected but welcomed disturbance from an upset yak." Enid reported.

"Enid, you are clear. Security cameras are now offline." Ian stated.

During the commotion, no one noticed three members of the burial party slip away through the gate, which had been left unguarded and open.

Swift and silent, Enid, Sam and Jon entered through the unlocked kitchen door on the side of the compound.

As soon as the three vanished, a member of the burial party, yelled and pointed and the small group dispersed onto the trail. Laughing the two guards never noticed the van or the two men that jumped out of it.

"The two guards are disposed of, sir," a member of Jackson's Alpha team relayed. "Guardhouse clear. We are proceeding to the control room inside the compound."

"Roger that." He countered as he waited in the shrubbery.

"All clear on the second floor. I am walking down the stairs to the hallway adjacent to the control center." Sam said when she heard a guard yelling. "Jackson, something is up. One of the guards walked away from his position in the control center and went through the steel doors of the tunnel."

"Jackson, we confirm what Sam relayed." Silence. "Control center is clear. Guard down."

"Roger." He entered with three members of his team as Jon, Enid and Sam joined them on the lower terrace.

"Listen up. Shelby is in the laser room with Peiling and Yong-Sun. Daniel is with Camden along with two guards retrieving elements from the vault. The guard that left this post, is most likely brought in to retrieve the unconscious Dr. Shing who was injured during the earthquake."

"Jon, I want you with me and my team in the tunnel. Enid, you stay here with Sam. Ian, bring in your team to cover the control room. Keep a man in the guard house."

"Roger, Jackson."

"Ian, we are going in with night vision. Keep those lights off."

"Confirmed. Get my agents, Jackson."

"We are going in dark and stealth."

CHAPTER 34

CAMDEN

A S HE OPENED the steel door with the retina scan, he noticed Daniel was twitching, his neck jerking sideways with beads of sweat on his brow. The two guards kept their weapons held staying between the door, and slightly behind Camden.

"Get that damn gun out of my face before I ram it up your ass." He yelled at the guard before turning to Daniel. "Two fucking guards, Daniel! With automatic M41 rifles." He heard two clicks in his ear. "I am not doing a damn thing until they are out of here."

"Leave the room but stay by the door." Daniel nodded at the guards. "Better?"

"Yes. Tell me what happened in there Daniel."

"Shing sabotaged the robot," Daniel responded. "After the explosion, when the lights came back on, he was lying on the floor." He pointed to the vault. "Open it now. Do I need to remind you. Peiling will kill Shelby."

He stood there. "Radiation. Your plan all along was to harness rare earth elements for destruction. Cesium and promethium combined will create a significant explosion but I doubt even these two elements can accomplish what you desire, Daniel."

"My people are blamed as the catalyst. We're told we should have foreseen a better future, anticipated these catastrophic floods with climate change. But what about your people?" Daniel pressed on. "Pakistan was embroiled in Afghanistan, aiding America to get rid of the Taliban. All while our people were starving."

"I am confused, Daniel. This has nothing do…"

"Must I spell it out?" He screamed. "You're a conceited, self-absorbed man. Afghanistan and Pakistan are destined to be engulfed in flames. Water can't purify their souls."

"Keep him talking." Jackson whispered. "Two guards down."

"You deceived us, Daniel. Shing refused to go along with your plan. Let me guess. Yong-Sun hit him with his gun. You knew all along what Peiling's plan was. Killing thousands, millions of innocents. Shing found out what you were doing and he refused. If he dies, his blood is on you."

The man changed before his eyes. "Blood on my hands? Oh, Camden you are hilarious. Daniel explained you're naivete. You're ethical consciousness. You see, I enjoy the feel of blood on my hands. That happens when a child endures the suffering of their mother. Murdered by one's father. I have had blood on my hands for generations."

"Who are you?"

"Oh, do tell."

"You were warned. Francium, although stable is delicate. Even the slightest miscalculation during the robot's loading or a tiny moisture droplet contaminating the container could result in an explosion." He paused, studying Daniel before asking. "Shing did not sabotage anything. Peiling did."

"No. You are wrong. Open." He spat.

"Oh? You think I am naïve? You, believe Peiling will pass the control of the robot over to you for detonation of your homeland, Daniel?" He stopped. "You are the foolish one."

"I am not Daniel. I will destroy my homeland and that of my father's people. They will feel the pain of hell on their skin as it melts away. I will be their leader."

"You believe that? Who exactly will you be the leader of? How many people are going to die and for what? Revenge? Daddy issues?" He stepped closer to the man. "But you are correct. Peiling will kill Shelby. Her blood will be on you, Daniel. Is that what you want?"

"You are the one who will kill Shelby if you don't open this vault." He was shaking. Twitching.

"You just said she is going to die anyway. I have no desire to help you, Daniel."

The twitching increased as he paced mumbling to himself. "I am not Daniel. I am Abdul. He is weak. He is nothing."

"Abdul? Really. You are weak. Peiling will never give you control. She and Yong-Sun are throwing you into the flames. If I die, you die. If Shelby dies, you die."

"Your girlfriend will be sacrificed for the greater good. Along with you," he mused. "If your abilities match your self-assuredness, I may even congratulate you for your assistance in this endeavor. Before you die. Ultimately, you'll grant me the satisfaction I've sought since childhood."

He didn't hear a word I said.

"Oh, I will exceed your estimation, Daniel. I will make sure you get what you deserve."

"I am Abdul. Daniel is gone. Open the vault, now." Daniel screamed and then he went quiet. "There's one more thing," he said politely. "To ensure my satisfaction and prevent you from coming up with any more tricks or excuses, I've taken the liberty of introducing a catalyst. This addition will ensure that your elements perform as expected."

There was a slight change again, in the man he knew as Daniel.

He began to slump and shake his head. And then, it happened again. The man stood straight, his shoulders back, as if he was inches taller. A smugness in his voice. He was no longer pacing.

With the comm in her ear, Sam whispered. "What the hell is he talking about?"

"A catalyst?" Ian questioned.

"The missing francium." Jackson stated. "It must be. But, why call it a catalyst."

"Mik, find out if there is another rare earth element that we do not know about. Or something else that could be used to…" Jon stammered.

"We know he is planning to cause an earthquake in Afghanistan and Pakistan using elements that are radioactive." Sam interjected.

"A catalyst can be anything even water when it comes to an element like francium." Jackson stated. "Quiet. Listen only."

"What about your mother Daniel?"

"I am not Daniel. I am Abdul. You know nothing of my mother."

"I know she loved you. She died protecting you, Daniel. For what? For you to murder innocent women and children. She gave you freedom to live a life she could not have. You disrespect her. You tarnish everything she stood for. You are your father."

"I am not my father. He mistreated my mother. He accused her of treason for educating other women. She was a university professor. He labeled her as a nushuz."

He saw another change as Daniel sat on the floor, his shoulders rolling forward. And then he saw the grown man, with his head bowed, put his thumb in his mouth.

"Mama," he cried. "I heard her sobbing, so I did a no-no."

"What did you do?"

"The door was open. She was hurt and crying and my father was holding her arms. Men were hurting her."

Daniels voice changed as he appeared to grow taller. Bolder, as he stood up.

"They raped her. Daniel was too weak to watch. Yella. she hides all the time. But I watched. I am the protector. I am Abdul. I will be the great leader of my people." He cried. "I was screaming at him. He hit me. He called me a little boy, not a man." He touched his cheek. "The mark he left on my cheek feeds my strength. He had a knife."

A high-pitched laugh escaped Daniel's lips sending chills down Camden's spine.

"I am not my father. I will be the savior of my people. Their ashes will be scattered across the earth to be reborn. To be cleansed."

"And the children that you murder? The innocents?"

"They must be sacrificed. It is the only way. My mother understands that." He nodded. "Yes. Their deaths won't be in vain," Daniel replied in a calm monotone voice. "Their innocence will be the seed for a new beginning—the dawn of a fresh world."

"Let me get this right. Peiling will destroy Three Gorges Dam so she too will be the savior."

"Yes. She is Nüwa. The floodwaters cleansing the earth, sweeping away the filth—the men who commit atrocities, who treat their own children like playthings. Their egos will drown and sink deep into the mud as the waters recede."

He noticed the man start to shake and a stutter in his voice. His shoulders rolled forward.

"Did anyone get the feeling that Daniel changed into another person?" Jackson asked.

"His voice changed because he did become another personality," Enid whispered. "The trauma he endured as a child. The only way he could endure was to became someone else. It is called dissociative identity disorder."

"Daniel, Shelby needs you. We need to protect Shelby. You care for her. You don't want to see her killed. She is an innocent. Daniel, listen to me. You must help her."

"Shelby," he whispered. "Yong-Sun will."

The man was changing before his eyes. "Yong-Sun will what, Daniel?"

The man was quiet, not moving, staring. "He appears to be in a trance." He whispered.

"Daniel, are you listening?"

Slowly, the man turned his head as he faced him.

"Peiling plans to kill you, Daniel. Do you understand that? She does not need you anymore. She has her twin to help her. You will burn with us. We must not give her the elements. We need to rescue Shelby. Do you understand?"

"I cannot fight him." He cried, holding his hands on either side of his head.

"Fight who? Daniel. Listen to me. Concentrate on Shelby."

In that instant, while he was distracting Daniel, he pushed the button to open the steel door.

"Perfect timing." He asked looking at Jackson. "Shelby?"

"She is holding her own. Peiling is furious and is arguing with Yong-Sun. Restrain him." Jackson ordered looking at the pitiful man pacing in the corner as Alpha 2 walked in.

"It appears Shelby has taken care of Yong-Sun." Jackson smiled. "Crap, Camden. We need to get that door open. Shelby wants some alone time with Peiling. Her exact words were, 'she's mine'."

As they walked out of the rock room into the dark silent tunnel, they heard Ian through their comms.

"Kent is with the President. We have our proof."

CHAPTER 35

SHELBY

CAMDEN STOOD IN front of the retina scan as Jackson raised his weapon. Before Peiling could react, Jackson's crimson laser sight zeroed in on her forehead.

"Don't do it, Peiling. My finger is itching to pull this trigger." Jackson looked at the woman.

Peiling squinted, her brow curling as her fingers danced over the keyboard, screaming in North Korean. Frustrated, she pounded her fist on the table, rising to her feet.

"No worries, Jackson," she said as she stepped towards the blonde anticipating her next move. "I got her. You bitch. You attacked my City and my State. My parents live in Anchorage."

With the speed of a viper, Peiling's arm jerked ready to strike as Shelby slammed the woman's throat with the outer edge of her hand. Peiling gaped at Shelby, her eyes wide like golf balls, as she staggered back into her chair, clutching her throat.

"I'm not who you presumed me to be," Shelby said calmly, as Peiling struggled for breath. "You've just witnessed restraint on my part. Crushing your windpipe would have been preferred, but we've got much to discuss, and it would be difficult for you to answer my questions with a crushed windpipe. Instead, it is only bruised."

Jackson lowered his weapon as Enid strode into the crowded room.

"Finally, we meet in the flesh. The lady with the hair on fire. Nice work, Shelby." Jackson grinned.

"Likewise." She hugged him."How is Shing?" She asked.

"He's alive. He is at the command center with Ian. A severe concussion at a minimum. Once he stabilizes, they will rush him to the nearest military hospital for treatment and debriefing. Unfortunately, he's still unconscious."

"And Yong-Sun?" Shelby inquired.

"We have him secured. Your version of morse code might go down in the FBI training manual."

"Thanks Ian. Glad you enjoyed that."

Camden looked up, his eyes meeting his mother's before being enveloped in a tight hug.

She held him tight as he reciprocated the embrace.

"I'm damn proud of you, Camden."

"Ian, the site's secure." Jackson reported as Jon and Sam walked into the room.

"That coffee you're sipping must pack a punch, considering your mug's scorching hot." Jon shook Camden's hand.

"Crickey, mate, they called in the big kahuna. Good to see you Jon. And yeah, that's one mug you don't want to mess with. You've got Mik with you, I assume?"

Mik piped up in Camden's ear. "Yep, I am here. Winter, Jackson's wife, and me managed to take control of that robot only a little late after the explosion. You need to tell us why that first robot went kaboom and that conversation ranga had with Peiling."

"Working on that. I assume Peiling did not seal the containment system. If she armed it with francium and promethium all it would take is a drop of moisture to cause it to explode. Shing's plan was to insert a virus into the communication system to the robot so Peiling could not take it over. Once it was it a safe spot, he blew it up."

"You guys glowing? That is a lot of radiation to let lose, man."

"Team is bringing in the monitor equipment now, Mik." Jackson responded.

"Speaking of which, I need to check on the remaining elements in the vault. The ones in that mug there are clean. The ones in the vault are contaminated with the bacterium."

"I want to hear about that." Jon responded.

"You want to join me?" Camden asked.

As Jon and Camden left the room, Camden asked. "Where's Daniel?"

"He is with Alpha team." Sam replied as she walked over to Shelby and hugged her friend.

"Who is ranga?" Shelby asked.

"Later Shelby." Sam said. "Shelby, this is the general, Enid. Camden's mom. It was her diversion plan that got us inside the compound."

"Enid. I am so grateful." She hugged the women. "You raised an amazing man."

"Yes, I did. He is a lot like his father. I am so happy to finally meet you. Red hair and all. And I cannot wait to hear about that move you made on Peiling. Sam tells me you two not only took Tai chi, but Krav Maga."

"Yes, and she fought me every movement in Tai chi and only agreed to learn if I taught her Krav Maga."

"One of the most difficult of the martial arts. Black belt. I assume?"

"Of course, why bother if you don't take it all the way. It has come in handy, several times." Sam giggled.

"Ian, we need a cleanup here." Jackson interjected.

"Already there."

While Camden and Jon were in the laser room, she explained to Jackson as Sam as Enid went to find Camden, about her conversation with Peiling.

"We picked that up, Shelby." Jackson responded. "We intentionally turned Sam's communication device off."

"Ian got that conversation?" She asked.

"Charles and my boss, Kent both got the intel. They are working that now."

"What? What did I miss out on?" Sam asked.

"In an earlier discussion with Daniel, Camden and I were trying to find out who financed this operation. He mentioned a senator but he had no idea what city the senator belonged to. He insinuated that the money was coming from the United States. A very powerful person in the United States."

"Wait a minute, Shel. When Daniel said city, what was the context of the discussion?" Sam asked.

"Now, I know he didn't mean a city but that was how we interpreted it."

"I got clean-up to do. Follow me."

"Jackson, remember when we were talking about the transfer of mining companies, and the Senator from Alaska who got voted in even after he was accused of illegal contributions?" Sam asked as they followed Jackson into the tunnel.

"Yes, I do and you were right."

Sam rolled her eyes. "I made a big deal because the Senator is the chairman of the CITI or the Cyber, Information Technologies, and Innovation Subcommittee. Shelby, did Peiling tell you that her money guy is the Senator? Is that what I missed?"

"I told Peiling that I knew who her investor was in ARKose. A powerful man in the U.S. and then I inferred that is was Daniel who told me and the reason is to destroy the mining industry in China." Shelby smirked. "All about control, greed and power. Using legends to support the reasoning to kill."

Enid joined Sam and Shelby as Camden and Jon waited for Jackson.

"Here is an update of that conversation you and Peiling shared." Enid explained. "Upon confirming that the Three Gorges Dam was among the intended targets, and after Ian heard the conversation between Shelby and Peiling, the FBI discovered a link between the congressman on the CITI subcommittee and ARKose. There was a trail of documentation including tape recordings and financial connections of the congressman's connections to the Stoney Mine, like you said Sam. But also, they found a connection between him, Peiling and ARKose." She hesitated. "And between others that hold high positions, not just in the U.S."

She asked Enid. "Where is Peiling and Daniel?"

"Jackson asked to keep them in two different rooms."

In that instant, Jon and Camden walked into the tunnel and saw the two women walking up to them. Placing her hands on each side of Camden's cheeks, she planted a brief yet passionate kiss on Camden's lips. "I love you, Camden."

"I've been waiting to hear those words since our first job in Nevada." He grinned and then whispered, "I love you back. Go with Sam. Jon and I will follow you."

Sam grabbed her friend's arm and slid hers through it as they walked side by side. Ian and Kent's voices buzzed in their ears with the procedural steps required to ensure the safe evacuation of everyone and everything they needed.

"Now I am included in the communication. We are being told to get the hell out of here." Sam laughed. "That was quite the kiss, my friend. Apparently, you have lots to tell me."

"Eejit," she swore. "I need to get out of this tunnel. And this place."

"You are avoiding the question."

"Yes, I am." She pondered. "Shing was only going to stop the robot infecting it with a virus. But it exploded. We had no idea they would proceed without us. Camden altered the elements using a protein from, believe it or not, an alder tree but they were still in his vault." She took a deep breath. "As, you know, it did not go as planned. Those were the elements that were planned to be used."

"What are you saying Shel?"

"Where did they get the elements? That was Camden's job."

Then she spoke into her comms. "Ian, Sam and I are heading to my laboratory to retrieve the computer and records."

"My team has already cleaned it, Shelby," Ian replied.

"Are our dorm rooms clean?"

"Roger. No evidence you and Camden were ever there."

As they entered the main reception room, Peiling shuffled past them with her hands and legs bound, escorted by two Alpha members when she spotted Ian.

"Glad to see you, Shelby." Ian shook his comrade's hand.

A small, remote-controlled vehicle used for transporting hazardous materials was followed by a half-dozen suited and armed men who walked past them, down the tunnel.

"Good news is the Chinese President confirmed ARKose was behind the plan to destroy Three Gorges Dam," Ian responded. "We have 45 minutes to get what we want and get out. Two of our guys will guard Peiling and Daniel until the Chinese show up. Orders are to give the Chinese those who are responsible and the evidence behind the proposed terrorist attack on the dam."

"Sir?" She questioned.

"We will comply and the Chinese will receive the evidence they need to establish guilt. Mik and Kent are working on that as we speak," he winked. "Understand, however, that you and Camden never existed here. We'll debrief everyone later, but for now, we must expedite our exit. Communications are to remain quiet." Ian said as he walked into the tunnel. "We are no doubt under surveillance by the Chinese military at this stage."

Sam heard men's voices echo against the tunnel walls. "Great job, Camden. It seemed touch and go there for a bit." Ian said.

Straining to listen, she could not hear the rest of the conversation until they were close to the entrance.

"Yes, she'd excel at it. We should discuss it further. But seriously, I can't believe Mik called her a rangy." Ian chuckled.

"The thing about Mik is that there's no filter between his brilliant mind and his mouth," Jon explained.

"If I know Irish, she won't let that comment slide," Camden chimed in. "I've seen the fire in those Irish eyes."

Unbeknownst to the men, Shelby and Sam were waiting to join them as they exited the tunnel. This time, the two women could hear every word the men said.

"Hello, gentlemen." Shelby greeted as she stepped out in front of the tunnel entrance. The four men came to a sudden halt, collectively silenced.

"Did they hear us?" Camden whispered to Jon as the two women walked away, arm in arm, laughing.

"Probably. Sam has ears like a wolf."

"Listen up, time for civilians, including Shelby and Camden to depart. Dress and meet Tenzin near the gate," Jackson said. "See you at the safehouse."

The team, made their way through the kitchen and reemerged through a side door, leaving the gate and proceeding down the road. Three women were slowly walking, dressed in long woolen coats with colorful aprons cinched around their waists. Each held a bucket, their faces shielded by thick woven hats as two men followed them. The two men were dressed in slate gray long-sleeved shirts and baggy black pants, each wearing a thick woolen hat.

As they approached a white delivery van, known in the area for transporting fresh produce and fruit, the small group stopped. One of the men slid open the side door and assisted the group inside, soon disappearing down a side street in Shigatse.

Once in the command room, the group watched the surveillance cameras of the compound overhead. Under the cover of darkness, two slate-black armored military vehicles adorned with white lettering and symbols parked in front of the now, dark compound. Two individuals with black hoods over their heads were ushered into one of the vehicles. The Chinese army loaded large military-grade boxes into the second vehicle and soon the two vehicles dissolved into the night.

CHAPTER 36

SAM

ENID WIPED AWAY the tears from both Camden's cheeks and her own. "I'll let you continue your work. Before I let him go, I want to express my gratitude to everyone in this room and in Anchorage, who played a part in bringing Camden back to me. Now, I need to change out of these dusty clothes, freshen up, and start planning a celebration. Ian, Kent, is that agreeable?"

Ian nodded, his eyes shimmering with emotion. "Yes, it is," Kent confirmed over the monitor. "The Chinese have received what they requested."

"Then I'll leave you to continue the briefing." Enid said, looking at her son, sharing a smile before she exited the room to prepare for the celebration ahead.

While the team was securing the compound, Enid secured lodging in a spacious private home near the Yarlung Tsangpo Jiang River. The property belonged to a significant contributor for the Tibetan foundation she volunteered for. This generous donor insisted her group stay there for as long as necessary in Shigatse.

From the moment they disembarked the LUNA jet, the

primary focus was to prevent an environmental crisis, prevent a war, and rescue Shelby and Camden. Enid understood all too well, the advantage adrenaline offered during perilous situations, but she also understood the toll it could take on the body once the danger subsided. Given the potential for a clash between the USA and China, the likelihood of a swift departure from Tibet was high. Amidst this tension, basic needs like sleep, food, and even showers were forgotten.

Enid closed the conference room door and leaned against it, pressing her hands together in a prayer gesture and closing her eyes. She began to walk towards her until Jon gestured for her to stop.

"Give her a few minutes, Sam."

"Enid is a rock. I'm in awe of this woman." She whispered, as Jon placed his arm around her shoulder. "How many times do you think she's been there? To be the rock. To be the light at the end of the dark tunnel."

"Too many times to count, I am sure," Jon replied in a hushed tone. "Right now, she is a mother grateful to have her son alive and well."

"They're a team. Part of our circle."

"Man, why do I always miss out on the gushy stuff, mate?"

"Seriously, Mik? You're eavesdropping now?" Jon laughed, shaking his head. "What's your ETA?" Jon realized his earpiece was still on. "Mik, I am turning this off. Call me and we can chat on the phone."

She laughed as Jon gave the ear piece to one of the agents, just as his phone buzzed. "Sam is with me and you are on speaker."

"Mik, thank you for bringing Shelby back to us. Although, I did have to tell her a wee lie about what ranga means. Be ready for that."

"Great. What did you tell her?"

"Aussie slang for a red-haired beauty."

"That works. I will stick with that. It will be nice to meet her even though she might hurt me. Jon, our ETA is to arrive at the Shigatse airport at 10:00 am tomorrow. On board will be Shelby's parents, Jacob and Winter. Charles and Kent got called to D.C."

"I assume they've got the cargo?" Jon asked.

"A little birdie told me Kent is personally overseeing the delivery. All good."

"That is a relief." She added.

"The path is clear, according to our contact in D.C." Jon confirmed

"Roger that," Mik took a deep breath before talking. "And Kent's invited our friend from the NSA to the meet and greet in D.C."

Slipping his phone into his pocket, Jon and Sam walked over to Enid.

"Are you ready Enid?" She asked.

"Yes. The car is down the street. Tenzin and his wife offered to swing by the restaurant to pick up the meal I ordered. Apparently, Tenzin's wife is also preparing a very special dessert for tonight's occasion." Enid stopped and took a deep breath. "Is everything ready for the crew arriving tomorrow?"

"Wheels will touch down at 10 a.m." Jon said as he kissed his wife's cheek.

"Is that some kind of code you two devised? A kiss for yes and two winks for, no? If not, it should be a thing after French Guiana and now," Enid exclaimed. "Actually, thinking about it, the business of mining is a hazardous career. Perhaps Camden should go back to climbing rocks instead of analyzing them."

"I can't help but agree, Enid." She remarked as she sat in the passenger seat of the SUV, with Enid at the wheel.

As they turned onto a shaded driveway bordered by tall, graceful bamboo, Himalayan pine, Tibetan cypress, and Chinese juniper, she pushed the button to roll her window down.

"The smell is so refreshing. There is a woodsy smokey smell."

An ornate black steel gate swung open after Enid entered a code into a keypad. At the end of the short driveway stood a spacious, one-story home with multiple sections, constructed from river rock in subdued tones of reddish-brown, black, and gray. The traditional Asian roofs over each section of the house were adorned with rounded red clay tiles, their graceful curves rising at the corners.

Bringing the vehicle to a stop, she stepped out of the passenger door onto worn, intricately carved, cement pavers. With her eyes closed she breathed the chilled air imbued with exotic fragrances of oranges, jasmine, and pine. Water dripping from aged stone fountains and the cheerful chirping of birds soothed her nervous system.

"Enid, this place is magical," she whispered. "It's perfect. After everything this place will provide much-needed peace and solace."

"This place has been a sanctuary for healing, a haven that unfortunately, has witnessed generations of pain. The foundation was established here when the owner lost his grandparents and parents to the horrors of genocide. It was part of his family's heritage, and when the time came, he returned to restore both the place and himself, to bring healing to others. It is magical." Enid squeezed her hand as they strolled amidst the pillars adorned in gold, red, and blue, guarded by two majestic golden lions, before stepping through the intricately carved solid wooden doors.

Jon observed the two women as they disappeared into the home.

"Jon, you won't believe how incredible this place is," she exclaimed, rushing out of the doorway. She kissed his cheek and then grabbed her backpack before slinging his worn, threadbare, canvas green duffel bag over her shoulder. "I love you."

"I love you more. And Sam," Jon said."

"Yes, my love?"

"I know my mum is proud of the man I have become because of the remarkable woman in my life."

"Probably but I bet she has always been proud of her loving

son," she blew him a kiss. "Now grab Enid's bag." He shook his head as he followed his wife.

"Isn't it amazing."

Jon held her as they stood mesmerized by the view through the wall of windows, stretching a staggering 15 feet from floor to ceiling, offering views of trees, gardens, and a tantalizing glimpse of the river beyond.

"Look at this." She held Jon's hand as they walked out on the deck. Sliding his arms around her small, firm waist, as he kissed her neck. She leaned into him, grasping his arms as tears welled up in her eyes.

"I was so afraid, Jon," she whispered. "I thought I would never see Shelby again."

"Nature is all about balance," Jon replied. "Death reminds us of the fragility of life and how crucial it is to fight every day for those we love and cherish the moments we have. You taught me that, remember?"

A flock of Black-necked cranes flew overhead, their high-pitched trumpeting breaking the stillness of the sky.

"Cranes are symbols of longevity." Enid noted, appearing with a tray of tea and small cakes. They're thought to possess wisdom that comes with age and many past lives."

"Unlike most humans who seem to have short memories. We often fail to learn from our history, missing out on such wisdom." She grasped the delicate China teacup, steaming with a scent of lemon and ginger.

"Yes. Strange how some of our life challenges become our gifts." Enid smiled. "I will show you your room. Freshen up, and then, we will set the mood for the rest of the crew. I am sure everyone will be starving after the aroma of spices permeate this house. My friend who owns this home knows the chef and owner of this quaint and marvelous café not far from here. He has prepared quite a meal."

After a long, hot shower that washed away the grime from their journey since leaving Anchorage, Sam and Jon found themselves sprawled on the spacious bed, overlooking a view of cypress trees and a fountain featuring a gargoyle-like creature, spewing water from its mouth.

"Now this is something I can get behind." Sam snuggled up to Jon. "If I weren't so hungry, I'd consider not moving from this spot. Maybe, for days."

"The few times I've been to China, I have only visited Lhasa twice and Shigatse once. Spending time with Enid has made me realize how little I understand about the people in the places I've visited." Jon contemplated, rubbing Sam's shoulder. "Growing up in Australia, I've heard about what the Tibetan people have endured under Chinese rule. But being here, I now recognize the stark differences between Tibetans and the Chinese. It's a challenging reality. I might know geology, but many times, I lack the understanding about the cultures, above the ground."

"It can be tough when your job involves so much travel. But now you have me." Sam giggled.

"Yes, and I was just about to say that—until I met you."

"There's no justifying what Peiling and Daniel did, but if you think about it, we're all just a step away from becoming monsters if our surroundings nurture evil and hatred." Sam rubbed the scar on Jon's back.

"Jackson remembered Peiling from graduate school as being introverted and isolated. Her anger and intelligence provided her solace, but it was her environment that ultimately led her to revenge."

"And it was a similar environment in the mining industry that drove Camden to join the FBI." Jon responded. The room was quiet with only the gurgling of the fountain and birds outside.

"I was in Cape Town for a meeting, and a group of us were having a drink afterwards at a local bar." Jon reflected. "When you're Capitol riots came on the television, the entire place went quiet, not a word spoken as we watched the news. You know, it wasn't that long ago when Apartheid took place, and it did not take much to reopen those wounds." Jon contemplated. "The authoritarian political culture in South Africa ensured that the political system was dominated by the white minority. But to witness this unfolding in the United States of America." He paused. "On a lighter note, she will say yes?" Jon asked.

"Oh yeah. She will."

As Jon put on a shirt, he turned slowly and looked at his wife. As she followed him into the hallway, she heard Shelby's laughter and then Enid's voice.

"Jon, could you show Camden and Shelby to their room?" Enid directed. "And Ian to his room. Sam, could you assist Tenzin with the food? Also, this is Tenzin's wife, Dacha."

She watched everyone as they gathered around the warmth of the substantial rock fireplace, chatting, as if the last few months were a distant memory. The shimmering orange sun gave way to the muted, violet night with the stars illuminating the darkness.

"Shine bright like a diamond," Shelby sang out, prompting her friend to respond. "We're beautiful like diamonds in…"

"The snow," she laughed. "The Alaska version."

"I've missed you, Sam." Shelby grinned.

"Were you ever going to tell me…"

"I believe I hear Enid calling my name." Shelby cut her off with laughter, while yelling across the room. "Ian, Sam has a question for you."

"What are you guys looking at?" Shelby asked Sam, as she put her head on Camden's shoulder. Enid and Camden were standing on either side of Tenzin.

Camden, his shaggy hair still damp, pointed at the picture in Tenzin's hand.

"This is the monument we erected for my son." Tenzin's eyes gleamed with pride.

Soon Jackson and Jon joined. "Wow, that is the most magnificent rock I've ever seen, Camden," Jackson held the photo. "Tenzin's son died during a climb on Mt. Everest. This guy was on the mountain when it happened."

"Camden carried my son, Chaka, on his back to bring him to his mother and me." Tenzin's voice softened. "It was a heroic yet perilous act. The Mountain was in a tantrum that day, my friend." Tenzin clinked his glass to Camden's.

"Camden discovered a chunk of ruby-red feldspar granite, an erratic the size of a small sedan." Tenzin paused. "He commissioned a local sculptor to fashion it into a condor, wings outstretched, gazing at the mighty mountain."

"Does Camden know what's inscribed on it?" Enid inquired.

"No. The words were not inscribed until later after the ceremony."

Camden seemed somewhat perplexed by the conversation.

"The engraving includes a quote, Chaka's favorite, and the dates." Enid clarified.

The group congregated around Enid's phone. "Dacha sent this to me while we were in the kitchen."

"Oh my, Camden, what a beautiful tribute from Tenzin's family." Shelby expressed, planting a kiss atop his head. "And what you did for his parents. For Chaka."

Misty-eyed, Dacha, standing beside her husband, held a package wrapped in shimmering silk woven with hues of gold, red, and blue.

Tenzin took the package from his wife and extended the gift to his friend. "For you, my friend."

Camden unwrapped the substantial gift, revealing another wrapped parcel atop a raw rock—the same granite feldspar that had been carved into the monument for Chaka. In the faint light of the room, the red and silver mica gleamed. The engraved words read:

Camden O'Connor
'Tragedy Should be Utilized as a Source of Strength'
Friend of Chaka, Family to Tenzin and Dacha
A Brave Man Who Brought Our Son Home from the
Great Mountain
Mt Everest May 2014

He unwrapped the smaller package. Inside was a hand carved gold frame adorned with colorful birds in green, red, and blue. Camden recognized the image of the monument, but it had changed. Above the familiar words he knew, there were new words inscribed — the same words engraved on the rock he now held, a gift from Tenzin.

Camden was rendered speechless. The emotions he had kept buried for the past few months surged forth. His legs felt unsteady, and he handed the weighty stone and the picture to Shelby, embracing Tenzin and his wife before succumbing to tears.

"Let's eat!" Enid yelled. "The food is getting cold. Don't forget your coats. It is chilly outside."

With tear-dampened cheeks and subdued laughter, chairs were pushed back and glasses refilled.

Resting her head on Jon's shoulder, she watched her circle of friends bundled in warm coats, gathered around the large wooden table under the stars, with candles casting a flickering glow. Embers of red floating to the heavens from the nearby fire encircled within the stone rock.

"Camden and Shelby are going to be alright." Jon kissed her cheek.

"Yes, and tomorrow, we'll start anew, stronger and more determined than ever," she declared. "I'm famished."

Once everyone was seated, Enid raised her glass.

"A night of celebration and gratitude. A night to embrace those we hold dear. To us and those yet to come. Now, let's savor this incredible meal."

Laughter filled the air, and eventually, she leaned back in her chair, sipping her wine. Her belly was full, her senses satisfied, and her gaze settled on her radiant best friend, as Enid and Dacha chatted in Tibetan.

Jackson nodded in agreement to whatever Jon was sharing with him, his eyes twinkling in the stimulating exchange. Plates were now empty and then Enid nodded, signaling a transition.

"If everyone has finished, please take your glass and gather around the fire place inside," Enid began. "Dacha has a special treat, a recipe passed down from her great-grandmother."

She began clearing plates as Shelby joined her. "Camden is very quiet, almost secretive," Shelby whispered. "I'm guessing you're in on it."

"Me? If I had a secret, I certainly wouldn't keep it from my best friend." Sam replied with a giggle.

"Oh man, how long are you going to tease me about this? I was sworn to secrecy, you know." Shelby laughed. "I mean, Charles made me swear on a Bible and everything. It's top-secret stuff, and if I told you…"

She burst into laughter. "If you told me, you would what? Make me do Tai chi? Wow, this dessert smells heavenly. Cinnamon, and is that orange? And those little chocolate wafer things with some kind of berry."

"And now you're using dessert as a distraction," Shelby shrugged. "Is that cocoa dusted on top of the berry?"

"Espresso!" She declared as she licked her finger, dusted with dark brown powder.

"Ladies," Enid interjected, standing with her hands on her hips. Dacha stood next to her, a broad grin stretching across her dark, cherubic face from dimple to dimple. Enid rolled her eyes and exchanged a few words in Tibetan with Dacha, leading to laughter. "If you're done sampling, please." She handed them each a plate and ushered them out of the kitchen.

After a tranquil interlude, everyone full, Jackson having polished off at least two servings of dessert, left with Camden following him. Shelby nudged Sam in the ribs, her voice hushed. "See, something's going on. Now Camden and Jackson disappear. If Ian follows suit, mark my words, I'm tailing them. And did you catch that? Enid exchanged a secret glance at Camden before those left."

"If it was a secret, you wouldn't have caught the glance." She stabbed her fork at a lone purple berry on Shelby's plate.

"I am a spy, you know. I catch everything. Would you like me to fetch you another serving?" Shelby offered.

"Would you?" Sam responded.

"Are you two always like this?" Jon said.

"Like what?" they both exclaimed, just as Camden and Jackson reentered the scene.

"Another toast." Jackson's voice boomed, prompting Sam to gather the remaining plates and follow Enid towards the kitchen area.

Carrying a tray of champagne glasses, Enid followed Sam with two bottles of champagne. Once everyone held a brimming glass of the effervescent golden liquid, Camden cleared his throat.

"These past few months have been quite the rollercoaster, and thankfully, every person in this room has been a part of it. I say 'thankfully' because, without any one of you, I'm not sure Irish and I would be standing here today."

"Jon, I know you can relate when I say this." Camden grinned. "Keeping this secret from my Irish has been a real challenge."

"I knew it!" Shelby exclaimed. "We're even now, Samantha."

"Before there is a cat fight…" Camden stated but was interrupted.

"We never fight." Sam and Shelby declared in unison.

Jackson approached Camden, presenting him with a small,

blue velvet box. "Good luck, man. You do realize those two are a package deal."

"Shel, let's do this. Will you please marry me, my Irish spitfire?" Camden knelt before her, opening the box.

"I'm going to kill you, Sam. Oh my god, that's the most incredible diamond I've ever seen, Camden." Shelby was left thunderstruck.

"It belonged to my grandmother. Enid's mom."

"You carry this rock around with you, Enid?"

"Oh, for… Shel, say YES before this bubbly loses its bubbles." She pleaded.

"Yes. I was just teasing. Yes, yes, and yes, I will marry you, Camden." She declared, clasping Camden's face with both hands and kissing him.

Camden slid the blue diamond ring onto Shelby's finger. As he stood up, he helped Shelby off the couch, and kissed her passionately, holding her close.

"Was it my flirting with Daniel?" Shelby's eyes sparkled.

"Nope, not Daniel."

"It was my witty charm and beauty."

"Nope," he quickly added, "Although you possess both those traits. It was this long haired, golden bear with small, coal-black eyes and very long claws."

"The moon bear."

"It is a good thing you said yes." Camden choked up as he looked into those green eyes. "Because we are not leaving this country until we solidify this."

Shelby looked around and locked onto Sam. "Always?"

"Always." She hugged her friend. "And the ceremony is tomorrow night."

"To Camden and Shelby." Enid toasted. "Drink up, now."

"She's not going to stop until she gets the story behind that ring." She warned Enid in a whisper. "Shelby's mom had a very difficult time not telling her daughter that she will be at her wedding."

"I am so grateful I was able to tell her parents the good news first. On all accounts," Enid said. "It should have been a strange conversation, but she was not shocked or surprised, it was like she knew her daughter was alive. After first being told Camden was gone, then, to be told he was alive was a lightning bolt into the gut. A good one, but never the less, a shock. Shelby's mother clung to faith and hope."

"Two mothers who had mourned together now share their happiness. You both connected at the wake because neither of you believed your children were gone."

"Yes."

"Here she comes."

"Please, Enid I have to know how you just happened to have this beautiful ring here," Shelby asked.

"My grandmother gave me this ring when Camden was born." Enid revealed, touching Shelby's hand. "Instead of keeping it locked away, I wore it around my neck." Enid retrieved a silver chain from beneath her blouse. "I never took it off the chain until today. When I met your parents at the wake in Anchorage, I felt the diamond grow warm against my skin. When they talked about you, I felt the diamond pulse. The first time Sam mentioned your name, sharing loving memories and stories about you and her," Enid's voice trembled. "It's hard to explain, but it was like holding a baby bird in your palm, feeling their tiny heart beat." Enid took Shelby's hand and cradled it between her palms. "I knew you and Camden would be safe, and you would be my daughter."

Enid embraced Shelby, while Camden held Enid's hand and Shelby held Sam's. No words were needed.

A new beginning. Sam whispered as she held her friends hand.

EPILOGUE

DEEP BELOW THE ground, in the darkness of a cold damp cell, the small thin shape trembled. The mind within cursed, disgusted with the weak frail body of the man while his intellect grew strong with focus and determination. The plan began to take shape. With careful preparation, he would be in control, shedding this affliction. His brilliance was waiting patiently until the time of his emergence. They promised the whimpering little boy would be transferred if he behaved and gave them what they needed. They will get exactly what they need. Be still. Patience, my love. They promised the weak creature his own lab if he cooperated. Blubbering fool. Soon, it will be soon when I destroy this weak creature, once and for all. The catalyst was well hidden and safe. He felt it calling. He shuddered remembering how it felt – its red skin, pulsating ever so slightly, like a human heart. Soon, my love.

GRATITUDE

Alaska will always be my home. Its land, people, animals, and sea have shaped me profoundly. This novel was inspired by my time on the Seward Peninsula, where local elders shared stories around the fire—powerful moments that reinforced my belief in storytelling as a tool for education and inspiration.

I am deeply grateful to the Indigenous communities who generously share their knowledge and wisdom, as well as to all those marginalized by the destruction of their lands. This novel seeks to honor their voices and the fragile beauty of our Earth.

Thank you to Julie Sharp, my dear friend who has always been there for me, for her expertise and invaluable insights into the chemical details of the story. And to Joe Moore, whose calm guidance and ecological expertise greatly enriched my understanding of Alaska's landscapes. To Dr. Chien-Lu Ping, my mentor and a global authority on permafrost soils, your wisdom brought depth and authenticity to this work, especially in capturing the Tibetan setting.

Special thanks to my niece Lori, my beta readers Suzan, Joe, Julie, Rebecca, and Emily, and my editors Elizabeth Thorpe and April Davila, for their invaluable feedback and support. To my writers' groups—Ventures in The Written Word and my Port Townsend Writers group—your camaraderie has been a constant source of encouragement.

Finally, heartfelt gratitude to Rebecca Bloom and Pamela Weiss, whose boundless creativity and dedication have been instrumental in this journey, from this novel to the adaptation of *The Understory*. Thank you for helping spread the message of environmental stewardship and resilience.

Michelle Schuman is the award-winning author of *The Understory: A Female Environmentalist in the Land of the Midnight Sun*. Her memoir is currently being adapted into a screenplay. When not researching methods of using nature to explode, kill and destroy, Michelle volunteers for the Marine Science Center, NW Marine Center, and a member of the Humane Society National Animal Rescue Team. After nearly four decades working in Alaska as a wildlife biologist, wetland scientist, and ecologist, her voice is one of authenticity in science-based thrillers. She currently resides in the PNW, in the rain shadow of the Olympic Mountains and the waters of the Salish Sea.

Stay tuned for
Michelle Schuman's next novel

THE CATALYST

CHAPTER 1

The naked, blistered-red body of a small-framed woman lay splayed on her back, arms and legs extended in a grotesque 'X.' Her long black hair fanned out around her head. From just below her breasts to above her belly button, a straight incision with four large sutures formed another 'X'— one of which had torn apart, leaving the remains of a single, shredded strand of intestine trailing into the sand. Two shiny black rocks, smooth like polished obsidian, filled the empty sockets where her eyes had once been.

Vultures soared above with wings stretched wide, riding the thermals directly over where the body had been found. Field technicians dressed in chocolate-chip camouflage documented the scene with meticulous precision.

Her skin felt as though it were shrinking, compressing against her bones as the relentless heat sucked every drop of moisture from her body. She thought of popcorn—sweet, salty, hot, melted butter popcorn that only exists in a movie theater. Every blood cell in her body felt ready to pop and hiss like kernels of dried corn in blistering oil.

"Burning hot out here in nowhere land," she muttered,

standing beside the 6'4" muscular frame of her friend and now work partner, Jackson. Her head slightly higher than his shoulder, her eyes remained fixed on the shimmering horizon. "How the hell did she get out here?"

North, south, east, west—every direction yielded endless tawny dunes against a soft blue, cloudless sky. Mirage-like waves floated in the distance, where the hot desert air mixed with cooler currents above. Silver shards of mica in the sand reflected in her mirrored sunglasses as the sun's rays caught the copper strands of her ponytail, glued to her sweat-soaked back.

"Unknown. If they hadn't been testing that new drone…" Jackson shook his head. "By the time someone realized she was missing, the vultures would've cleaned up the evidence."

She turned to face him. "Why are we here, Jackson?"

He cocked his head, gesturing toward the open-walled tent where the technicians worked. She followed him. Standing over the body, she noticed that the left hand lay open, palm skyward, with the thumb resting against the tips of the fingers, forming a teacup shape. A yellow marker rested in her palm.

"That," Jackson pointed at the outstretched hand, "is why we're here." He nodded toward a technician who handed him a sealed plastic bag. Opening it, he passed it to Shelby. Inside was a red crystalline rock, roughly the size of a lime. Shelby removed her sunglasses, staring at the item as her face paled. Jackson nudged her as they stepped back as the technicians gently placed the body into a body bag, and carried it to the transport vehicle. She watched as the vehicle disappeared into the mirage.

"Daniel," she whispered, remembering the last word he had said before his arrest: catalyst. Daniel, the sociopath geologist with ARKose, a mining company sampling geothermal springs for rare earth elements in Tibet.

Carved in precise, black block letters on the rock was one word: CATALYST.

"How? He's in a Chinese prison."

"He escaped ten days ago during a transfer."

"Why here? In the Jordanian desert?"

"No idea. Tower 22 has fewer than 350 U.S. Army and Air Force personnel, mostly National Guard. The Iraqi border's six miles that way," Jackson nodded toward the horizon. "And over there's the border between Jordan and Syria. Twelve miles from here is al-Tanf, a smaller U.S. garrison suspected of monitoring weapon shipments for Iran." He rubbed his chin, speckled with more gray than black, stubble these days.

"If it is Daniel, this doesn't fit his MO."

"A Chinese prison could change anyone," she pointed. "What's the rock?"

"I sent Camden a picture. He thinks it's tourmaline."

"Tourmaline? I am not sure I have heard of it." She bit her lip. Camden had been in Malaysia for weeks. "You know we were supposed to meet in Hawaii in a few days? For our honeymoon."

"Almost a year late?" Jackson shrugged. "I know, Shel. Sorry."

"Duty calls." She touched the blue diamond on her ring finger. "Tell me about tourmaline."

As they walked back to the dune buggy, Jackson explained what Camden had told him.

"Tourmaline is prized for its variety of colors. A single crystal can contain multiple hues—the rarer the combination, the more valuable. The Paraiba variety, neon blue to greenish-blue, can fetch over $10,000 per carat."

"When Daniel mentioned a catalyst," She gripped the buggy's bar. "We thought he meant a chemical to enhance plutonium or francium reactivity. But this rock?"

"Not as valuable with one color, but…"

"Are you telling me someone died over jewelry?"

She recalled how Daniel had discovered the largest francium deposit on Earth at ARKose's Alaskan mine.

"He knew something," she murmured. "Something we missed at the hot springs in Tibet."

He stopped the buggy in front of their barracks. "Clean up and I will meet you in the mess hall."

After much needed water and something to eat, a young technician escorted them, to a makeshift autopsy room inside, where they were instructed to don the heavy lead-lined suits. On the autopsy table, the body's ribcage was spread wide. Where the heart should have been lay a translucent object, glowing with a pulsating red aura.

Jackson stood by the surgeon without saying a word as another technician took photos documenting what they were seeing.

"It's hot," said a masked voice. "Rad is level 3. There should've been blood everywhere at the scene. Her heart was surgically removed."

"Private Santos," another voice added. "Was three months pregnant. She was scheduled to go home in two weeks." The man shook his head. "I am her CO."

Jackson nodded as he carefully lifted the object with shielded gloves, placing it in a lead container Shelby held. The pulsation slowed, then stopped. No words were necessary as they shed their suits and walked into a small conference room. The object safely sealed.

Jackson sat down in front of the monitor as Camden looked up from his work, his blonde hair disheveled. "I see Daniel's made something new. A crystalline, radioactive tourmaline. It's as if he embedded a pinprick of francium or cesium inside the gem."

Shelby's voice dropped. "It looks like a heart."

Camden's smile faded. "Tourmaline has symbolic meaning. It's thought to protect against negativity, enhance creativity. Different colors mean different things. Red…"

"Stop." She raised her hand then began rubbing her temples. "I know what you are thinking Cam."

Camden continued. "Rubellite Tourmaline is tied to passion and fire. It's energy, life. It represents the path between the heart and the base chakra."

"He won't hurt me," she said, glancing at Camden. "He blames you. You are the one in danger. And Sam."